The Sick Box

AN ENTRY FOR THE

Stephen Leacock Award

FOR HUMOUR FOR

2022

The Sick Box

Matthew Fries

First Edition

Cover art by Aimee White

Library and Archives Canada Cataloguing in Publication

Title: The sick box / Matthew Fries.
Names: Fries, Matthew, 1971- author.
Identifiers: Canadiana (print) 20200196510 | Canadiana (ebook) 20200196529 | ISBN 9781989225288 (softcover) | ISBN 9781989225295 (PDF)
Classification: LCC PS8611.R533 S53 2020 | DDC C813/.6—dc23

6

It was in the age of Gamagin when the Nakara Corporation's management team conducted the first of its "Sisyphus" studies. After facilitating many focus groups and restructuring the team countless times, the Sisyphus report (phase one) came back with the conclusion: "Motivational art in the workplace increases productivity and enhances morale while reducing stress on male employees age 25 to 55."

Thus, a project plan was struck, and a risk manager was hired to lead a new team. After an eon of debate, and long nights poring over building maps with the facilities manager, procurement services finally had some numbers to work with. The Nakara Corporation sent out requests for tender. Months were spent in negotiation, and in spite of a well-publicized police investigation into collusion, a contract was drawn up with a company called The Black Circle Society. The first of the art arrived quickly, and the carpentry department, a division of plant operations, donned their green uniforms and took up their levels and drills like soldiers called to arms. They worked tirelessly to frame and hang the art, but the project was stalled twice due to contract negotiations with the union and another time due to vendor bankruptcy.

Legend has it that there are still thousands, upon thousands, of truckloads of motivational art sitting in crates in the Nakara facilities warehouse. While many have been driven mad by the endless task of framing and hanging all the art, management at Nakara feel confident that the completion of the project is on the horizon. Graphs have been drawn, spreadsheets crafted, and projections for the completion date fall sometime between the end of the age of Bushyasta and the beginning of the age of Drekavak.

All sorts of photographs were used for the motivational poster art (verdant forests, racing motorcycles, soaring eagles, sailboats at full tilt, frying eggs), but inscribed beneath each and every photograph was the same sort of motivational message, the same kind of mundane greeting card sentiments and quotes void of all context that serve to gaslight only the thickest numbskulls and most shameless boot-lickers that the office cubicles can contain. The poster on my wall depicted a lone mountain climber ascending a snowy peak of unknown proportions. In the distance, an endless range of smaller peaks flowed all the way to the horizon. It was captioned, in capital letters:

"ONLY THOSE WHO RISK THE PERILS OF THE JOURNEY CAN REACH THE HEIGHTS OF SUCCESS. *Susan Jones*."

What a load of shit, I thought as I stared at those snow-capped peaks.

That is when I noticed that the red light on my phone was lit up. I had somehow missed a call.

"Sigh," I sighed, and pressed the VTRC (Voicemail Telephone Retrieval Code) and listened to the mechanical voice on the answering service. "You have two waiting messages. To listen to your messages, press six."

I pressed six. "Beep"

"Sorry, I didn't get that. Please try again."

I pressed six again. "Beep."

"Sorry, I didn't get that. Please try again."

"Come on," I spat beneath my breath. I pressed the worn six button again. "Beep."

"To hear your message, please press six."

"What a piece of garbage," I muttered and pressed six.

"Sorry, I didn't get that. Please try again."

I took a deep breath and pressed six again. "Beep."

"Sorry, I didn't get that. Please try again."

"God! What an asshole you are."

"Hey, can you watch your language please?"

"..." For a moment I thought the phone had answered me but quickly realized that it was Lucy, the woman in the cubicle next to mine, who had spoken. Lucy popped her head over the partition that separated us. She glared at me.

"What?" I said.

"Whadya you mean what? We're at work," Lucy said.

"No, I mean, like what for? Why, Lucy? Tell me why I should watch my language."

"Code 17. Section 9 point 2 in the employee code of conduct handbook," Lucy said. "*Thou shalt not use offensive language in the workplace.* I will talk to Mr. Bauer and he will write you up."

"I'm so scared, Lucy," I said. "We're in Hell already. Case you hadn't noticed. How are they going to make my life any worse?"

Lucy grimaced, her lipstick smeared over a festering herpes sore, and she sat down, loudly typing away on her computer. *Peck. Peck. Peck.*

I went back to concentrating on the phone. *Where was I? Oh yeah, of course.* "Six. Okay. Bloody six. How many times should I press it? Why can't IT fix this phone system?"

I heard a click and some static on the other end of the phone. Either the connection had dropped, or the system was kicking over to the answering service. I pinned the receiver in the crook of my neck, and I picked up the photograph of Alice off my desk. Using bent paper clips that I had mangled specifically for this purpose and some tacks, I hooked Alice overtop of the mountainscape.

The picture of Alice was the only thing I had left of my life before the Nakara Corporation. I don't even really know how I came to have the picture. One day it appeared on my desk. I didn't ask any questions. Alice was about seven years old in the photograph, and she wore pigtails and a flowered dress that my mother had made for her. She was all long arms and tanned skinny legs and a crooked smile. My little sister, Alice.

I heard a click on the phone. "Message one." An androgynous, robotic sounding voice began to speak: "This is not a test. There has been an NLED breech."

Unbelievable. Zombies. Can this day get any worse? I wondered.

666

The worst thing about Hell are the NLED breeches. The NLED breeches and the acronyms. I hate them both. For clarification: NLED = Non-Living Eternal Dead, deemed a proper noun, by Satan's own team of grammarians (a group even more corrupt and morally bankrupt than Hell's Olympic committee). NLED, or zombies, as they are more commonly known.

When we were children, Alice (poor little Alice with her trailer trash name and scraped knees) used to call them "shombies."

"The shombies are coming," she would shout.

And everyone would say, "Isn't she adorable," as she squealed with delight and ran away from all the mispronounced threats that were on her tail, her ribboned pigtails trailing behind her like streamers, her tiny feet flitting across the lawn so quickly and lightly that she appeared to be running on hot coals.

Alice thought it was fun to invent threats and then run away from them.

Also in pursuit of her were scorpions, "orpians."

"The orpians are coming," and "cereal" killers, which she thought were the funniest thing ever because she could not imagine what a cereal killer would do to her and why she should be scared of them. And what did they have against cereal anyway? My father put all these ideas in her head. (The zombies. The scorpions. The cereal killers.) He thought she was the most adorable thing ever.

If Alice only knew that when you die you can actually go to Hell, and although Hell feels, and looks, just like the world that you were used to, there are horrible, unspeakable threats here. Oh, Alice. My poor dear, sweet, dullard Alice. Those were more innocent days. Who knew what tortures the future held?

When she was very young, Alice also refused to believe in the existence of mosquitoes. She laughed herself sick whenever anyone told her that there were, in fact, real live bugs in the world that would use their needle noses to puncture one's skin and drink one's blood.

We all have to grow up at some time.

I suppose that is what dying and waking up in Hell was like for me, much the same way Alice must have felt when she recognized her first mosquito bite: "The filthy bastards were telling the truth all along!"

666

"There has been an NLED breech on the first floor. Do not panic. Follow your NLEDZSW and move to your designated SZ. I repeat: This is not a test. There has been a NLED breech. Stay calm and remember your training."

Luckily, I had just finished the ZWHAAST (Zombie Workplace Hazard Avoidance Application Safety Training) refresher course and could decode the acronyms as "Non-Living Eternal Dead (NLED), Non-Living Eternal Dead Zombie Safety Warden (NLEDZSW), and the very simple, Safety Zone (SZ). My stomach grumbled.

Of course, I suddenly had to use the washroom.

It's a humiliating thing to admit, but let's be honest here because Hell is Hell and zombies are zombies, and there is no way to sugarcoat it: Zombies usually descend upon you when you have to go to the washroom or are already seated on the toilet. They are kind of like Hell's version of telephone solicitors.

Or, I suppose, an argument can be made that you have to go to the washroom because the zombies are attacking. What came first, the zombies or the feces? It doesn't really matter because either way it adds an extra layer of unpleasantness to the whole being eaten alive scenario, and I cannot begin to relate how many times I have settled down in the toilet stall at work, or at home in my cozy bathroom, only to smell the moaning hordes approaching. Then it's time to wipe up quickly (by the way, the toilet paper in Hell is like fine grit sandpaper, so maybe think about amending your wicked ways before it is too late), pull up your undies, grab the nearest chainsaw, and make for high ground. Because nobody wants to be eaten alive while they are having a poo.

Well, I suppose there might be some perverts out there who would like it. It is Hell, after all.

By my estimation, I had maybe two or three minutes to get to the safety door before the zombies made it up the stairwell to the 31st floor. They would soon come streaming into our little warren of cubicles and begin gorging upon the flesh of the two hundred or so mid-level staff members who were housed there.

In a perfect universe, I would have just hung up the phone and ran for the exit; however, this was Hell, and Hell is the furthest thing from perfect. If I did not listen to the second call, I would be flayed by giant fire-breathing ants. (It was written in the corporate discipline policy.)

The voice on the phone continued: "To delete the message, press six. To save it, press six. To donate six dollars to the United Way, press six. To skip to the next message, press six."

I pressed six.

"Message two. BEEP."

I started gathering my things and putting on my coat while I listened to the second message.

"Mrs. Floyd. This is Professor Norris from the Outreach Team. I've got some compelling content for you. We've actualized your sick box. We'd like to offer you a promotion. The rubber's hit the road on this one, Mrs. Floyd, so we'll have to deliver the peripherals posthaste here. The proposal has been tabled, and the metrics are exceptional. We're taking this one to the next level! We'd like you to report upstairs. Come to reception on the 200th floor and enquire for Professor Norris. The girls will deliver you behind the curtain. Be seeing you, Mrs. Floyd."

My heart nearly stopped. I couldn't believe it.

"To hear your message again, press six."

After years of toiling in the warren of cubicles, this was

Glenda was an elderly woman who always wore a pink shawl to ward off the frigid air conditioner that blasted cold air at us day in and day out. She kept tins of potpourri all over her organized desk and grew African violets under lamps. I was not friendly with her, but Glenda had an awful time figuring out how to send emails, so I often helped her with her computer.

"Dentist appointment," I lied.

"Again?" she said. "You just went last week."

I wondered what evil act(s) had sealed her fate and condemned Glenda to Hell for eternity?

"Do you know how to open a dot zip file?" Glenda asked. "I keep clicking on it and nothing happens."

"Sorry. Dentist appointment," I told her.

"I marked all those emails as urgent, like you said, with the little exclamation mark, but nobody got back to me." Glenda's face was pinched tight with worry and her horns looked dull and old. "Darren said they might be in my spam folder? Do you know which one is the spam folder? How do I get there?"

I sighed. "It just says 'spam.' It's right there on the left-hand side."

Glenda moved in close to her computer screen, her nose craned upwards and her gaze cast down over her reading glasses. "Here?" she asked. Her hand working the mouse, the arrow icon skittering all around her trash folder.

"Yes, there," I said, feeling like I wanted to slap her. I thought I heard something bang above me.

"I should go," I told her. "The dentist wants me to maximize my benefits. They're trying out a new whitening treatment on me. They say it will help my self-esteem. Our insurance covers it. You should try it."

"They say that stuff burns," Glenda replied.

I smiled at her. "Only for a few days," I said.

"And causes cancer," Glenda said.

"What's a little cancer? You can't die twice, eh?"

"I only wish," Glenda said, and we shared a laugh.

"Be seeing you," I said, and I started towards the exit. Glenda got back to her mail.

All the horned heads in the office were working quietly, answering emails, face down into their keyboards, typing with an angry and tense clickity click click that filled the warren with a sound not unlike that of swarming locusts. The red lights on their phones were lit up, but they were all too busy working to check their messages.

The fools.

When I got to the exit, I noticed something wasn't right. The door wasn't shut all the way.

There was a wriggling foot holding it open. I did not recognize the foot, per se, but I did recognize Mary Leamington's shoe. She was famous around the office for wearing pink loafers. She had the desk right next to the exit. Her cubicle was empty.

I opened the door and saw a young zombie, maybe a ten-year-old, gnawing on Mary's neck, blood frothing from Mary's jugular, spurting in the zombie's face as it bit and chewed. Mary had on her orange safety vest and the red trucker cap that identified her as the NLEDZSW.

"Oh, Mary," I said. "Some safety warden you are."

With her last bit of energy, Mary lifted her blood-soaked hand and raised her middle finger at me.

Someone let out a shriek. All over the office, my co-workers popped up their heads, and began sniffing. A zombie leg had cracked through a ceiling tile. They began moving, gathering their water bottles, house keys, and bicycle helmets. I did not have much time. I took my letter opener from my pocket and I stabbed the little zombie in the eye. He fell back against the wall. "You can't die twice," I muttered.

From the stairwell beneath me, I heard them coming. It smelled like a large horde. Their tattered clothes and reeking flesh crested the landing of the 30th floor. I looked down from the 31st. One mean looking female actually caught my eye and growled at me. She was a big girl and liked to eat. If she was to have her way, I was to be her main course for this evening.

Inside the warren, my co-workers were scrambling towards me as a zombie burst through the ceiling tile and crashed to the floor in a cloud of asbestos and other fire retardant, cancer causing, dust particles. Leading the pack was a boy named Kevin, a quick young study just transferred into Accounts from the Call Centre. He was cunning, handsome, and quite evil, a true sociopath, but too fresh, too naive. We all might have been working for Kevin when he was alive, but here in Hell, you needed to be downright ruthless if you wanted to survive. It's eat or be eaten. (Most times quite literally.) I kicked Mary's foot out of the way, and waved him towards me.

"Quick. Quick. This way."

I held the door open for him, and just as he was within arm's reach, I took a firm hold of Kevin's necktie and spun him towards the stairs. I let go of the tie. Kevin cartwheeled down the stairs into the thrashing mound of zombies, and as the horde set upon him, I saw him mouth the words, "Why, Floyd? Why?"

"Why?"

Why indeed?

Us Hell veterans call it the "buddy system." It's a simple premise. If things look rough, throw them your buddy. You know, in retrospect, that is one thing I can appreciate about Hell: You always know where you stand.

I slammed the heavy steel door shut, catching someone's manicured and painted fingernails in it as I did so. The person on the other end of the fingernails screamed as I pulled the lock pin from the door latch, locking the door on them. I stepped over Mary's body on my way up the stairs to the executive floor to meet Professor Norris and start work on a new project; but as I did so, I felt a hand grab my calf. The little zombie that had eaten Mary had one tiny little bite left in him.

With the letter opener jutting from his punctured eyeball, and with a vice-like grip, he pulled my foot towards him. He tore off my shoe and was about to bite into my heel, just like someone biting into a crisp new apple. With my free foot, I booted and punctured the zombie's head repeatedly until it was mush, and he was still, mostly, except for the teeth chattering in a final death shudder upon the flesh of my foot.

"Fuckin' jerk," I said. "I just bought those pumps!"

One of my shoes was lying on the floor beside the

carnage that had been Mary, and the other, still on my foot, was covered in gore.

But this was no time to worry about my shoes. The horde had nearly consumed Kevin, and I was next on the menu. Again, I started up the stairs, wondering, *What happens to your soul when you turn into a zombie?*

Gargle, went my stomach.

I heard a voice. Someone was calling out across the 666 dimensions. Someone was speaking. (Not to me, mind you, but speaking nonetheless.) And this voice was different. It was not hollow and maniacal, it was not full of phony platitudes and promises of, "I'll get you those contracts tomorrow. First thing. I promise." It was the voice of a man, a living man, not a demon, not one of my own kind.

666

I found myself looking through a rectangular box out onto a room. Inside the box, everything was black. On the other side, there was light.

"Well, they call it that for a good reason," the voice said.

His voice (it was a him) was so…well, alive…and warm, alive, deep, and comforting, like an announcer in a documentary film. He looked nice, mostly because he was alive and didn't have horns or a long red swishing tail, beautiful to me, with green eyes and friendly hands. And he was alive. Did I mention that he was alive? Like, alive for real.

I could see him and a woman standing and staring at the box. I pushed my head out of the blackness, and as I did so, I felt the pricks of my horns pierce the mathematical fabric, the thinnest dimensional tear. My right arm followed. Then the left. I pulled myself through. The woman and the man did not even notice. At first, I did not think that I was going to fit, but my body did not seem to have any substance. I appeared to be nothing but a shadowy ether floating in an attic loft. I saw sunlight streaming through a couple of windows at either end, and a cat scurried across the floor and down the steps. There was a desk and old beer cans sitting on top of numerous dusty bookshelves.

The man was still speaking to the woman and pointing at the rectangular-shaped object that birthed me. I floated up behind them to see what it was.

"Because you got it when you got sick," the man said.

My sick box.

"They come in all shapes and sizes. Roman Catholic priests used them to administer last rites. You just nail it to your wall, like Christ on a cross, and you wait to get sick and die. It's got every creepy thing one needs to shed this mortal coil and ascend into God's heavenly skies. You've got your picture of the holy mother cradling the lolling head of our bleeding Lord and Saviour, you've got your holy water, your crucifix, candles, holy anointing oil, and, of course, your trusty bible. What else? Plates, napkins. I'm not sure what those are for."

"It's like some kind of gruesome picnic basket," the woman responded.

"Ha. Yeah," the man said.

"What did you buy it for?" the woman asked.

"To keep the old deer head company."

Throughout the loft, on the floor and hanging on the walls, were oddities, rarities, collectables, hoardables, an assortment of strange items, such as deer head with eyes painted neon green, old lanyards hanging from its antlers, and at the end of each lanyard an old ticket, backstage passes to concerts (Bruce Springsteen, Teenage Head, Tito Jackson) and tickets for events (Beerfest 89, Ox Roast 2006, a ticket to game five of the 1976 ALCS); there was a model of the Death Star from Star Wars hanging from the ceiling and spinning in some unseen breeze; a golden Buddha statue that someone had turned into a lamp shedding its sacrilegious light on a child-sized cardboard cutout of Alfred E. Neuman; there was a disco ball; two child-sized alien mannequins robed in silver, with dark, piercing, oblong eyes that seemed to stare right through you; and my sick box.

I wanted to touch it, but I could not.

The woman smiled. "But who is preparing to eat?" she asked.

What a nasty thing to say, I thought. I wished I had my body with me, so I could push her down the stairs.

"I bought it at a yard sale," the man said.

It was horrible to see it again. It made me sad. I wondered how far it had travelled? Who took it from me after I died? Was it my sister, Alice? Mom? Dad? What circumstances led to its clearing house dismissal? It was the last attempt to save my soul. I died staring at that sick box, dreaming about a muscled old Caucasian man with a long white beard and a staff. He was dressed in immaculately clean white robes. A germaphobic bro wizard. I thought he was coming for me, His heart full of mercy. What a fool I was. It was the last thing I ever saw on Earth, and someone sold it at a garage sale. It made me so mad.

"Alice?" I said.

"Did you hear something?" the man asked.

It was you, wasn't it, Alice? I wondered. *You never loved me again, did you? Not after what happened. You sold it.*

And now this man with the green eyes had it, had pillaged it from a heap of rusty golf clubs and dog-eared moldy books.

The woman ran her fingers over the edges of my sick box. I could feel her filthy hands, I could feel her spiky, pointed and painted nails as if they were trailing over my own skin. If I could have dragged her to the window and tossed her out onto the street, turn her neck 90 degrees, I would have.

"So any idea when Dana will be home?" she asked.

Did you really hate me this much, Alice? I wondered. *Did I deserve this?*

I heard some shuffling coming from downstairs, the opening and closing of doors. "Ben.

Ben! We're home. Where are you?"

"Speak of the devil," Ben said. "Up here!" he shouted down the stairs.

"Is Alexis here? I got the pork chops," a woman's voice called. "Sorry we're late. Mallory had to use the toilet at the mall."

There was a massive windy sucking sound coming from my sick box. I was being pulled into it.

"Daddy!" a child's voice called.

"UP HERE!"

"Daddy!"

"The rubber's hit the road." The words of Professor Norris swam in my head. The pressure from my sick box was building, and I was being pulled closer to it.

"Mallory?" Alexis asked. "I finally get to meet Mallory?"

"Yes. That's Mallory," Ben said.

"DADDY!"

"Yes, honey. We're upstairs! In the attic," Ben shouted.

"What are you doing?" The child's sweet voice was getting closer. She climbed up the attic steps using her hands and feet as if she were climbing a ladder. She was a little pixie, her long dark hair hung down her back, she had pointy ears, gleaming green eyes, and a dark complexion. She wore a floral print dress and sandals. Her knees were scraped, and she had thick eyebrows, tiny pearly white teeth, and a smile that warmed my heart. It was easy to love her, and in a way, she reminded me of my own dear sister, Alice. Just because all little girls reminded me of sweet Alice. Sweet Alice, the betrayer.

"What are you doing, Daddy?" She stood at the top of the stairs, five (or six) years old maybe.

"Hi, baby. We're just up here having fun without you."

"Daddy…" she was used to good-natured teasing from her dad.

"I'm just joking. I'm just joking. This is Miss Warrington from Mommy's acting group. Remember Mommy invited her to supper?"

"No."

Ben winked at Alexis. "Well, anyway. Can you say, 'Hello,' to her?"

"No."

"Pardon me?"

"No. I won't," the little girl said.

Alexis fidgeted a little, hung her head as she turned a little red in the face. "It's okay, Ben," she said.

"I'm sorry, Alexis. She's usually very outgoing," Ben said. Then he turned to address Mallory. "Well, that is your decision, Mallory. You can say hello to whomever you want, but I think you are being rude. Are you okay, honey? You look a little green around the gills."

Mallory said nothing.

"Can you please just shake Miss Warrington's hand?"

Mallory hung her head and took a step towards Alexis. She stuck out her arm, her limp outstretched hand like a dead swallow.

Alexis got down on one knee and took the little girl's hand to shake. "Hi, Mallory. I have heard so much about you. Your Mommy and I are friends from the theatre."

Mallory raised her head and opened her mouth wide. Alexis Donaldson's scream filled the entire house.

"Oh, my GOD!" Ben shouted.

"What is going on up there? What happened?" Dana asked from downstairs.

"Dana. Get some paper towels. Quick. Jesus Christ! I am so sorry, Alexis. Hold still."

"What happened?" Dana shouted.

"Mallory threw up all over Alexis. Get some paper towels. Forget it! Get the shop vac. It's everywhere!"

"Holy shit!" Alexis shouted, dripping with vomit.

"Jesus H. CHRIST!" Ben did not know where to begin. "Are you okay, Mal?"

"Daddy, my belly hurts."

"Good Lord, that's a lot of puke. I'm so sorry, Alexis. We'll get you cleaned up. Run downstairs, Mallory, and wash up in the bathroom. Your Mommy will help you.

"Christ, it stinks!" Alexis said. "Get me a towel!"

"Jesus Murphy," Ben said.

Mallory turned, paused, and before she slid down the stairs on her bum, she smiled at me. Green chunky vomit that smelled of zombie scat painted her chin. And I was sucked down my sick box, back to Hell, to a washroom. Soft music was playing. The Muzak version of Don McLean's American Pie (a song in constant rotation in Hell.)

666

I put my foot on the counter to take a better look at the zombie bite. There was a red mark just above my heel, near my tendon. It was about an inch long, the exact size of a tooth. A pinhead's worth of dark red blood had gathered and congealed at the one edge. It appeared that I might have been infected, but I was not sure.

I took my long winter coat and hung it, along with my purse, on a hook by the washroom door. I removed my ripped pantyhose and threw them into the trash. I turned on the tap, the hot water, and hiked up my skirt. Standing on one leg, I rested my shin on the counter and stuck my heel in the sink. The tap ran scalding hot for a second, then freezing cold, then scalding hot, then back to freezing cold, but I withstood the annoyance and tried to wash away the zombie poison. I didn't know if this would work or not, but it was the only thing I could think of. After a couple minutes of this, I took my foot out from under the tap and dried off with scratchy brown paper towels from the dispenser. I straightened my skirt and checked my hair in the mirror. I would need a comb, lipstick, and a bit of blush, maybe some eyeshadow, some new shoes and pantyhose.

I thought I heard someone laugh. Giggle. And in the reflection of the mirror, I saw what appeared to be a crooked eye peering out from the beneath a stall door.

The giggle came again.

"Hello?" I said.

"Hello," a man's voice came from behind the stall door as he shifted position.

"What are you doing in here? This is the women's washroom!" I started backing towards the exit.

"Don't worry," the voice said. Whoever was speaking had a southern drawl. "I am your mentor, but you are the gift of you," the voice said.

Great. A helpful pervert, I thought as I started searching through my purse for my letter opener but quickly remembered that I left it sticking out of the little zombie's eyeball.

I heard the lock on the stall door slide back. The door flung open. There was a little man standing on the toilet seat. He could not have been taller than four feet. He was naked from the waist down (except for his socks and shoes), with an erection jutting out at me. Cords for his video camera were strung about his neck. His stubby fingers worked the zoom on a camcorder with a flashing red light on it. He was zooming in on my face.

"Get away from me, you weirdo!" I shouted.

"I am the gift of me!" he said. A greasy horseshoe of short black hair ringed his ears and horns while his bald head gleamed in the fluorescent lights of the washroom. His well-trimmed black moustache squiggled above his anus-like lips as he spoke again, "I am the gift of me!" And he hopped down from the toilet and ran for the exit, nearly knocking me over, dragging all his cords and video camera equipment behind him.

As he reached for the door handle the door swung open and he was nearly knocked down.

"Oh my God!" the woman who opened the door said. "Did somebody die in here?"

She was a slim woman with a large bust wearing a ridiculously coiffed, frosty-lilac-coloured wig; her skin was deeply (and impossibly) tanned; and she smelled like she had been snorkeling in a vat at the Avon factory. Her eyeshadow was so thickly layered that you could barely see her eyes beneath eyebrows penciled on her forehead like circumflexes. Her lipstick was frosted and sparkled, and so thickly shellacked on her collagen-injected lips that I questioned whether she might just have come from a stage performance somewhere.

"You little pervert. Are you up to no good again?" she shouted.

The little man laughed and ran past her with his bare ass and camera equipment.

The woman walked into the washroom. She saw me standing there. "Did he assault you?" She put a comforting hand on my forearm.

She was much shorter than me, and if her hanging gizzard neck was any indication, significantly older, although it was hard to tell because of all her makeup.

"No. I'm fine" I said. "Thank you."

"I swear that little pig has more yellow folders than anyone else on the floor."

"Yellow folders?" I asked.

"Sexual harassment folders." She took her hand away and started preening in the mirror, picking away at her giant lilac wig. "Well, well, well, I don't recognize you," she said. "First day on the floor?" She asked but did not wait for a response. "Yeah, I mean, we can put up with a little bit of it. A joke's a joke, right? But that one takes it too far. Frankly, he abuses his position. Just file a grievance with HR, and they'll open a yellow folder on him." She reached into her pocket, bent in closer to the mirror, and started smearing a tube of lipstick on her lips.

"And then what?" I asked.

"Well, what, by golly, do you mean?" She smacked her lips and admired herself in the mirror, pushing her pug nose into a wrinkled bunch and using a bit of tissue to wipe lipstick off her gleaming white dentures.

"What happens then? After the yellow folder is started?"

"Well, you do a bunch of paperwork. It takes a while. It all has to be signed. And then they put the folder in his permanent file."

"Right. But what does that do?"

"What do you mean, dear? His permanent folder will follow him for eternity!"

"So?"

"So? What are you saying? Am I missing something? What do you mean, so?"

"Well, so what?" I said. "So what if the folder follows him around for eternity? Will he be punished?"

"Oh, dear," the woman said. "You're one of those, are you?"

"One of those whats?"

She took a deep breath. "I think we get off on the wrong foot. Let's start over. Hi, I'm Elizabeth," the woman said, finally introducing herself. "My friends call me Betty."

"Hi, Betty. I'm Karen. Karen Floyd."

"I said my friends call me Betty. You can call me Elizabeth. Ha ha." She laughed. "Just teasing. Come on. You can take a joke, can't you? Big girl like you must be used to a little teasing. You have to be able to take a joke if you're going to work with us."

"Sure, of course I can take a joke," I said. "Ha. Yeah, I'm fine. First day, you know."

"Well then. We're all just a little crazy up here. Never mind us," Betty said. "You'll get used to it soon enough. Give it a week and we'll be best buddies."

"Who is us?" I asked.

"Are you Ted B's new assistant?" Betty answered my question with a question. She turned to me and stuck out her red ruffled sleeves, offering to shake my hand. "Don't let the rumours get to you. Ted's a sweet guy. He really is. And he knows where all the bodies are hidden, if you get my drift."

I took her hand and shook hard, watching the rest of the ruffles on her red outfit shift and shiver with my effort. "Ted B? No." I said as I let go of her. "I'll be working on a project. Professor Norris called me about a portfolio."

Betty released my hand and stepped back. "Well. Whadya you know? By golly. Look at you. A portfolio. Well well well." Her eyes suddenly seemed to go black. "Well well. I say. Look at you. Running with the big dogs. What happened to your foot?"

"My foot?" I tried to hide my bitten foot behind the other. "Nothing. Why do you ask?"

"Where are your shoes?"

"I think that little pervert took them," I said. "He must have a thing for feet."

"Did he bite you?"

"No."

"Your foot. It's bleeding," Betty said.

"No. It's fine."

"Yes. It is bleeding." Betty moved closer to me, her hot breath stinking of coffee and menthol cigarettes, and she whispered into my ear, "I can smell blood."

"Smell blood?" I backed away.

"Among other things," Betty said.

"No. Sorry. You are mistaken, Elizabeth."

"Well. I'm sure it's fine. You can call me Betty. Never mind what I said before. I was just joking. Come on, don't you like jokes?" Betty asked. "I tell ya what: Why don't you go sit on the couches in the lobby and wait for me. When I am through freshening up, I'll give you a quick tour and take you right over to Professor Norris. You can borrow my walking shoes. What size are you?"

"Nine and a half."

She looked down at my feet. "Whew. Big girl. Nobody's going to mistake you for Cinderella, eh? There might be some men's runners in the lost and found. I'll check." Betty laughed. "Big girl. Big dog."

I smiled, laughed along with her a little. "Thanks. Thanks for your help," I said. "I think that would be wonderful."

"Well, okay then?" Betty said.

I imagined Betty with a letter opener jutting from her eye socket and rivers of mascara and blood running down her cheek as she screamed and tried to claw blindly at my face.

Laughing loudly, I turned to her, "Yeah, okay. Cinderella, that's a good one," I said. "Never heard that one before. Ha." And with that, I turned and left Betty alone in the washroom.

666

I stepped out of the blackness of my sick box into the attic loft. I had no idea how it happened, but I was back in the earthly realm. Somehow, I would have to learn how to control this. I followed the sound of voices, down the dark attic stairs and through a door to the upstairs hallway.

"Yeah. That's it. I'm telling you, Alexis. We could do it! I'm not even joking."

I saw Mallory. She was in her parent's bedroom watching the television. She was also listening to her father speaking from downstairs.

I wondered if Mallory could see me?

We heard the tipsy laughter of her mother and the woman that Mallory had barfed on, Alexis, the necks of wine bottles tinkling on the edges of wine glasses. Mallory turned down the sound on the television with the remote. She pulled back the covers and sat up in her parent's bed, the TV casting a blue light over the entire room. Her hair was washed and her yellow nightgown smelled of laundry detergent.

She ran on her tiptoes to the hallway where a mirror was affixed to the wall by the stairs.

She peered around the corner and listened to the adults.

"That's it, then. That's what I'll do for a second career. We'll start up Ms. Vicki again, eh, Dana? Whadya say?"

"As if, Ben," Dana laughed.

Mallory backed away and looked at herself in the mirror. Posing with her hands on her hip and then flexing her biceps, she played muscle man. I walked, well sort of floated, behind her and also looked into the mirror to see if I could recognize myself, to see if I had changed at all. Unlike the last time I was here, I felt like I had some substance and I was in control of it.

In the mirror I looked cartoonish, with big round sad eyes that sparkled and a long devil tail that swished to and fro. Tiny fangs jutted from my smiling mouth. My head was round as a beach ball, my body even more so. I even had little cat whiskers, a cute button nose, and a bright red bow tied to my right horn. I was evil light, a Hello Kitty doll with a black heart. Not exactly what I expected, but yes indeed, I was something, perhaps not the same woman that I was in Hell, but something.

.

Mallory looked up at me, frightened by my sudden appearance (no matter how cute I was).

I smiled at her.

"Are you a dream?" she whispered at the mirror.

"Kind of," I told her, smiling.

Mallory smiled back.

She was so adorable; I could have just eaten her up right then and there. (Hindsight being twenty-twenty, maybe I should have done just that.)

Mallory waved, and I waved back. I placed my gigantic puffy mitt of a hand over her head and her hair stood straight on end. She laughed out loud and clapped her hands. I took my hand away and the hair fell flat. "Do it again," she said. "Do it again."

From downstairs, Ben's voice rose in wild excitement. "Alexis. As God is my witness, there is no reason to question the morality of it."

"Ben, sit down. Have you had too much to drink?" the voice I knew as Dana said.

"Shhh" I raised my balloon index finger to my lips. Together, Mallory and I eavesdropped on the adults. I had not had this much fun in what felt like a million years.

Ben continued: "Pshaw. People do it every day. There's not one honest person left on the planet. And show business is the worst of all."

Dana scoffed. "Oh, as if. What do you know about show business?"

Ben kept on. "Hold on. Hold on. Hear me out. Let me tell you, ever since Milli Vanilli got railroaded, people in the entertainment business saw the flaws in their game and fixed them. Lip syncing is bad, but only if you are two black men from Germany whose grasp of the English language is marginal. If you are white and young and attractive, and you say the right things in a TV interview, then feel free to use autotune and lip sync the hell out of every song someone writes for you."

Dana took another shot at him. "Ben, I think that joint went straight to your head. You're rambling."

"It's fine, Dana," Alexis said. "He's hilarious."

"No. Hold on, Dana. Listen to me here. Hear me out." Ben's voice deepened. "All the sheeple want is an answer to the question: "Why do I hurt?" And they don't care if the answer comes in a can, or is flash frozen, or it's just add water. You know what I'm saying? It's not orange juice. It's better. It's sugar and chemicals. It's the drink of astronauts. What could be better than that?"

"Alexis, next time we'll smoke the joint alone." The girls laughed.

Ben rambled on, "I used to write an advice column for the university paper. Like I was saying. People loved it. I called it Dear Ms. Vicki. Now that I'm unemployed, I should start it up again. You could be Ms. Vicki, Alexis. You could be my Milli Vanilli. What a great idea."

"Jesus, Ben," Dana said. "She's a talented actress. She doesn't need to be Ms. Vicki. I'm sorry, Alexis. He didn't mean to insult you."

"It's fine," Alexis said. "He's funny. Besides, it's the first professional role I've been offered since I left acting school. You're funny, Ben."

"He's not being funny," Dana countered. "He's serious. He's been talking about Ms. Vicki for a few weeks now. Haven't you, Ben?"

"Listen. Hear me out," Ben said." It's not a bad idea. We get a cable access show."

"Cable access? Isn't that full of losers?" either Dana or Alexis said. I could not tell because the two girls were laughing so hard.

Ben ignored the question: "From there, we move to network TV. Think of the potential. Self-help gurus get PAID. Big time. You know how much people would pay to attend a Ms. Vicki conference? We'll hold it out by the airport and sell T-shirts for thirty bucks apiece. Ten bucks for a ham and cheese sandwich. We're going to make some serious coin. We're going to build the Ms. Vicki brand."

"You know what, Alexis. Just ignore him. He's nuts. What you are doing, Ben, is accepting that severance package work offered you, and first thing Monday morning, you are signing up for that Risk Management course. Forget about silly Ms. Vicki. Just sit down."

"Ag. You are the most unsupportive spouse in the world," Ben said.

"Come on now, children," Alexis laughed. "Are my clothes dry yet?"

"You're not a dream," Mallory said, staring at me in the mirror momentarily before sticking her fingers in her mouth and pulling apart her lips, sticking out her tongue, and waggling it at me. I did the same. My mouth opened wide, huge, and instead of my tongue, a vision appeared in the entire length of the mirror, a vision of Ferris wheels, bumper cars, fun houses, and endless carnival lights, with toothless and tattooed barkers hacking on cigarettes and calling upon the unwitting rubes to come on up and 'win a prize.' Circus music played and balloons of myriad colours went floating up, up to the endless red sky. I shut my mouth. The vision disappeared. Mallory stood in awe.

How did I do that? I wondered. There were so many

questions that I wanted answers for, but I knew that I would never get them.

From downstairs we heard: "But you can't develop a cult of personality without a face. Alexis Warrington, YOU should be the face of Ms. Vicki. Listen, I already contacted this guy from Dream Makers Publishing House."

"You DID not!" Dana said.

Ben ignored her: "He said my best option is to do a POD book, that's print on demand book, and then we control the supply. We fill orders. We get it into bookstores. After that, we dive headlong into the cesspool that is North American culture. What is a cult but a slice of culture? I'm not playing games here. We can turn Ms. Vicki into a cult. Not a bad cult either. Not the kind of cult where people take a razor to their genitals while singing Kumbaya. We're not going to encourage 12-year-olds to marry sixty-year-old men. We're not building secret bunkers and stockpiling weapons behind barbed wire fences. Cult. Culture. It is a cult of personality. It's all laid out for us. It's advertising. It's branding. It's a look. It's a way of life. With the fashion sense of a dictator and a ream of corny slogans. We take the profits from the book and we re-invest it. We hold two-day conferences out by the airport. We fill a stage with flamboyant designers, prophets of clean-living and holistic medicine, faith-filled celebrities, folksy life coaches, rare and exotic gurus. We follow this up with a timely hug, and send the crowds tearing into their wallets in a pitched frenzy."

"Okay, Ben. You are officially nuts," Alexis said. "But you do have a way with words. I will give you that."

Dana laughed, this shrill, emasculating laugh that seemed to send a shudder through the entire house.

"Slogans. Catch phrases. That's what it's all about." Ben ignored them both because at this point he was really only talking to himself anyway. "Injecting nonsensical pseudo spiritual venom into the veins of a society that desperately needs our help. We're all so sad. And they will find such solace in what Ms. Vicki will have to say. An honest woman, her anti-intellectual homespun verve, her mental ramblings and ebullient laugh. She'll say things like, 'We are you," and "Your journey begins today,' or 'Set goals in life, but know that one goal is never enough to win a game.' I just made that up now. I have an entire booklet of them. Over four hundred nonsensical catchphrases."

Alexis laughed loudly.

"Ben, I've really had enough of this talk. I'm serious," Dana said. "You are signing up for the Risk Management course if I have to drag you down there myself and you're getting a new job. I'm sorry Alexis. Thank you for

47

entertaining my insane husband, but it's time to get back to reality. I want to apologize. We were supposed to meet tonight to discuss our little community theatre's production of The King and I, and here you are half-naked in a robe watching my drunken, stoned husband making a fool of himself. You have been barfed on by my daughter and bored to tears by this silly man of mine. I am sorry."

"Dana, it's fine," Alexis said. "Ben. I love the way you think. I believe people should take chances, and if Ms. Vicki is truly your dream you should go for it. It's your passion. I can tell. We're all gifted in our own way."

Dan laughed. "Yeah, he's gifted all right. He's very special."

Ben's tone raised in excitement. "See. See, Dana. I tell you, I am. I am gifted. And you can laugh at me all you want, but for years you've been given the gift of me! You don't see that. You never have. I should write that one down. The gift of me. Where's that pen?"

Mallory took her fist and raised it in the mirror. I raised my arm and fist as well in this game of copycat. She smiled. I smiled. She tried to wink. I tried to wink. Then with her fist presented, she slowly raised her middle finger. I laughed. My entire belly nearly burst with laughter.

"What was that?" Dana was startled.

"I don't know."

"What a creepy sound."

"It sounded like howling wolves," Alexis said.

"Coming from inside the house?" Dana wondered. "You need to check those pipes, Ben. I told you there was something wrong with the plumbing."

"It's fine. Just finish your wine."

"It's freezing in here all of a sudden. What's your AC turned to?"

"Ben, can you go check on Mallory?"

"And what's that smell?"

"Oh, come on. She's fine," Ben said. "She's asleep. What's going to happen to her? You know what we should do? We should play Scattergories."

"Ben. Please," Dana implored.

Mallory scooted back to her bed, her tiny feet flitting across the hardwood floors (oh, Alice), stuffing herself beneath the covers.

Left standing alone in the mirror, I looked at myself. I was no longer that cartoonish devil, the Hello Kitty devil. My eyes glowed a fearsome yellow with red pupils, and my teeth were grey and pointed. Although most of my body was in shadow, I could make out my cloven hooves and the dry, greyish-green naked skin that hung reluctantly to my bony frame. The worst were my fingers and hands, bony with flesh that seemed to be melting off, no blood, no muscle or sinew, just hanging grey skin. I had had such nice hands when I was alive.

Ben came up the stairs past me. "Mallory, did you hear a noise?"

Mallory, feigning sleep, turned towards him. "Daddy?" she said.

"I thought you were asleep. What are you watching?"

"Caillou."

"Is it good?"

"Yes."

"That's hard to believe. You can't sleep in Mom and Dad's bed tonight, okay Mal?" Ben reached down and kissed her on the head.

"Awwww. Please, Daddy. Please."

"Come on now. Enough of that. What did I tell you about begging? Does your belly still hurt?"

"Maybe," Mallory said. "My foot hurts now. It's itchy. I think something is biting me."

"Scooch over." Ben sat on the edge of the bed as Mallory made room for him. "Nothing is biting you. Let me see." Ben took Mallory's foot from beneath the covers and began rubbing it.

"Daddy," Mallory asked.

"Yes, baby?"

"When I grow up, you and I will be married." Mallory started squirming and fidgeting nervously. "And you are going to be young forever. We will have a wedding and have babies. I want a girl, but God will probably never give me a girl. So I should lie to God and tell him that I want a boy and then he will make me a girl." An evil smile blossomed over her face as she said it.

A host cut in my own deceitful image.

"That sounds great, Mallory," Ben said. "But I've got some bad news. You can't marry your Daddy. I am already married to Mommy."

"But I love you."

"Mommy loves me too, though, and we are already married, so I can't marry anybody else. There's laws you know."

"If you and Mommy love each other so much then why do you two shout at each other?"

"Mommies and Daddies sometimes fight. It's normal."

"Why don't you go to work anymore, Daddy?"

"Daddy had some problems at work. But he's going to take a course in Risk Management and get a better job. Or maybe he will write a book or something. Who knows? But you shouldn't worry. Maybe even one day we'll live in a big mansion in a nice neighbourhood and we'll have a pool and a games room with a ping pong table and pinball machines and a big screen TV to watch the baseball games on. And Granny and Papa can visit anytime and go swimming with you. You'll go to good schools where there's a kiss and ride. And you'll go to university."

"But I don't want to move. I like our house. Don't leave me, Daddy. Sleep with me."

"I won't leave you. I'll never leave you. If I leave you, I would die. My heart would split in two. But you can't marry me. Okay? You'll have to grow up and find a nice person to marry. Someone smart and gentle and kind who treats you with respect. But I love you, and I will always be your Daddy."

"And you'll never leave me?"

"Never."

"Never ever?"

"I will never leave you. Not even the biggest monster in the world could take me away from you. Nothing in Heaven, or Hell, could ever take you away from me."

"I love you, Daddy."

"I love you too. Now, get to bed. Little girls should not be up this late."

"Will you sleep with me tonight? I'm scared."

"Honey, how many times do I have to tell you? There's nothing to be scared of. This is your house. It is the safest place in the world. I am going to do the dishes, and I'll be up in a while. You go sleep in your own bed with your stuffies and your dollies. There is nothing to be scared of. Think nice thoughts."

"My foot hurts, Daddy. Can you rub it? On the heel. It feels like something is biting me."

From downstairs: "Ben," Dana called up. "Alexis's clothes are dry. She's going home."

"Shoot," Ben said to Mallory. "I wanted to play Scattergories." He turned his head and yelled, "I'll be right down." Back to Mallory: "I'll come and rub your foot later, baby. I have to go. Our guest is leaving. There's nothing to be scared of." Ben took the TV remote from the nightstand and turned off the television. He picked up Mallory in his arms and carried her to her room. Setting her gently in her bed, he pulled the covers up to her neck and kissed her on the forehead. "Goodnight, baby." He turned, and left the room, flipping the light switch as he went. "I love you."

As Ben left, he walked right past me. I was standing in the corner of Mallory's room, watching him. It felt like I should probably be getting back to the office, but there was something that I needed to do. Mallory's room was so bland. Such a dull room for Mallory to sleep in. There were no pictures on the wall, the flooring was dull old wooden planks, and the walls were yellow. I thought maybe it would be a good idea to surprise Mallory. I noticed a box of crayons on the floor by her dresser, and I bent to grab them. The first time I reached for them, my hand passed right through, but the second time, I concentrated a little harder and I was able to pick them up. That had to be a good sign. I was getting closer to the earthly realm. My plan was to draw some nice pictures for my poor host. Something to cheer her up. If the horror movies I watched when I was alive were any indication, the next few weeks were not going to be pleasant for her. She might need some cheering up.

It was dark in the room, but the streetlight shining through the window cast enough light for me to draw my wall mural. I drew little flowers, and rainbows, farmhouses, trees with birds in them. I drew kittens dressed in pretty long dresses, carrying parasols. They strolled arm in arm beside their farmer cat husbands. Oversized mice were dancing and strumming on fiddles. A cartoon utopia. When I was done, I stood back and admired the sweet drawing. *I never want to go back to Hell*, I told myself.

"Wake up."

"No," I said. "I don't want to."

"Wake up."

666

"Wake up."

"Huh?"

"Karen. Wake up."

My eyes slowly became accustomed to the light in the executive lobby. Somehow, I had fallen asleep on their couches. My body was back to normal: two horns, one devil tail, a woman's body with shaved armpits and legs dressed in proper beige business attire - minus the shoes.

"Did you fall asleep?" Betty asked.

"No. No," I said. "I'm fine."

"Good. Because that's not the kind of first impression you want to make." Betty's mountainous head of lilac-coloured hair seemed to tower over me as I sat up and checked my surroundings.

In front of me, three receptionists sat behind what could only be described as a dais. One was beautiful and young. She was eating miniature cupcakes from a plastic tray and laughing as she twirled her blond hair around her earpiece.

"Of course, I'm as cute as I sound," I heard her say.

The receptionist on the opposite end of the young one was old and wrinkled. She had a pink wash in her permed hair. Raising her palsied hand and pointing her finger, she said, "Let me transfer you," striking her finger downwards to stab the buttons on her switchboard.

Between the two was a middle-aged woman eating carrot and celery sticks from a giant Tupperware container. She worked frantically pressing buttons, tears of self-pity streaming down her face as she shifted from one call to the next. "Naraka Corporation. Please hold. Naraka Corporation. Please hold. Naraka Corporation. Please hold." Her face was getting a little fat, I noticed, and she appeared to be going bald. She wore a lot of makeup and sweated beneath spotlights that lit up the company sign high above the dais. In massive gold and silver letters it read "NARAKA CORPORATION."

A steady stream of men in jumpsuits came out from a door by the young woman. They were pushing wheelbarrows, and in the wheelbarrows, they had shovels. They walked behind the dais with their wheelbarrows and began shoveling some mystery substance up off the floor. Once their wheelbarrows were full, they wheeled them off through a door on the other end by the old woman.

It was an unusual scene, even for Hell, and I wondered what department the wheelbarrow men worked for.

"You were asleep." Betty's fingers, more like talons, rested on my shoulder. "I'm surprised all of you fit on that couch. You must be tired."

"Sorry," I said, brushing Betty's hand off my shoulder. I stood and straightened my skirt. "Let me show you around," Betty said. She started walking and I followed, my bare feet brushing along the lush golden carpet emblazoned with the company logo, NARAKA, in the deepest vermillion, with a three-headed fire-breathing beast, reptile, canine, porcine, holding a battle axe in one hand and its giant erection in the other.

As we walked towards a doorway, I got a chance to peer behind the dais. Behind the dais was the lower half of a very large goat that branched out into the three torsos of the young woman, the old woman, and the middle-aged woman. They were all one beast, and a steady stream of large pebbled feces dropped from its rear end. That's what the men with the wheelbarrows and shovels were picking up and wheeling away.

"Follow me," Betty said. "It's time for the potluck."

"Potluck?"

What did you bring?" Betty asked.

"Well, nothing...I just got...I didn't know about any..."

"Well, Hell low, lovely Betty," one of the wheelbarrow men said as he stopped to chat. "Hell low to you too, Ron," Betty responded. "How are we doing today?"

"Not too bad. Not too bad." Ron's wheelbarrow was teeming with goat turds.

As Betty stopped to chit chat, I noticed a letter opener resting on the corner of the receptionist's desk, and I reached up to grab it. Thankfully, no one noticed as I stuffed the letter opener up my sleeve.

"Nakara Corporation. Please hold."

"Well, keep up the good work, Ron. Nice seeing you again."

"Okay. Have a good day, then."

"That was Ron," Betty said as we started walking again. "His wife's having an affair with his supervisor. Everybody knows but him. So what'd you bring for the potluck?"

"Well, nothing. I didn't know there was a potluck," I said.

Betty sighed, "Don't you read your emails, Karen? You have to keep up with your emails around here, honey, or you'll be eaten alive. Like, I mean it. They throw you in a pit with giant flesh-eating rats. And there's plenty of you to eat, so it might take a while."

"I don't even have a computer yet. How could I read my emails?" I said to Betty.

"Listen, Karen." Betty stopped me as we stood by the elevators. "It's Karen, right?"

Elevators, I wondered. *I didn't know there were elevators in this building. I just walked up 170 flights of stairs.*

"Yeah. Karen."

"Listen, Karen. You might have been a firecracker in that call centre downstairs, but this is the big time. The executive floor."

"I was in sales."

"Well, whatever. Up here, they play hardball, big girl. No excuses. I'll tell you right now, no one, least of all Professor Norris, has time for excuses. Tuesday and Wednesdays, and every third Friday, there's a potluck. It's organized by the social committee. Put it on your calendar. All social committee events are mandatory. It's team building. Bad things happen if you don't attend. And this is a Friday too. The Boss is at this one. She always comes to the Friday potlucks."

"The Boss?" My knees shook.

"Yes, the Boss. The Boss of Bosses. The Slayer of Men.

The Great Deceiver. The Quarterback and Coach. The
Purveyor of Grief and Pestilence. Evil incarnate. Our great
and fearless leader, Satan. The Nameless Terror."

A shiver ran down my spine. "Well, what do I do?"

"I tell you what. I've got some Little Wanda cakes in my
office. You know Little Wanda, right? Looks like you've
made a box or two vanish in your time eh, big girl? Am I
right?" Betty laughed, "My husband, Richard, loves them.
He always tells me that he is having an affair with Little
Wanda. It's fine. Come to my office. We'll unwrap them,
put them on a plate, and nobody will know the difference.
They'll think you baked them."

"And you have shoes?"

"Yes, I'll get you some shoes too."

I didn't see how passing the Little Wanda cakes off as
home baking was going to be possible. (Little Wanda cakes
were the only sweets you could get in Hell. They had the
texture of memory foam and tasted like carpet cleaner
covered in a layer of cheap waxy chocolate). But I had no
one else to trust and no information to base my own
decisions on. My fate was in the hands of this woman,
Betty, so I followed her down the hallway to her office. We
passed a window on the way. It was snowing heavily, as
usual. It would be a tough bike ride home tonight. If

quitting time, five o'clock, ever came, which most days it did not.

"Who did this?"

Someone was shouting. I heard someone shouting. Maybe from behind one of the doors in the hallway? Maybe from outside even? It was difficult to tell. Betty's mouth was moving, but all I heard was:

"Come on! We know you did this!"

666

Have you ever, in your life, experienced one of those times where you thought you were helping someone, you thought you were doing someone a favour, and it turned out to be an unmitigated disaster? All the creamed corn you made from scratch attracted wasps and ruined the picnic? The person you knitted the scarf for was deathly allergic to that cheap yarn you bought at the liquidation store? Their throat swelled up, and they ended up in hospital? The Christmas decorations you made started the house on fire? The joke you played made your sister cry? You weren't being mean. It was just funny. Everyone was supposed to laugh.

"Come on! We know you did this!"

In the morning light of the earthly realm, I crawled from my sick box and followed the sound of voices to Mallory's room.

Mallory looked like a toy blending into the sea of dolls and stuffies on her bed. A single tear streamed down her sorrowful face. Dana, Ben, and Mallory were all staring at the mural I had drawn on the wall. *Oops*, I thought, as I too took a look.

"Who did this?" Dana said to Mallory.

"What do you mean who did this?" Ben jumped in. "Mallory did it. Who else? Mal, you are going to be punished for this."

"I didn't do it. The Hello Kitty did it."

"Oh, okay. You're blaming it on your stuffy now? Stuffies get up in the middle of the night, take your crayons and draw all over your wall?" Ben said.

"No. The one in the mirror," Mallory countered. "She was bigger than me and had a tail. And horns on her head. She's magic. She makes clowns appear. Bad clowns with sharp knives. And they use cigarettes."

"Cigarettes? Where the Hell are you coming up with this stuff?" Dana petitioned the universe for answers.

"Come on, Mallory. What did I tell you about lying?" Ben railed. "You lie to me again and it's no TV until after lunch!"

"I'm NOT LYING." Mallory flung herself down on her pillow.

"Ben. Look at this. Do you really think that she did this? I don't think my daughter would do this," Dana said.

"Could do this."

"But she did, honey. Who else did it? Me? You? Do you think the cat did it? Or someone broke in here last night and drew all over the wall?"

Dana looked very confused. "I don't know, Ben. I just don't know. But how could she do all this? She's just learning to read. She still can't write her letters properly. And look: It clearly says right there on the wall, *Karen. Right there. Karen is coming.* It says. Right there. Look. Read it. Mallory still writes her Ks backwards. I tried to teach her the proper way to do it the other day. But look. There's a perfect K. Right there. Look at it. Karen. Who the hell is Karen? There's no way Mallory could have written that. And to further my point, Mallory's drawings are of rainbows and flowers and everyone is holding hands. There are birds in the sky. She is not Hieronymus Bosch. Look here. There are flowers sticking out that cat's ass, and speaking of asses, that one is about to be sodomized, and that cat there is going to be beheaded. Look, the white one. And to my knowledge, this child has never seen anyone's giant, erect penis, either. At least, she better not have! All the cats have giant penises and testicles. And tits. Tits everywhere. Did she just make that up? Oh, God. Is this worse than I thought? Is someone molesting her? One of your creep friends? Who's that piece of filth you had over here the other weekend? The one you knew in university? Brad? What's his number? Maybe he did this?"

Ben rolled his eyes. "Jesus Christ, Brad did not do this. He's on a fishing trip. There was no one in here last night, and Mallory is not being molested. She did this, Dana. Mallory, just admit that you did this."

Mallory's face turned all red, and she summoned all her strength to rail against the machine that was her parents. "NO. I DIDN'T DO IT. THE HELLO KITTY DID."

I thought I'd drawn a nice painting, sigh, with happy little farmer cats in a field. Nothing ever goes right for me. The cats were supposed to be tending to farmland and strolling arm in arm on cobbled paths, but somehow, the kittens and flowers I drew turned into giant phalluses and cats sodomizing other cats. Fart bubbles coming out of their arses with stink lines. I guess what I learned in that online 'Professional Communications' course was true: "The most important thing about communication is hearing what could be said." Poor Mallory. I would make it up to her. She was staring at me now. She pointed at me.

"She's right there," Mallory said. "She looks like a sheep now."

Dana wasn't listening to her. She was trying to tear Ben

another asshole. "Why do you always have to be right, Ben? What do you get out of it? You wanna win? Go ahead and win. It doesn't solve any of our problems if I can't have a say."

The serve.

"She's right there!" Mallory repeated herself.

"Win?"

The volley.

"This is lunacy, Dana. No one broke in here and drew on the wall. Maybe she copied it from a picture? Search around. She did have that one book that your sister got her for Christmas. We never really looked at it. Pam is so weird. Who knows what kind of filth she got her. Mallory, where's that book that Aunt Pam got you for Christmas?"

"Daddy! She's right there."

"Who's there. Pam? What are you talking about? Where?"

Dana started again. "Leave Pam out of it. I can't help it if you don't like Pam. And I can't explain it, Ben, but something happened in here. My daughter has never seen a beheading before, or a cat with a giant erection. And God help me if she has. You don't just make crap like this up."

"THERE!" Mallory said.

"I understand your feelings, Dana. She must have seen it

on the internet or something. I want to help you work through this…'

"Don't talk to me like I need counselling, Ms. Vicki!" Dana barked. "Something weird happened here, Ben, and you need to get your head out of the fucking clouds. You bring all this garage sale stuff home. We don't know what it is or who had it before."

"What are you saying?"

"That weird piece of shit box, that sick box. What is that fucking thing, anyway? I don't like it. It's fucking weird."

"HEY!" Ben scolded her. "Watch your language in front of our daughter!"

"BULLSHIT!" Dana shouted. "Every time we have a fight you talk to me like I am mentally ill. I don't want that. I don't want that box, but you brought it home anyway. It's creepy. And you're so condescending. I need you to back me up. I need you to go to work. I need you to stop shooting me down in front of my daughter. She needs to learn to respect me. I am not a crazy person who needs counselling. Maybe you're the one who needs help? You ever think of that? Your newfound obsession with this old column you wrote in the university newspaper fifteen years ago is weird."

"Oh, come on. You never give me any support. I lost my

job, you know. Are you aware of that? Huh? How about a little sympathy? A little respect. A kind word would go a long way. All you ever tell me is to pick myself up and get another job. It's not that easy you know. Maybe reminiscing about good times when I was a happy productive human being is all I have left."

"You know you made an ass of yourself last night in front of my friend!"

Ben said nothing.

"Listen." Dana took a deep breath. "I'm sorry, Ben. I didn't mean that. You were fine. This is upsetting though. There is no way that our daughter drew this. So that leaves us with some very upsetting questions: Who was in here last night? Should we call the police?"

"Jesus, Dana," Ben said. "Nobody was in here. Stop it. It's normal for kids to draw on the wall. They all do it. You're losing it."

Men are so stupid.

Mallory's loud whimpering cut through the room.

"Mallory, it's okay," Ben said. "Stop crying. Dana, come on. Look at what you are doing here. Stop it."

Dana did not stop. "Stop? Me? Stop? I should stop? I need help? I'm the one that needs help?"

"Yeah, stop," Ben said. "Why are you attacking me?

Why has this become personal? Look what you've done, Dana. She's crying now. Mallory, it's all right."

"Maybe, if I need so much 'help,' as you say, why don't you help me then? Huh? Ben. Help me. You wanna help me? And help your daughter? Help her. She needs clothes and money for her lunches when she goes to school in the fall. She needs toys for her birthday. And swimming lessons. How are we going to pay our mortgage with one income? You selfish jerk. Why aren't you in the unemployment line right now? Why aren't you signing up for that Risk Management course? Because you got downsized, right? You told me you got downsized. You're eligible for unemployment insurance, right? Or was that a lie? Did you get fired? I think maybe you got fired."

Ben stood still and just shook his head. He was having one of those man moments. Those moments when a man realizes that he is in way deeper than he ever thought he'd get. He was thinking: *Why did I have a family? Why did I get married? Why did I buy a house? Why didn't I just run off to Hollywood when I was young and slim and had a full head of hair?* He was wondering how it all happened, how this simple event, of a kid drawing on her wall, something all kids do, turned into a screaming match in front of his weeping five-year old? None of this was healthy, but he could take none of it back. He couldn't make this go away. It had already happened, and the damage was done. Permanently done. I'd seen that look on men's faces before.

"Dana, come on. Why would I lie about something like that? Why would I lie at all? I don't want to take that risk management course. It sounds boring. I'll find something else. I promise. Mallory. It's okay." Ben sat on the bed. "Do you need your bucket, hon? You look a little green. Do you need to go to the washroom? You going to puke again?"

Dana kept on at his heels: "Because I am your wife, and I know you. I can tell when you are lying. Something's not right. I can call them you know. I can call your work."

"Don't do that, Dana. Listen, this is all about your aggression towards me. I know the job thing seems tough right now, but life's about living. You're going to thank me one day. I know it. Sometimes a person just has to stop and take a breath."

"Life's about living? Your life's about living. Apparently. Because my life is about working and paying the mortgage while you piss around the house and ignore your responsibilities."

A retching sound filled the room (mercifully, in my mind, for it was much easier on the ears than the bickering of those two).

"Oh, God! There she goes again." Ben scrambled to the other side of the bed, grabbing a bucket.

"Get her to the washroom. QUICK," Dana shouted.

"For God sakes. How much puke is in this kid?" Ben was gagging and trying to look away from Mallory as she spewed green vomit into a black bucket. When she was finished, she laid back on her pillow, her face a greyish green, tears running down her cheeks.

"Go downstairs and get another bucket," Dana said, hurrying to the child's side. "Get some towels. The Clorox. Ben, should we take her to the emergency room?"

"I don't know. I think so. Yes. I think so."

"Fine. Pack her bag. And hurry up. Oh my, God. It reeks. Empty that bucket."

Ben followed orders and left the room with the puke bucket.

"Momma?"

"Yes, dear?" Dana said, holding Mallory tightly to her breast and wiping off her chin with a tissue.

"My foot hurts."

"I know, baby. Where?"

"The bottom. On the heel. The heel. It hurts. She is biting me."

(Biting is such a strong word. Nibbling, maybe? I

couldn't help myself. She was just so damn cute.)

"No, honey. Nothing is biting you."

"Yes, she is biting me."

"We're going to take you to the doctor.

Ben called from downstairs: "DANA. Where's her bag?"

"I'm going to go help Daddy, okay?" Dana said. "Okay? Is this you, Mallory Justine? Am I really talking to you?"

"Yes, Momma."

"Why did you draw on the wall?"

"I didn't do it."

"Well, if you didn't do it, who did?"

"Karen."

"Who's Karen?"

"She's the one biting my foot."

"Why is she doing that? Who is she?"

"She wants to become me. I don't want to share you with her, Momma. She wants to be a little girl too. Like me. She wants me to share myself. She came last night. I thought she was nice. But maybe she's not."

"MALLORY? What do you mean? I don't understand. Stop crying, baby, and talk to Momma."

"Dana! Where are the goddamn car keys?"

Dana took Mallory in her arms and hugged her tightly.

I heard Ben's feet on the stairs, and he came bounding

back into the room carrying a little Hello Kitty suitcase.

"Okay, let's go," he said.

666

"Come on. Can you keep up? It must feel good for you to get some exercise. Don't worry. We'll whip you into shape up here. Let's go. Come on. We don't want to be late for the potluck."

If there's anything worse than a work potluck, I don't know what it is. Wait. Zombies. They are worse, but not by much. Worst things about Hell:

1. Zombies
2. Acronyms
3. Potlucks

I hurried behind Betty, struggling to keep up with her. I was carrying a tray of brownies that looked like they were made of plastic and belonged in a child's playset. The tray itself might have actually been tastier. This was no way to make a good first impression on the rest of the team.

Betty, a good twenty yards ahead of me, veered left into a room. I followed her into the lunchroom, ill-fitting men's size ten running shoes that we poached from the lost and found slapping on my feet.

There was a nervous energy in the lunchroom. Call it discomfort, uneasiness. People seemed jittery and the room smelled of brewed coffee and bad breath. I could almost taste it. To a man, this group needed a mint. My zombie-bitten foot started to throb, and I felt self-conscious. I tried to shrink myself, to little or no avail.

Betty abandoned me in favour of her friends almost immediately. She was a shotgun blast of pleasantries: "Oh, hi. How are you, dear? Nice to see you. How's your husband? Did he find work yet? And look at you? Where've you been hiding yourself? Still going to Waist Watchers. It shows. You look amazing. How's the kids? Still working on the Lindwood Deal? And what direction is that heading? And your lab work? Thanks for organizing this. The social committee is doing such a great job. Yes, everything is wonderful. Oh, Sam. So nice to see you. Why it's been, what? An hour or more? Ha ha ha. Look, it's my partner in crime. No. We put the Warren file on the backburner for now. Tom's digging up the peripherals. We'll move on it in the morning. Rhonda, you look beautiful as always." The words and conversations all indistinguishable from one another as Betty was swept away, absorbed into the foul stew of conversational platitudes.

I set my tray down beside Betty's. I noticed there were little white cards folded like a pup tent and placed on top of the cellophane that covered each and every dish. On the cards, everyone had written their name. "Prepared by *Joe Smith,* Accounting Team." I took a card off the table and wrote my name on it. "Prepared by Karen Floyd, External Communications Team," and I switched it with the card on Betty's dish.

If you want to spend the rest of eternity working in Food Services and making minimum wage, you can be fair-minded and trusting, make all the safe choices, but if you want to succeed, you have to make a few enemies along the way. Such is my theory about survival in business.

There was no doubt that Betty was trying to screw me with those brownies anyway. I just returned her serve.

A man standing beside me nodded. "Hi," he said. He had obviously seen what I had done.

"Hi," I said back, pretending that nothing had happened.

"Your first day on the executive floor?" He asked, small talking it up.

I did not answer.

"Mine too." He was an older man, with a slim body and

a freshly shaven chin. He was dressed in a tailored blue suit jacket with a shiny red lining. He sported a painfully obvious, and dusty, toupee over his horns.

The door opened suddenly, and someone shouted, "Avert your eyes!"

The entire room fell to bended knee.

"Hail Satan! Hail Satan!" The drone began.

"Oh, my," a voice said. "Please stand. Stop being silly. We are all equal here, people."

I was in the same room as Satan. It did not seem real.

"Come on everyone, stand up. Stand up. No one deserves this much attention or adoration. Stand up." Her voice was loud and seemed friendly.

"Hail, Satan."

"Come on, people. Stand up. There's no need for this. Please. Just stand up."

The man with the toupee shuffled from his genuflecting to two feet and stood up.

"YOU!" Satan's friendly voice changed to an enraged wail. "Don't you love me?"

"Hail Satan," up went the chant.

"How could you do that? I only want what is mine. Thomas. Thomas Ambler. Yes, I know you. I know all my staff. Why do you wear that wig on your head? What are you hiding?"

"This is my hair!"

"Liar! I can read your thoughts. I can see them. They are sick. You are sick. Paranoid. Distrustful. With low self-esteem. Yet you scored ten out of ten on the narcissist test. When you were alive you wrote a treatise. A ream of paper full of your thoughts. Full of perversions and scenes of violence and you made jokes about people's lives, as if you were superior to them. It was negative. You are a pessimist. This is why you are here, coward."

"No. A realist. I am a realist."

"HAIL SATAN."

"Narcissistic. Pig. You have a bad attitude. LIES. DECEPTION. HYPOCRITE. BAD ATTITUDE. PESSIMIST. COWARD."

"No one ever read it. My wife wouldn't even read it. It was a satire! I swear it. Life is beautiful. I want it back."

"That's what they all say. And I say this to you, Mr. Thomas Ambler, I say this: Your satire is vicious and evil, nothing but poorly veiled hostility towards the world. You would be so much happier if you just acted like everyone else."

"But ..."

"All I want is your love. How could you do this to me?

Take him. Teach him to love me. Take him for the test."

"NO!" The man named Ambler cried as I watched him being dragged away on his heels. "No."

"Adjust his attitude. It is for the best," Satan said.

Other than a brief scuffle in the doorway, the faint cries of Mr. Thomas Ambler shouting, "NO NO NO," the bitter weeping of Satan, and the crunching of potato chips being eaten, there was no sound in the lunchroom. I stayed genuflecting and staring at the ground until I heard others around me stand, and when it was clear that no one else was going to be taken away, I stood and got my first glimpse of Her and Her entourage.

Before me, the great beast, Satan, stood. A big woman, a giant woman in fact, three feet taller than the tallest man in the room and every bit as wide as a Volkswagen. She wore a Hawaiian-printed muumuu, and her jet-black, afro hair was combed painfully straight, burned to a crisp with straightening chemicals and a flat iron. Her skin changed colour depending on who she was standing next to: from white to brown to bluish black. On her shoulder rode the bald man who had filmed me in the washroom. Surrounding Satan were a number of characters wearing expensive-looking grey suits and sporting fearsome dog masks. (Or were they masks?) There was a Doberman, a pit bull, and a Chihuahua.

"Well," Satan said. "Let's get past this unpleasantness. Before we begin the lunch inspection, let's send a little wisdom the way of Mr. Thomas Ambler, for we are not born broken, someone, or something, breaks us along our journey. Mr. Ambler, go back to being perfect, seek out love, know that the universe has a plan for you, and find your pieces. Without them, you cannot glue yourself back together."

There was a pause, as if she were waiting for a chorus to sing "amen," but there was none of that.

"People," Satan continued, "he will take the colours test and find his pieces. It is not a punishment. It is a gift." She slowly waddled over to the table where all the dishes rested.

Everyone got out of Her way as quickly as they were able to. "What do we have here?" Satan took the name off the first dish and read. "Laura Boyd. Finance. Let's see what you brought, Laura." She peeled back the cellophane covering the dish. "Oh, that smells wonderful. What is that? Kale salad. With Raisins. And what are those? Walnuts?"

"Yes," came a meek voice at the back of the room that belonged to Laura Boyd (I assumed). She was a mousey thing with thin brown hair who shuddered when she was called upon. "We drove all night to get them. We were attacked by a zombie horde in the parking lot of the megaplex. Our son lost his arm at the elbow."

"That's wonderful, Laura. Thank you so much. I am so happy to see that you care so much about your team. Thank you. See, people! See? Remember this for your performance review, Laura."

"Hail Satan," Laura said.

"Oh, stop. What else do we have? Pete Starr. What did you bring this time, Pete? It's your quinoa salad with the light Russian dressing. (Russian salad dressing was all you could get in Hell.) Oh, it's such an appetizing colour. You know that's one of my favorites. Thank you. And Mike from HR. What did you bring? A green salad. You know, you can't go wrong with a nice green salad. And you brought a nice Russian dressing. My favorite. Again. It's like my birthday. And let's see here: Full fat. Oh my! How decadent. Oh, it sounds delectable, but Mike, although I appreciate the effort, maybe next time, let's go for the light Russian dressing. You know a full fat dressing can lead to obesity and heart disease. It's a good try, but we must eat healthy if we want to live for the rest of eternity. And I want all my team to be healthy. You've got a lot of work to do. And what do we have here? Betty. Oh, Betty. My best girl, Betty. What wonderful concoction have you brought us today? Your hair looks wonderful, by the way. What do I see? A treat? How bold. Let me guess. Healthy, flourless brownies, made with pumpkin mash and sweetened with agave? They look a little weird. Are these store bought?"

"Brownies? No. No. No," Betty said. "No. I didn't bring brownies. Mine's the minted broccoli with chia seeds. Zero fat. Zero fat! Zero carbs."

"No, Betty. Your name is on the brownies," Satan said." See?"

"No. That's not mine."

"Are these? They can't be?" Satan peeled off the edge of the plastic wrap and picked up a brownie between her index finger and thumb. She brought it to her nose and sniffed. "Sugar? ARGH! NO!" She dropped it as if it were a hot turd. "How dare you, Elizabeth. How dare you! Are you trying to kill me?"

"No. I wouldn't. I swear it. She did it." Betty pointed at me, twitching with hatred, vitriolic bombs of spittle exploding from her lips. "She switched names. I would never. Hail Satan!"

"All hail Satan!" I shouted.

"You, Betty Mick, are trying to kill me. You know what is in that? Triglycerides, sugar, salt. Wheat! Wheat is the silent killer. Researchers at The Health Institute for Natural Research discovered that wheat is the cause of 100 different deadly diseases. Typhus, Hang Sang disease, Rubella, Ingsmare Barre disease, and the main cause of Wheat Belly. No one should be eating wheat. What you have brought to me is diabetes in the shape of a rectangle. You might as well have served us a packet of **cigarettes**."

"AG!" Everyone gasped at the word.

It was then that I noticed where the sound of the chip munching was coming from. Satan had two faces. Yes, she had two faces. I had never seen that before, and it was quite startling.

While one face, the face she spoke from, could be seen in the normal place faces should be, between her forehead and her throat, the other one was at the back of her head, well hidden beneath the straightened hair; and the reason the little bald man was riding on the back of the beast was due to the fact that he, the little bald man, was responsible for shoving food (potato chips for the moment) into the mouth of the second face.

"What is it? Why do you hate me? You want me dead!" Satan railed. "You want my legs amputated, my heart to stop. You want me to DIE. USURPER! You want me to get Ehlers–Danlos syndrome."

"NO. It's not me. She's bit. Karen. She's the one who did it. She switched names."

"LIAR!" Satan screeched. "Take her for the colours test!"

"NO. NO." Betty's cries were shrill and piercing. Two dog-faced minions grabbed her and began dragging her away. "She's been bit," Betty shouted. "She'll kill us all. She's bit. She's the liar. I'll get you, Karen Floyd. I will get even with you."

"What colour is your world, Elizabeth? What colour is your world?" Satan cried. "You need help. Don't bring her back until she is a pink."

"NO. NO. NO. Check her foot. She's bit," I heard Betty's distant cry from the hallway. "No. No. No. Please, God, NO."

I looked around nervously. No one seemed to care much about Betty's cries. They were hungry and just wanted to eat. At the front of the cafeteria, past all the lunch tables, a little enclave, formerly hidden by darkness, came to light. In the enclave, in front of a wall of windows looking out onto the howling, and constant, wind and snow of Hell, sat Satan's throne. The throne was large enough to fit Satan's giant ass and seemed to be made of writhing snakes, rat kings, and bones, grouped and tangled together to form the shape of a chair. Satan went and sat in the big throne. A giant fiery pentagram with a hologram of her glowing, smiling face in the centre of it, suddenly formed above her. The tiny bald man got up on a stepladder behind Satan, lugging a sack with him. He hung the sack on the corner of the fiery pentagram and reached his hand in to grab a handful of chocolate bars. One by one, he unwrapped the chocolate bars and started feeding Satan's second face. While he was doing this, Satan's front face said, "Chip," in reference to the one dog-faced man who looked like a Doberman Pinscher, "fetch me a plate of Laura's salad with the walnuts, will you? It smells wonderful. Not too much dressing. On the side, maybe. Remember, people, small portions. Make sure you only take a teaspoon of dressing. Even if it is low fat, the eggs might raise your cholesterol." The smell of fried chicken suddenly filled the room. "And before we eat, I would like you to all do something for me," Satan continued. "When you go home tonight, write your dreams down on a piece of paper. Then burn them in a fire. Watch the smoke rise up to the sky and be at peace. Write down your dreams again. The same dreams. Lock them in a box. Throw away the key and then throw the box into a lake. Now, one last time. Write down your dreams again and place them in an envelope and give them to the person you love most. Tell them that you will love them forever. That is enough. For as long as you keep your promise, those dreams will never fade."

"..." And again, a pregnant pause filled the room. I felt like we were supposed to sing "amen," but no one was doing it. I wondered where Satan expected people to start a fire or to find a lake; most everyone lived in apartment buildings and all the lakes had been paved over.

"That's from the newest issue of the magazine," Satan offered. "Do you love it?"

"All hail Satan!"

"We must work to inspire, people. That is why we were put here."

Chip came to her and, averting his eyes from The Beast, handed over the salad.

"Oh," she said. "Chip, dear. That is too much. Oh well, it's Friday. Might as well live it up. Right people? Go ahead and eat, people. Don't wait for me." I could smell pizza as the bald man took a pizza box out of his sack. "Chip, will you fetch me a diet soda, please?"

Everyone then jostled for a spot in line. Plates and knives and forks were spread out. I was near the very back.

"I am just so full. I cannot eat this much," Satan said, her plate untouched, and she pushed her salad around with her plastic fork. Chicken wing bones rained to the floor behind her throne. "Oh. I am just so full. I can't finish all this delicious salad. Laura, the kale salad is delicious. You will have to give me the recipe. We'll put it in the magazine."

"Follow me," a voice behind me said.

"Why would I do that?" I asked.

"I'm Professor Norris."

666

"Who keeps texting you?"

Again, I entered the earthly realm via my sick box, but instead of walking about the Matthews' house in search of voices, I was instantly transported to the side of my precious Mallory. (Don't ask me how this stuff works.)

Dana put her phone back into her purse. "Nobody," Dana said. "My sister. Where's that doctor? How long have we been here?"

Ben checked his watch. "Ten hours."

"Jesus, I should have just tried to pick up a shift. I could have been paid for this. Where's that doctor?"

"He'll be here. It's probably just an allergic reaction to something," Ben said.

They were standing in a curtained waiting room at the hospital. Mallory was asleep on a hospital bed while Ben and Dana sat on chairs in the corner. I found myself standing on the opposite side of Mallory. I could see through a gap in the curtain. Across the way, in another curtained room, a woman was leaning against her bed. Blood-soaked meters of gauze were wrapped around her arm. She was slim with ropey muscles and a sinuous, veiny neck, like an athlete, perhaps a cyclist, or a hockey player, someone to whom strength and endurance were important. There was a look of absolute determination and resolve on her pinched yet attractive face. She was pretending that everything was normal and that she was not in the hospital, and she was not scared, and her bleeding arm was merely a blip on the radar, an inconvenience, a light scratch. Her arm itself, however, betrayed her, for it trembled and shook with fear of losing a section or perhaps all of itself to the medical waste barrel. The detached (or soon to be detached) two ignored each other. All of which seemed perfectly reasonable. Sometimes it is only about the flesh.

The sounds of the rhythmically beeping machines and soft-soled footsteps of the nurses wheeling gurneys and wheelchairs all about the premises seemed like a hypnotic dirge.

"Well, at least we are out of triage."

"What does your sister want, anyway?" Ben asked.

"Nothing."

"Dear Ms. Vicki, I am scared my wife is having an

affair. We've been trapped together in a cave for 10 hours, and she is refusing to be honest about who is texting her."

"She wants to know how Mallory is, okay?"

"Again. Dear Ms. Vicki. My sister-in-law suddenly gives a shit about my daughter. No. Seriously, who are you texting? It's not good to keep secrets in a marriage, Dana."

"Christ, can we leave Ms. Vicki out of this, please?" Dana said. "I am getting sick of her."

I wondered how their bickering would go over on the executive floor? The dog-faced security guards would have definitely taken them for the colours test by now. I stroked Mallory's sleeping forearm and watched the goose pimples rise along her skin. My touch must have felt so cold to her. She looked peaceful when she was sleeping, though, and I could not resist. I could watch her sleep all day.

A nurse wheeling a man in a wheelchair stopped across from us and turned the man so that the back of his wheelchair was facing the wall and the man could see in our little curtained enclave. The man immediately locked eyes upon me. His jaw dropped. The loose skin on his hoary face began to flap as he struggled to scream. He raised his ancient bony arm and pointed his finger at me, struggling to get the word "help," (or whatever he was trying to say) out of his cancerous throat.

"What is wrong with this old guy?" Dana asked.

"What?"

"Him. That guy pointing in here. What's his problem? Go shut the curtain all the way."

No sooner had Ben shut the curtain and sat down again than the doctor came whisking in, pushing the curtain aside and leaving it half closed, so we could see the rude old man still pointing at me and shaking.

"Well, what seems to be the trouble here?" the doctor asked. He was a young man with shoulder-length curly black hair. His lab coat was weighed down by countless pens and prescription pads, and his pockets rattled with pill bottles as he walked.

"Hi, Doctor," Dana, said. "Our daughter has been throwing up a lot. Very green vomit. And she seems to have developed body odour too. She smells like a teenager who hasn't had a shower in a week. That's new. And her complexion. Why does she look so green?"

The doctor removed the stethoscope from around his neck.

"We didn't know if we should bring her or not?" Ben said. "She's probably having an allergic reaction to something."

Dana huffed, loudly. "Should we wake her?" she asked.

"No. It's fine," the young doctor said. I scooched away from Mallory to make room for him. He turned Mallory over and listened to her heartbeat. I wondered if he could also hear mine. A part of me was in there with her. I'm not sure what percentage, and I am not sure if it had a heartbeat, but it may have. Probably, for now, I thought, it would be better if I went undetected anyway.

Dana's phone chirped with another text.

"Can you shut that damn thing off?" Ben scolded her.

"Fine." Dana pulled her phone out of her purse and swiped and poked at the screen a few times before she set it in her lap.

"Who are you texting anyway?"

"Nobody," Dana spat.

"And you say the vomit is green?" the doctor asked.

"Like pea soup," Dana told him.

"Allergies are strange," the doctor said.

"See. I told you," Ben said.

If Dana's evil eye had been capable of actual murder, instead of wishful thinking, Ben would have been a dead man.

"Especially dairy allergies," the doctor continued. "Usually body odour in young children can be attributed to dairy allergies. You can have her tested if you like. I'll write the form up for you, but the tests are very unreliable. It's kind of a crap shoot if the thing is right. The best thing to do is to remove dairy from her diet and see if she improves. Buy her some probiotics at the health food store. If it doesn't clear up, then bring her to your family doctor for further testing. I'll go do that paperwork. You wait here. Pretty girl, by the way."

"Thank you."

"Allergies. See, I told you. It's nothing to be worried about."

"Doctor, wait." Dana stopped the doctor before he swished out from behind our curtain. "Mallory's been acting weird lately. Last night she drew all over the wall of her bedroom. She drew horrible things, like penises and cats with pentagrams on their foreheads. She wrote words that she couldn't possibly know how to spell."

"Well, I'm sorry to hear that, Mrs. Becker. I believe you can get some stuff at the hardware store that will take crayon off walls."

"It's Matthews."

The doctor checked his chart, flipping up a page. "Are you sure?" he asked.

"Yes, quite certain, Doctor. Well, how do you explain the words she wrote. She wrote the word "shit pants." She's never used that word. She couldn't have known the word shit. How? And she tells me that someone is biting her leg. I think she needs psychological help."

Ben jumped in. "Dana. Come on. That's the last thing we need. She probably saw it on TV. Maybe she changed the channel when we weren't looking? I am perfectly capable of handling this myself."

"Handling what? We don't even know what is going on with her," Dana said.

"It is normal behaviour for a child to write on the wall," Ben said.

"Ben! No, it is not. Not like she did."

"I'm not a psychologist, ma'am," the doctor interrupted, "and certainly not a child psychologist. I am an ER physician. I can have the nurse bring you some pamphlets, but I can only diagnose her physical ailments. I do have a younger sister who drew on the wall when she was a child. It seems to be a compulsion for children. It's quite normal, as far as I understand it. Especially for girls. Nice meeting you all. Goodbye." And he disappeared through the curtain.

"Pamphlets," Dana scoffed. "Like what? So you think your child is crazy? Or maybe he'll get me an advance copy of *Dear Ms. Vicki.*"

"Why don't you just quit ragging on me?" Ben said.

Dana's phone chirped again.

"Okay. I thought you turned that off. Who the Hell is sending you a million texts? Is it that woman from my work? She's just a gossip. I told you not to speak with her. She's crazy."

"Pam? No. It's not Pam. And even it if was, you can't tell me who I can speak to. She was my friend. Just because you quit doesn't mean I can't speak to someone."

"Downsized. I got downsized. I didn't quit. If it's not Pam, and I know it's not your sister, then who is it?"

"Fine," Dana broke down. "It's ALEXIS, all right. She is concerned about Mallory."

"Alexis? From the theatre? From dinner? Are you guys besties now or something?"

"Fuck you. How dare you be so condescending."

"Oh, come on. It just seems odd, is all. You've been in two shows with her at the theatre, we had her over for supper once, and all of a sudden you're texting her about private family matters."

"Well, you seemed to like her enough when she was sitting on our couch. In a robe. Half-naked! But if I want to be friends with her it's '*odd.*' Why? Why is it odd? Can't women become friends?"

"Seems desperate to me. You haven't known her that

long."

"Maybe it is desperate, Ben. I have no one to talk to. Maybe my whole life is desperate. I need a friend. You used to be my friend, but all you do is scold me now. Treat me like I am crazy."

"This is ridiculous,' Ben said. "Pack up her stuff. Let's be ready to go when the doctor comes back."

"..." Dana was silent.

"A milk allergy," Ben said. "See, I said that. I told you."

"Don't you dare," Dana said.

A nurse breezed into the room. "Here are your pamphlets," she said, tossing them on the bed.

"Thank you, Ms.?"

"Norris. Paging Dr. Norris."

"Thank you Professor Norr..."

666

He was an older man, tall and slim, with a thinning head of hair that he dyed an orangish-brown. The creased skin on his face and hands was oily with spray-on tan. His buck teeth were unnaturally white and jutted slightly from his mouth. When he was not speaking, the two front teeth rested easily on his bottom lip, making permanent indentations in the dry and cracked pink flesh of a heavy smoker.

"Professor Norris," he said. "Yes. Finally. Pleased to meet you, Karen. Let me show you to your office. Follow me."

I followed Professor Norris out of the cafeteria. I was happy to get away from Satan and the rest of the executive team.

"You seemed to slip away for a second there," Professor Norris said as we walked down the carpeted hallway. "You've already seen her, haven't you? You've travelled?

Left Hell?"

"Yes," I told him. "The mother might be starting to suspect something."

"And the father?"

"Clueless."

"Typical," Professor Norris said. "Listen, Karen. Let me tell you where we stand on this. We're working to continually foster cross-functional strategic protocols here. To architect, develop, and deploy a functional cross-unit infrastructure with designs on world domination methodologies."

"Okay."

"With a rapidiously aggregated market of goal-oriented human capital, we feel that we can holistically monetize distributed systems and get a foothold...no...we feel that we can get total linkage in the market. Satan is on board here, so with you in place in your new position, the rubber has hit the road. We're thinking outside the box on this one."

"You can count on me, Professor."

As we were walking, we passed a large glassed-in room. Behind the glass I saw Betty struggling with the dog-faced security. She was thrown into a chair and strapped down. A number of men in lab coats buzzed around her, affixing wires to her temple and her back. The smeared makeup on her face made her look like she was melting.

"Ah," Professor Norris said. "The colours test. My own invention. If you will allow me to brag a bit. And this is what we call the psychometric coaching laboratory. Dynamically harnessing the cutting-edge technologies of psychology and upswings in human capital methodology, we determine personality types and then assign a colour scheme. From there we can maintain mind source metrics and tailor functionalized human source practices for future betterment. It's mandatory for all staff. Have you had yours?"

Betty was squirming in her chair as the scientists removed her shoes and started pointing bright white lights at her. One lifted her skirt and placed a giant iron bar across her knees. Her eyes looked wild, scanning the room for an escape door. I almost felt sorry for her.

"Yes. Yes, of course I have," I lied. "First thing I did when I jumped on board. I couldn't wait to find out who I am."

"NOOOO," we heard Betty wail through the glass as one of the lab monkeys (a monkey in a lab coat) set a pencil down on the table in front of her.

"So melodramatic," Professor Norris said in reference to

Betty. "I am a Mauve. A deep thinker and born leader. What are you?"

"Oh, um. A Green."

"Really? Which shade?"

"Chartreuse."

"Oh, excellent." Professor Norris pulled out a notepad from the breast pocket of his coat, scribbling something down. I noticed that he was left-handed. I always notice when people are left-handed because my father was left-handed. "We should get along well then. I was scared you were going to say seafoam. Then I'd have to make you redundant."

After a brief, tense, moment and me checking to see whether or not my letter opener was still in my pocket, we shared a laugh. (Well, maybe not a laugh. More of a nervous cackle.)

The questions started coming from behind the glass, played on giant speakers that we could hear in the hallway. A woman's voice with a received pronunciation accent asked slowly and calmly: "You are most attuned to a work methodology that is:

   A. Structure focused

   B. Goal oriented

   C. Sequential

D. Knowledge triggered"

"No. NO. I swear I will do anything. Please, I can't make it."

"Choose a word, or phrase, that best describes your emotional state in conflict:

A. King Kong

B. Morning Glory

C. Restricted

D. Calculated"

"I'll give you anything. I have money," Betty said. "Make it stop!"

"She'll be here a while," Professor Norris said. "Let's move along."

"Are you best described as: A. A perpetual learner who likes to feel challenged at work? B."

"OH, GOD. PLEASE GOD NO!"

As we walked further, I thought I could feel my little Mallory inside of me. I thought maybe she could see through my eyes and hear as Professor Norris spoke. I felt her uneasy displeasure at being forced into the workaday world of adults. It only made sense that a piece of her was in me, even if it was only the smallest piece. We were becoming one.

"So, Professor, I was hoping that you could give me an

idea of what needs to be done? What I am shooting for?" I asked.

"Ah, here's your office," Norris said.

It was a small windowless office, which was fine with me. I was sick and tired of watching the snow fly outside anyway. The carpet was old and worn. On the wall there was a poster. An endless mountainscape with a beautiful rising sun, the likes of which no one in Hell would ever see, puffy white clouds, and the green untouched forest spreading down the mountain sides towards a rushing river. The scene was framed with a black border, and in a heavily scripted caption beneath the picture: *The beauty in you is your spirit.*

As I crossed the threshold of my new office, an iron cage slammed behind me. Professor Norris was on the other side of the bars standing in the hallway.

"Here are your keys," he said as he reached through the bars. "IT will engage you post evening to administrate your resources. Hope you don't mind staying late. In the meanwhile, if you could target that data," he nudged his head towards the corner and a tower of banker boxes all teeming with files, "and fabricate some distinctively adaptive initiatives and put them in a positive framework to deliver to the board of directors on Monday."

"Monday?"

"Mrs. Floyd, the board meetings are the rock that the talent stream at The Nakara Corporation runs around. The production arena is growing the resources for our takeover. You will play a most important role in this. Make sure you are prepared to deliver the peripherals to the board. Monday. Okay, Mrs. Floyd? Monday."

"Certainly, sir. Monday it is then. I'll be ready by Monday." It was Friday.

Sometimes I wondered if home was nothing more than a mirage or a false memory, a shadow of something that once existed.

"Of course, you will," Professor Norris said, "your master set is green." He turned to walk away but stopped. "Oh, by the way, Mrs. Floyd."

"Yes?"

"There is no chartreuse."

"..." Letter opener.

"But there is now. I like the cut of your jib, Floyd. You'll do well here."

As Professor Norris walked away, I suddenly felt like he had told me nothing about my job and what I was supposed to do, what the 'deliverables,' or the 'peripherals', as he called them, were. I combed the recesses of my brain, trying to remember the things I learned in my online course, "The Rosetta Stone to Success. Translating the speech of our Superiors. What they mean and why they say what they say," but came up blank. I had never met anyone as confusing as Professor Norris before, and I didn't dare ask him to clarify for fear he thought I was stupid.

The answers were in the files. They had to be. I went over and picked up one of the banker boxes and set it on my L-shaped desk. I pulled out my chair from beneath. It was not a regular office chair like I was used to. It was more deluxe. It had handles on the back of it, and giant wheels the size of bicycle tires, and two little places to put your feet. The basket seat and back could have even been real leather. I thought, *Girl, you've finally made it. Your own office with your own wheeled chair.*

I sat and pulled the lid off the banker box. It was full of files. None of them were labelled. There was a name on the underside of the box lid. Hepburn P. I started leafing through the files. At first glance, a lot of the file folders were Xerox copies of old Archie comics. Jughead was in trouble with Moose. On one page someone had taken an eraser and tried to rub out Veronica's sweater, to see her breasts, I presume? As if the illustrator had first drawn her naked and then dressed her in a sweater. I wondered what sort of imbecile this Hepburn P. was, and I wondered what these files had to do with me.

I pulled out what appeared to be a photograph. The photograph was of me. Taken when I was alive. I was lying in bed, wasted and worn from chemo. A skeleton beneath the white sheets. On the wall in front of me was my sick box. It was open, and the candles were burning. I remembered. It was summer. It was very hot out. Even back then they were preparing for me. You'd think if they had been planning this possession for that long that they would have left me with some sort of instructions. I sighed and sat down in my wheeled chair.

666

It was hot in the loft, and as I crawled through my sick box, I heard the sound of a motor running. I followed the sound down to the living room. An old fan was blowing where Mallory played with her dolls, bashing them together, as if they were fighting one another. An orange cat slept on a basket of unfolded laundry. Ben stuck his head out of the kitchen and into the living room.

"Mallory. Come here. It's time for your probiotics."

"No," Mallory said.

"Yes. The doctor said they would help your belly. You haven't thrown up in a week. It's good for you. They are working."

The cat (Gregory, or Gregsie as I had heard him called) jumped from the basket of laundry, stretched and stepped around a warzone of Barbie bodies and overturned Barbie vehicles, a boat, a car, a scooter. It sniffed at a crust of discarded toast and jam that was stuck to the floor before

sauntering over to a bowl of cat food in the kitchen.
Digging his nose into the bowl, spilling kibble about the
floor, Gregory sat and began to crunch away.

I got down on my knees across from Mallory.

"I missed you," I said. "How long have I been gone? I've
been hard at work."

She looked at me and hissed like a cat. Inside her mouth,
she was sporting a set of plastic vampire teeth.

"What is that noise?" Ben asked from the kitchen.
Again, he stuck his head into the living room. He had a wet
dishrag in his hand, his forearms covered in soap. "Mallory,
can you please pick up some of your toys? The house is a
complete bomb. Mommy is going to kill us when she gets
home.

Mallory's eyes did not leave mine. "Hissss," she went.

"After that, we are going to meet Uncle Don for lunch.
Okay? So pick up your toys, and let's go get dressed." He
disappeared back into the kitchen.

I picked up a Barbie and a Ken and pressed their thick
plastic lips together.

"Hissss," Mallory said.

From the kitchen I could hear Ben: "Mallory, would you
please stop hissing? You are not a cat. And take those
vampire teeth out. You're going to get gum disease."

"Hissss," went Mallory.

I put the Ken and Barbie back down as I heard what was obviously a tower of dishes fall to the floor, some smashing.

"OH, COME ON!" said Ben as Gregory came tearing down the hall and up the stairs.

That is when the phone rang. I went to the kitchen door to watch. Ben checked the number on the telephone and cursed beneath his breath. He inhaled deeply, wiped his soapy hands on a dish towel, and answered the phone.

"Hello."

"..."

"Yes. Speaking."

"..."

With the phone pinned between his ear and shoulder, Ben crouched and began picking up the smashed porcelain.

"You can't do that to me. I've got a family," Ben said.

"..."

"No, but I need it. We need the money. This can't be right."

"..."

"This is not fair. I know I quit, but I thought I would still qualify for benefits."

"..."

"I know. But what about the training? Can I at least take the training? What about the Risk Management course?"

"..."

"Right. Okay, I understand that benefits are for people who need them. I need them. I fucking need them, do you understand?"

"..."

"No. Don't hang up. Good faith. I hear you. What if I contacted my former employer and asked to take a leave of absence? For psychological reasons?"

"..."

"Then I would qualify for benefits?"

"..."

"Okay, I will get back to you."

Ben hung up the phone. "Come on, Mallory. Go upstairs and get dressed and get your coat. We're going out to meet Uncle Don for lunch."

'Out? Did he say out?' I had not been out in a very, very long time.

"And take those teeth out of your mouth. You won't be able to eat your lunch with those in."

"We're going out," I said to Mallory, all smiles.

"Hissss," said Mallory.

666

"GET OUT. You're fired. Pack thine shit and get your cursed self out of here!"

One of the executives down the hall was shouting at his secretary.

"Seductress!"

I had been up all night working on my report for the board meeting and listening to him berate her.

"You can't fire me," I heard her shout. "Just because you died in the 1500s doesn't mean you can treat women like dirt. It might be Hell, but we're past that stage. Trust me."

"Out, vile wench! WITCH. Or I will burn thee at the stake."

"Talk to my union steward about it. I'm entitled to one sick day a month and I'm taking it."

"A pox on you! I need those reports, She-Devil!"

"A pox. I got a pox," she said. "That's right. I'm not going to be in on Thursday. I got the pox."

That's right. You tell him, sister, I thought.

"Harpy!"

"Right here, buddy. Right here," she shouted.

It was tough to focus with that going on, but The Nakara Corporation had an open-cage policy. We were not allowed to shut our office cages during core hours (7:00 am to 6:00 am). I consoled myself with thoughts of life in the earthly realm, prospects of it anyway, which were getting better by the second.

I was just emptying the last banker box in my office, trying to find some hint, some clue that would help me possess the body of little Mallory Matthews. The files were spread all over my desk and the floor. I had found all sorts of coloured folders labelled with folder tags saying things like, "budget, peripherals, procedures, tax codes, yearly revenue," etcetera, but none of the Hepburn P. files appeared to be of much use. Most of the folders were full of comics and pornographic anime, which obviously would not help me. There were some startling pictures of me as well. Pictures of me when I was alive on earth: getting ready for work, driving on the expressway, sipping coffee, changing into my nightgown, dying. It was difficult to look at those pictures, difficult to see myself wasting the short life that I had had. If those pictures were any indication, all

I ever did was get drunk, sing karaoke, and work. Nonetheless, the prophecy had been foretold years prior to my arrival in Hell. Some demon had taken these pictures.

Hepburn P. knew this day was coming. But how did he get to Earth? And how did he get a camera? And how was I to make sense of all this? Who was Hepburn P.? And what the Hell did any of this (the anime, the Archie comics, the Mad magazines) have to do with anything? And why didn't the dumb so-and-so leave me any information about how to break through?

It wasn't until I was nearly at the bottom of the last banker box that I found what I had been looking for. It was a slim file stuck to the bottom of the box. Buried beneath a near mountain of Archie comics and pornographic anime. It was difficult, and gross, to pick up, the green folder ripping away as it came loose.

The file was labelled, "Peripherals." Inside it, I found a few pictures of people that I knew. These were not pictures of Archie and Jughead or Veronica and Moose. These were pictures of Ben and Dana on their wedding day, shoving a piece of cake into one another's face. There were pictures taken on a beach somewhere. Ben was wearing a straw hat, and Dana had on a pink bathing suit. Blue water stretched endlessly behind them as stray dogs romped in the surf.

Mixed drinks crept into the frame of each and every shot. Then came the pictures of Mallory.

From Dana's balloonish belly and much laughter at her baby shower to Mallory's birth. Then Mallory's first birthday party, Halloween, Christmas, a cycle of holidays and birthdays, and in each picture Dana and Ben looked a little fatter and older and more tired as the years rumbled on. As Mallory became taller and more vibrant. I couldn't help but think that she was feeding off them, taking something away from them in order to grow herself. Maybe this was me rationalizing my new role as the possessor? Or maybe it was true. The family dynamic was a symbiotic one. The parental units happily give away all their youth and energy so that their offspring can thrive.

The narrative went on and on like this for five years, with Mallory looking less and less like a baby with each passing year and her parents aging alongside of her, creeping up towards forty. Dana and Ben were always smiling and happy, though. Another thought crossed my mind. Maybe somewhere deep inside them, they knew that raising this vessel for Satan was what they were put on Earth to do. I wondered at what my own father used to say about my sister and me. "It's tough to teach children that they are not the center of the universe, when, in fact, they most certainly are."

In the folder were also a few typed pages. I read:

Paul Hepburn on Ben Matthews (full report to follow at The Board presentation):

Objective: The purpose of this report is to get a brief overview of the couple that will produce a wife for Paul Hepburn. The takeover of the earthly realm will begin in earnest only when Paul Hepburn has possessed the boy child, Jeremy Marshall, and Jeremy has subsequently grown to adulthood without:

    A. Undergoing an exorcism

    B. Drowning at a bush party

    C. Being thrown in jail for an extended period

    D. Obtaining spiritual enlightenment and becoming a

        a. Priest

        b. Rabbi

        c. Yogi

        d. Swami

        e. Elder

Or essentially any form of cult leader. (Such as some false prophecies, and sensationalized newspaper articles, have borne witness to.) The possession of an unbaptized girl child will begin stage 30 (see my previous report on

*staging the takeover and report 7b on planting a porthole).
All is dependant on whether or not we can reach Stage 29,
Know Thine Enemy.*

Action Items:

   A. Know thine enemy

   B. Find another portal for Karen

   C. Foil any religiosity or freak conversion attempts

   D. Possess an unbaptized daughter

   *E. Meet me in the earthly realm; you must find me,
     Karen*

   F. Hire Molly Hatchet for the inauguration

I could feel a shiver run down my spine. I was part of a
prophecy. And a big one too. I felt great courage and pride
(something that I was not used to feeling) in the important
work I was doing for The Nakara Corporation, and I knew
that I couldn't let anyone down, especially myself. My leg,
however, was beginning to itch. I went to scratch my calf
and some skin peeled away. A line of dark poisonous
infection was starting at my heel and running up towards
my heart. I would soon become a zombie. I wondered how
much time I had left. I had to get to work. I read on.

*Know thine enemy. As all prophecies foretell, in the
taking of a child, the parents are a demon's number one
hurdle when it comes to possession. In the early stages of*

demonic possession, we have little control over our actions or the bodies of the children we possess. Hell always seems to creep in, bits of evil seep through hypothetical window sills and leaky doors in the quantum fabric separating the realms, and this may have strange effects on the child you are possessing. Take note that such phenomenon, which I call 'soft rot,' can occur and alert parental units to the demonic workings of supernatural, unholy forces, and this can result in unwanted results, such as exorcism. If your host is experiencing any of the symptoms listed below, please take action:

A. Excessive vomiting

B. Walking on the walls or ceiling

C. Speaking in tongues, dead languages, or Hawaiian

D. Foul body odour

E. Murderous rampages

There is little we can do to stop soft rot, but what we CAN do is pay close attention to the weaknesses of the parents. Divide and conquer. If they are not a cohesive unit, you may be able to find shelter in the love of one or the other. But don't let the squabbles and family fights fool you, spouses are difficult to separate.

Just when you think you might have a foothold this

happens:

ENOUGH

<Dana Matthews> scorpio.1987@gmail.com

To: <Ben Matthews> vicki_can_help@gmail.com

*Ben, I've had enough. I'm sorry we are fighting. I'm
sorry about what happened at lunch today. I should have
told you. That felt awkward, and it was uncomfortable. I
wasn't trying to hide anything. It was a last-minute thing,
like I said. I'm sorry. You know, we really have to stick
together here for our child. I know she is sick, and I know
you love her and want to take care of her. That is what I
want too. Let's not fight anymore. Okay? Have I ever told
you about Ringo Chan? His real name was Xinhua, or
something like that. His Canadian name was Ringo. Maybe
his parents liked the Beatles. I don't know. As you can
imagine, in that tiny little shithole of a town I grew up in,
everybody made fun of Ringo Chan. But I liked him. He
was my friend. He and I were the only ethnics in town, so I
guess we found solace in that. He used to come over to my
house to play IQ 2000, this trivia game for kids. Do you
remember it? Have you ever played it? We should get it.
Can you still get it? Maybe we will see it at a garage sale?*

*Anyway, we would play IQ 2000 and ride our bikes
together. One day my dad asked him to stay for supper. We*

had spaghetti with meatballs. In his South African accent, he started telling Ringo about Cape Town. Then he asked Ringo all kinds of questions about his family and what sorts of things his parents made for supper. He told Ringo that he really liked his parent's restaurant (because, of course, the only Chinese family in town owned the only Chinese restaurant in town), and he asked Ringo if he ate that good restaurant food all the time? Ringo's responses to my dad were a series of 'yes, sirs' and 'no, sirs' followed by one-word answers. 'Chicken.' 'Noodles.' 'Rice.'

He was a nice boy but nervous in front of my tall and imposing father. So we ate our supper quickly, and I petitioned Ringo to leave right away because I was worried that Dad (a big fan of The Beatles, as you know) would question Ringo about his bizarre Canadian name.

After supper, we went on one of our bike rides and we stopped at the convenience store.

Ringo had money, and he said he was going to buy a big bag of cheezies, my favourite, for dessert. (Only kids would eat cheezies for dessert.) I had forgotten to ask Dad for money, and I was uncomfortable with the purchase of the large bag of cheezies. Ringo knew that I didn't have money. We got on our bikes with the cheezies and started riding again. Ringo stopped near a tree by the bridge, and we put our bikes down on the ground. I didn't feel like I should eat the cheezies because I didn't help pay for them, so I only took a few from the bag when Ringo opened it. What I really wanted to do was gorge on them, to shove them into my mouth one after the other, like Ringo was doing, but I did not. And he kept offering them to me, like some gracious monk offering spiritual enlightenment to the unwashed. I wanted to spit in his face, tell him to shove his cheezies up his ass as he lorded them over me. And then he went to put his hand on my knee, his fingers all stained orange with cheezie dust. I slapped it away, got on my bike, and rode home as quickly as I could. I remember slamming the door and going to up to my room and kicking some things around the room, tossing some books to the floor. No one heard me. No one came to my aid. I never spoke to Ringo again. I hated him. And he stayed away from me too. He was embarrassed, I guess.

Why am I telling you this again?

Maybe life is not as predictable as we think it is. We expect too much ordinary.

Anyway, love you. And I look forward to seeing you tonight. I am sorry about everything.

Maybe we can put her to bed early and even have a poke?

Dana.

<Ben Matthews>vicki_can_help@gmail.com

To: <Dana Matthews> scorpio.1987@gmail.com

Ha. His name was really Ringo Chan? How strange.
Yeah, I am sorry too. I'll see you tonight. Really looking
forward to it. I will cook something nice for dinner.
Spaghetti? Hope you didn't eat too much at lunch.

We'll figure this out. Okay? Love you, babe. Great idea
about the poke too.

BM

I set the file down on my desk. "Divide and conquer,
huh? That's the plan, eh, Hepburn P.? Wherever you are."

I sighed and rested my cheek on the pile of files spread
out on my desk. I wanted to fall asleep and never wake up,
but my horns made it impossible to form a flat surface
between my ear and the files. My neck began to ache. Rest
was not possible. I felt my zombie-bit leg pulsating as the
blood worked its way towards my heart. A tear streamed
down the bridge of my nose and landed softly on my pillow
of files, carrying with it the universal question that we all
ask ourselves hundreds of times each and every day, dead
or alive, Heaven or Hell: *"What am I going to do now?"*

But that was self-pity, and that movie didn't play in Hell.
One thing about demons and monsters was that they don't roll

over. No, because just when you thought the movie was over and that the horrible, relentlessly stalking beast had been expunged, blown to smithereens, riddled with bullets, cast out by prayer, there you see it again, the shadow, the horror, plodding towards the heroine to rip her soul asunder. And life was just like a horror movie. Yes, if the movies taught us anything it was that bad guys can take a punch and get up off the mat, angrier and meaner. I lifted myself up and turned on my computer. The home screen popped up. There was a cat, hanging from a branch, its grip slipping as its hindquarters dangled over some precipice, and the words, "HANG IN THERE," in capital letters at the bottom of the screen.

The computer took a minute or two to load and then I opened the browser, Internet Exploder, (the only browser available in Hell) and typed in the Yahoo (the only search engine in Hell) search bar, "How long does it take a person to turn into a zombie?" The little wheel spun and spun and spun until I decided that the application was hung, and my computer was frozen.

I panicked for a moment and prayed that I had saved the fan letter that I had been writing to Andy Kaufman. I shut the computer down and leaned back in my wheeled chair.

What was I going to do? I needed a plan. I needed a presentation ready for the board of directors. After about fifteen minutes, my computer started working again. I moved my cursor around the screen a bit before I opened an excel spreadsheet and started a new workbook.

I had learned in my training class, "The Art of the Proposal," that everything began and ended with numbers. So that is where I would have to start: crunching the numbers. Any numbers that I could think of I would crunch them. I started digging through the files, looking for numbers: Mallory's age, plus the number of fangs in God's mouth, divided by the number of kilometres that Ben, the avid cyclist, rode in a week, multiplied by Dana's final exam mark in grade twelve history class. SUM column one. Column two row six. I began again, highlighting and making nice orderly rows and columns, using the skills I had learned in my extended learning course, "The Subtle Art of Beautiful Spreadsheets."

"It's a thing of beauty, I say. A thing of real beauty."

Ben sighed so loudly that I thought I could feel his breath on my arm. I was going back to the earthly realm.

"Don, why do you have to admire every beer, wine, or whiskey as if it was going to be the last?"

"It's a thing of beauty I say. A thing of real beauty."

And I named the file, the now infamous name, "The Cheezie Report," and I saved it. Twice.

666

'Admire every beer, wine, or whiskey as if it could be the last.' What a great credo, I thought. I wish I had done that when I was alive. (I mean, there's a motivational poster that I could get behind.)

In that brief moment between the realms (kind of like the second between sleep and wakefulness, before one's eyes are open and the next hour could go either way: it could be breakfast time, or you could go back to that dream about the exploding geese and the kung fu robot) I could hear music. And it wasn't American Pie. It couldn't be. It was the music of the angels. *Was I in Heaven?* I wondered. Loud riffing guitars, double bass drums, a screeching singer…rock music!

And the smells. It smelled so good, and then, pop! Shat out of my sick box and jettisoned across the city and plopped into a booth in a restaurant called Zeke's Roadhouse.

I watched as Ben's friend, Don, wiped away his frothy beer mustache with the back of his sleeve and smiled as he set his pint down. "Whew, somebody's in a mood," he said.

Don was a short, balding man wearing a cheap brown suit. He had a badge alligator-clipped to his breast jacket pocket (sewn closed) that read, "Radio Roundup Manager, Sergio Aragones."

"Yeah, well. This Mister Mom shit is getting old fast," Ben said.

"Your food will be right out." The waitress, a thin twenty-something blonde who had a tattoo on the back of her neck and wore a stained and greasy uniform, pitched up at the side of the table. She peeled a pint of lager and a Shirley Temple off her tray and set them down in front of Ben and Mallory. She smiled.

Ben reached over and switched the beer that she had set down in front of Mallory with the Shirley Temple that she had set down in front of him.

"Oh, my God," the waitress smacked her forehead (so hard that it left a red mark). "Did I just do that?"

"She hasn't developed a taste for beer yet, eh, hon?" Don laughed.

"So, sorry," the waitress said. "Your food will be right out." She turned and wormed her way through the gathering lunch crowd, back to the kitchen.

Don smiled and had another gulp of his beer. "I should ask that one out on a date. Dull as a bag of hammers."

"You should," Ben replied. "If that is what you are looking for in a woman...Sergio."

Don scoffed. "They're still making mine, okay? It's a brand-new promotion. Least I got a job."

"Touché," Ben said.

I watched the men take their beers up and give a nod to each other in a silent cheers, and the beers looked so wet and delicious that the pain of the closeness nearly crushed me.

Hey, all you witches and Satanists out there: If you want to call a demon out of the pits of everlasting damnation, you can forget about the talismans, the slaying of prostitutes, the cannibalism of unbaptized babies, vampirism, and invocations. Forget about dancing nude in front of a roaring bonfire, the goats with the creepy eyes, the mutilation of the chickens, ancient Sumerian tablets. Forget about all that stuff you've seen at the movie theatre. Just offer up the sacrifice of a pint of beer and a plate of Buffalo wings at the gates of Hell and the evil masses, who haven't seen the inside of a bar in an era, will flood the earth.

The golden bitter of the lager, and the deep, dark black-as-pitch stout in their sweating glasses made me crave dearly for life again; and the smell of the food, the melting cheeses, and the searing meats, were almost too much to bear. I felt like throwing my future away, just for one slice of pizza, but I knew that I must not. It was not like giving up on a diet. I would have been jeopardizing my career. I had already made one regretful decision in my existence, and I was not about to screw up a second chance at life by making another one.

But, oh, in that moment, I so badly wanted to take Don and Ben and smack their heads together, as if I were Moe, and they were Curly and Larry, only I wanted to crush Ben and Don's skulls when I did it, crush their skulls and drink their beers. Then, having gone well over the edge, forever destroying any chance to complete my assignment, I would have just had to massacre every single person in the restaurant with flying scissor kicks and razor-sharp talons, gutting and gouging with my horned head. I would have gobbled their food and drinks down one after another and lay there bloated and sated in a slippery mess of their blood and crushed organs until Satan herself came roaring to drag me back to Hell, a failure, a delighted, smiling, fat failure. If they only knew how close they were to death, their petty issues might not have felt so dire.

"Yeah, well, you're the one who quit your job," Don countered. "Jesus Christ, it's cold in here. Do you feel that? Feels like I'm sitting next to an iceberg. And something stinks. What is that smell? Smells like rotting meat. You smell that?"

"I don't feel it. I don't smell it," Ben responded.

"You feel it, Mallory?" Don asked. Mallory kept her head down, playing with her colouring book. She did not respond. She knew it was me, and she was sick of trying to explain everything and then getting in trouble for making up lies. The poor dear.

"What's up with her? She looks all green. You not feeling well, Mal?" Don asked.

"..." Mallory did not answer.

"Honey, please answer Uncle Don when he speaks to you."

Mallory shrugged her shoulders. "No," she told him.

"Mallory might stink a bit," Ben said. "It's the dairy allergy. It causes really bad body odour. The doctor says that the allergens have to come out somewhere. In her, apparently, they exit as B.O. She'll feel better when we get the dairy out of her system. She's on probiotics. And we're getting her some antiperspirant today."

Don shifted a little further towards the edge of the seat. "They must have the air conditioning cranked in here. That doesn't bother you?"

"No, Don. I don't feel cold."

I began to become a little self-conscious. I raised my arm and sniffed at my armpits. Of course, there was no deodorant in Hell, but I didn't think I stunk that badly. I tried my best to stay clean. I looked over at Mallory and smiled. She raised her head and snarled back at me. I imagined how beautiful she would be when she became a teenager. I would take such good care of my body this time around. I would eat right and get to the gym three times a week. I wouldn't be the fat girl at the prom. The kids would never call me a "pear Kare" or anything like that ever again. I imagined all the showers I would take with real soap. And I could nearly feel the cold roll-on antiperspirant pressed against my shaved armpit. Imagine that: having a second chance at being a teenager again. My heart sailed at the thought. The things I would do right this time. I would get a job at a cool record store and use the money I made to buy expensive perfumes that came in pretty bottles. Did they even have records anymore? Course they did.

"I swear to God, it reeks in here," Don said. "I can't believe you can't smell that."

In time, I thought. *In time.*

We were sitting in a booth. Mallory was sitting beside her dad and Don, Ben's friend, was sitting beside me. A sign above the bar read, "Lunch with the Amazing Larry! Mondays to Fridays." On the walls everywhere were pictures of sports heroes. I never really cared for sports when I was alive. Maybe, on my second go around, I might give them a chance though. I could back a winner. It was fun when your team won something. In Hell there was only one professional sports league, frisbee golf, but no matter who you cheered for your favourite player always seemed to finish last.

The restaurant was full of people, and the dull roar of their chatting and chewing filled the room. They were being entertained by a magician, The Amazing Larry, I assumed. He was dressed in ripped blue jeans and a tight black shirt. Silver chains dangled from his neck. As the diners chewed on their food like a herd of cows in a pasture and slurped up their drinks with bendy straws, the magician, the necromancer (he was going to Hell for sure; tons of those ridiculous bastards end up in Hell…tons) went from table to table making things appear and disappear. The lunch crowd, more interested in their dusted chicken wings and mozzarella sticks than they were in card tricks and linking rings, paid him little mind.

"Did you really quit your job?" Don asked. "I'm not so sure that was a good idea if you did. Like, are you sure they won't take you back?" Don took a sip of his beer.

"Yeah, well. I did," Ben said. "And no, they won't. I couldn't take it anymore."

"Take? What is there to take?"

"It was an omen."

My ears perked up.

"I saw this guy," Ben continued, "and it seemed like no one else even noticed him. Like he wasn't alive at all. He was just walking through the crowd with his head down, and he didn't bump into anyone, and no one bumped into him. He was walking away from me. He seemed short too. Like, shorter than me. You know what I mean?"

"Yeah, man. Short people make me want to quit my job all the time."

"No. Listen, asshole. That's not the point. He was carrying a plastic container full of sushi. Probably taking it back to his office to eat. Alone. Again. Like he probably did every day of his life. His pants were disheveled and unkempt, out of fashion, too long for his shrinking body. He had, like, a monk haircut. You know, bald on top with a horseshoe of hair over his ears. And it was all shaggy and various shades of grey. A greasy old skullet. He looked so sad, and he walked with his left foot at an odd angle. It was like he hadn't lived a life. More like he'd been attacked by life. And I thought, 'My God. My God it's me. That is me in the future. I've shrunk and gone bald.' And I thought to myself, 'What can I do to stop this? I don't want to be a loser my entire life. This is not what life is for? I cannot accept that this is why I was put here on this earth.' And I walked to my office, sent an email to my supervisor, cc'ed the director, and I told them I quit. And I went home."

Don took a gulp of his beer before saying, "You hate sushi. I ask you all the time to go out for sushi, and you always say no."

"That's not the point."

"Okay, fine then. So where'd the guy go? Who was he? Did you ever find out?"

"Yeah, man. He was me. He was a vision of me from the future. He was an omen. I told you. I believe that."

If it was an omen it was not an omen sent by Nakara. Nothing in the banker boxes said anything about a tonsured old man carrying sushi. *Has someone else thrown Her hat into the ring here?* I wondered.

"Who had the steak? Rare?" The waitress was back.

"That's her." Ben gently took Mallory's crayon from her

hand and moved her colouring book aside.

"Here you go, dear." The waitress set the plate of food down in front of Mallory. "I have never seen anyone her age order a rare steak. They usually order cheesy tots or the pizza."

"Yeah. She's got a dairy thing," Ben said. "She's taking probiotics."

"And you had the perogies?" The waitress smiled at Don as she set his food down.

"Thank you, my dear."

"And are you sure you don't want anything, sir?" the waitress asked Ben.

"Maybe another draft," Ben said. Taking a slurp of his beer before he cut Mallory's steak for her.

"Thanks, hon," Don said as the waitress walked away. "Mmmm. I'd like to get a taste of her perogies."

"What does that even mean?" Ben asked.

Don shoved a forkful of pierogi smeared with sour cream and onions into his mouth and leered cretinously, as if Ben knew exactly what perverse act he had been referring to.

I liked this Don. He was a man after my own heart: bawdy and quick with a knife and fork.

"Well, as long as you're comfortable with your decision

to quit your job, who am I to judge, eh?" Don said. "One schizophrenic moment can change anyone's life, I suppose. Jesus Christ, it sure is rare," Don mouthed around a hunk of pierogi and bacon.

"It's all she'll eat lately," Ben said. "Rare steak. Ever since she got sick. Rare steak every night. She doesn't want the cheap cuts either. Rib eyes and New York strip. It's costing me a fortune."

Why do people talk about children as if they are not even in the room? I wondered as I wiped a long string of drool from my bottom lip.

Mallory sidled up next to her father and rested her head on his arm as he cut her steak, the red beef blood seeping from the flesh where the serrated steak knife sawed away.

"Oh, no. Not the Amazing Larry," Don said.

The necromancer veered towards our table.

He had changed costumes in the past ten minutes and was now wearing a long black trench coat. Smiling at Mallory the magician reached to the back of his head and whipped his jet-black hair out from the hair tie that had bound it in a ponytail. As his long hair fell about his shoulders, he took the hair tie up to his mouth and breathed into it. It was a blue balloon. He blew it up, and with a few quick twists of his fingers, he made a rabbit. He set the rabbit down in front of Mallory's plate.

Ben clapped in an exaggerated manner, trying to get Mallory to smile. Don chewed. The magician held his index finger up to his mouth, suggesting that everyone shush. He pulled open one side of his trench coat and shook it. He pulled open the other side of the trench coat and shook it. He then took the trench coat off and shook it violently in the air, nearly hitting the people at the table across from us. They glared at him angrily. He put the trench coat over his forearm, smoothed it out on both sides like a sophisticated gentleman, and straightened an imaginary tie.

Don, as if the magician were an oafish imbecile who had just figured out how to flick boogers, offered up an exaggerated thumbs up of encouragement and shoved a wad of pierogi and sour cream into his mouth.

The magician set the trench coat on the floor and motioned for Don to move over. Don was nearly in my lap. He kept sniffing at the air. The necromancer stared at Mallory and raised his fist. He counted down with his fingers. One. Two. Three. Four. And finally, the thumb. He sprung up, smiling, and whisked the coat from the floor where a white rabbit sat eating a carrot.

This guy was going to Hell for certain. Maybe even

sooner than I thought.

Ben and Don clapped while Mallory watched. She looked at me. I shrugged my shoulders, indicating that I had nothing to do with it. She looked back at the rabbit and smiled. Ben, who saw her smile, nearly burst wide open. She had been in such a funk since the possession started. The magician picked the animal up by the scruff and presented it to the table. Then the animal looked my way and what happened next was a fairly natural occurrence. I mean, this is what usually happens when a little bunny sees a demon. A shock cut through it and it wriggled and squirmed, biting at the magician and scratching his arm. The magician yelped in pain. He dropped the rabbit to the floor and cried out in shock. Blood was streaming down his fingers as he ran off to find someone who could dress his wound.

"What the Hell?" Ben said.

Don shoved the final bite of pierogi into his yawning gob.

The entire restaurant was laughing and whispering, passing the news on to those who had not seen what had happened. The waitresses gathered around the magician with the first aid kit. The rabbit sat still on the floor for a moment, recovering from its fall, and then it hopped underneath the table and scrambled up onto the seat beside me. It began grinding its teeth (the bunny version of purring).

It just wanted to be with one of its own kind. Bunnies may seem cute, but for some reason (reasons that I did not come to understand until much later), they love demons and fear angels greatly, and that little rabbit, henceforth to be known as "Todd," just wanted to be safe and be by my side.

Of course, the only person who noticed this was Mallory. She watched me stroke Todd on the nose, and although I enjoyed the feel of the rabbit's soft fur, I recognized an opportunity. Picking up Todd, I set him on the table and pushed him towards Mallory. Todd hopped down onto her lap, positioned himself, and sat. Mallory smiled at me. I smiled back and mouthed the words:

"We are in this together."

"What in Christ just happened there?" Ben asked.

"I don't know," Don answered on behalf of the universe. "Somebody should phone the board of health on this place, though. CHEQUE PLEASE."

"Finish up your lunch and get your coat on, Mallory. We're getting out of here. And put that rabbit down. He bites."

Instead of listening to her father, Mallory pointed across

the restaurant and said, "Mommy. Mommy."

"Mommy is at work, honey. She'll be home tonight." Ben stabbed at Mallory's steak with his fork, taking a bite for himself. "Now eat up before that nasty magician comes back."

Don craned his neck to face the direction that Mallory was pointing. "No. No. Look, Ben. It is Mommy. That's Dana. And she's with somebody. Who is that? She looks familiar."

"What?" Ben squinted to see.

I turned as well, and there she was. Mommy. I remembered the email that I had read. The one about Ringo Chan. Dana must have written it sometime shortly after this lunch. And Dana was with someone. Divide and conquer.

"Alexis! What the Hell is she doing here?" Ben asked.

"Is that the Alexis you told me about?" Don asked. "Is it? You weren't kidding. She is hot."

"Pay that bill and meet me outside," Ben said.

"What about the steak? Your beers? I'm not paying for everything."

"Get a doggie bag. I'll pay you back. It's a business lunch. I'll write it off," Ben said.

"Write it off what? You don't even have a job. How are you going to pay me back?"

"I might get some severance."

"Right. Severance," Don said. "CHEQUE PLEASE. What about your beer?"

"Chug it."

"Yes, sir. You're the boss."

Ben stood and started towards Dana and Alexis.

Mallory, still cradling Todd in her arms, scooched past him and ran towards her mother.

I floated above, drifting over the cacophony of diners.

Just as Dana took a menu from her waitress, Mallory ran up to her. "Momma. Momma. Look what I have."

"Baby? Mallory? What are you doing here?" Dana went to hug her daughter but stopped when she saw the rabbit. "Ben?"

"Fancy meeting you guys here. I thought you were working today?" Ben said, approaching the table. "Alexis. We meet again."

"Ben!" Alexis said. "Nice to see you. Why don't you sit down and join us?"

"No. I am sorry, Alexis. I can't do that. We just finished our lunch."

There was a long awkward pause. Even Mallory did not know what to say.

Dana finally spoke: "What is this that you have here,

Mallory?"

"It's a bunny, Mommy." Mallory said. "It likes me but hates the magician. It bit him."

"Bit him! Oh, my. Ben? Should she have that thing?"

"No. Mommy's right, Mallory. Put the rabbit down."

"His name is …" Mallory, realizing that she didn't know the rabbit's name, craned her head upwards to enquire.

"Todd," I said.

"Todd. His name is Todd."

"Well, Ben. Can you please take Todd from her and give it back to the magician?" Dana said.

"Of course. Mallory, put Todd on the floor. So what are you guys doing here? I'm surprised to see you. Dana, you didn't mention anything about meeting Alexis for lunch."

"It was a last-minute thing, Ben. Who are you here with? You didn't mention that you were going out for lunch either."

"Is it okay with you, Ben?" Alexis said. "I'm not trying to steal your wife or anything. Ha." Dana laughed.

Ben did not laugh. "No. It's fine. It's fine, Alexis. I'm here with Don. Who else? Always with Don."

"Mallory, can you please put the rabbit down?" Dana politely asked her daughter.

"Mallory, put the rabbit down," Ben said more firmly.

"Let the nice waitresses take care of it. It belongs to that magician."

"No."

"Mallory. Put it down."

"NO."

"Mallory. Do what your father says."

"NO."

Ben sighed. "No sense making a scene," he said. "I'll talk to her outside. Um, I'll see you tonight, I guess. When you get home from work? Should I make something? The food's good here. You'll still be hungry, right? What should I make?"

"Whatever you make is fine, Ben. Just no more steak, please. I'll see you tonight," Dana said.

"Okay."

Ben reached down and pecked Dana on the cheek, but he lingered for another moment, standing, hovering persistently.

"Come close, child," Alexis said. She was glaring at Mallory.

Mallory looked to her father for guidance.

Ben shrugged his shoulders.

Mallory took a step towards Alexis.

"I'm going to show you a trick. Look at me," Alexis told

her. "Look right into my eyes."

I felt something pulling me into Mallory. My breath came in short unsatisfying bursts. I could feel Mallory's heart beating.

"Do you feel my energy?" Alexis said as she put her hands over Mallory's ears. "Feel how hot your ears are becoming. Look right into my eyes."

I could see through Mallory's eyes, and I was looking directly at Alexis Warrington, her eyeballs suddenly flooded with blackness. Then she blinked and pulled away, and everything returned to normal. I was floating above the crowd.

"Wow, what was that?" Ben said. "What did you see, Mallory?"

Mallory shrugged her shoulders. "Nothing," she said.

"Well, we should go, I guess," Ben said.

"Okay. Love you guys. I don't want to see that rabbit at home either," Dana said. "You'll have to find that magician and give him back his rabbit, Mallory."

Ben smiled. He looked out the window. "Speak of the Devil," he said.

The magician was sitting on the bumper of an ambulance, and a paramedic was wrapping gauze around his hand.

"And he shall appear," Alexis finished the sentence. Her complexion was pale, and her forehead beaded with sweat.

"Let's give that magician back his rabbit, Mallory. See you at home, Dana. And, Alexis, nice seeing you again. Let's have another dinner party. That was fun. Okay?"

"No," Mallory said.

"Yes." Ben and Mallory started to walk, Ben prodding the skulking Mallory on before him.

I hung back momentarily, trying to make sense of what had just happened. Mallory might have seen nothing, but I had.

"What did you see?" Dana asked.

"Hell," Alexis said.

Dana's hand went to cover her mouth, and a tear streamed down her cheek.

"Fuck," I said and headed for the door, following Ben and Mallory. I was going to have to do something about those women before it was too late.

The daylight was warm, but it made my eyes sting. I had not seen real sunlight for too many years to count. Summer was a horrible thing to have missed. It was probably summer all the time in Heaven, warm summer, with birds singing and people frolicking in the grass. Yes, I believe there is a lot of frolicking in Heaven. At least that is the way it was always presented to us in Sunday school. Frolicking and worship. Frolicking and worship.

Ben was talking to the magician in the parking lot. "You can keep it," the magician said.

Ben piped up: "No way, man. It's your rabbit. You keep it."

The necromancer looked at a ball of gauze where his hand had been. "I got a gig tonight at the Registry. What am I going to do? I'll have to cancel. That's a big lick for me, you know. I don't want that damn rabbit anywhere near me. Take him home. He's no good to me. Or let him loose in the grass. I don't want him anymore. Once they taste blood, they lose their chops."

"Chops? Are you insane?" Ben asked. "What are you talking about? Listen, Larry? Larry, right? Mind if I call you Larry?"

The Amazing Larry did not respond, just sat staring at his bandaged hand.

"Larry, I don't care whether you want it or not. It's yours, and you're taking it."

"He nearly took my finger off," Larry said.

"He's going to need stitches," the paramedic added as he helped the magician into the back of the ambulance. "Wait here," he said to Ben. "I'll call animal control. We'll need to test that thing for rabies. Lock it in your car or something."

"What the Hell?" Ben said. "MALLORY. PUT THAT DAMN RABBIT DOWN NOW! How the Hell did I get involved in this shit?"

As the magician got into the back of the ambulance, he turned to Ben and spoke: "He doesn't have rabies or anything else. He has all his shots. His name's Todd. You can ask them inside. They wouldn't let me bring him into the restaurant if he had rabies. The bartender has all the paperwork on him. He's a nice rabbit. I don't know what got into him."

The ambulance door shut. The paramedic jumped into the front seat, and with the lights flashing, pulled away.

Don was leaning against the back of Ben's Pontiac Vibe smoking a cigarette. "I figured it out," he said.

"What did you figure out?" Ben asked. "Move aside. Mallory, toss that rabbit in the grass."

"No."

"Well, set it down then. The ambulance man said you had to set it down."

"No. He didn't."

"Yes, he did. He told me that you should set it down while we wait for animal control. What did you figure out, Don?"

Mallory checked my way for advice.

"He's not going anywhere," I told her. "Put him down."

"It's her," Don said.

"Who?" Ben asked. "Who's her?"

"Alexis."

"Okay. What about her? Who is she?"

"She's the naked reiki girl."

"What?"

"Yeah, the naked reiki girl. She has her own website. She does naked reiki sessions on the internet. Well, she's not totally naked. Pretty close though."

Ben coughed. "You know, you're not seventeen anymore. Why are you consumed by sex? It's all you can think about. Why don't you meet somebody instead of constantly trolling the internet for porno? Alexis is a perfectly nice girl. She is not doing naked anything on the internet. Especially not naked Rape E?"

"Ray kee," Don corrected him. "I'll send you the link. That's her. I'm telling you."

That is when the man with the dog walked by.

He was wearing jean shorts, a Phish T-shirt, and a white bucket hat, stained yellow with sweat around the brim. He oozed marijuana and patchouli from his pores. The dog took one look at Todd the rabbit, preparing to chase it, then looked at me (because, of course, the rabbit was standing at my feet), and with a yelp, tore off out of the parking lot into a nearby field.

"HENDRIX!" the man called after the dog. "HENDRIX! Man, that's my dog." He looked to us for assistance.

"Keep the thing on a leash if you don't want it running away," Don told him.

"A leash, man. Yeah. Right on. We're born with a leash on, man. I'm not imposing that on my fur brother, man. HENDRIX," He called again. "Dudes. It's your guy's rabbit, man. That thing probably has rabies."

"It doesn't have rabies," Ben said.

"Hendrix. Dude, come back." The hippy ran off after the dog. "HENDRIX!"

"Bloody hippies," Ben scoffed. "I swear this town is overrun with them. Ever since that drum factory opened up."

"Pain in my ass," Don concurred. "You don't have to tell me. Asinine drum circles everywhere you go." Don looked at Mallory and the rabbit and said, "Whadya going to do with the bunny?"

"Nothing," Ben said. "We're going to leave it in the grass. It'll be happy in the wilderness."

Mallory, sensing impending doom, picked up the rabbit

again and cradled it in her arms.

"We can't keep that rabbit, Mallory. It's not ours."

Mallory looked to me for help, and tears began to stream down her face.

666

My eyes burned with strain. I had been working on The Cheezie Report for days, or so it felt like. I was exhausted. My leg, to the knee, was turning a greyish green, and it felt like it was made out of wood. Yes, the end was near. I knew it. I saved my spreadsheet again. I was in the habit of saving my work every 10 minutes or so, in case of the inevitable computer crash, and, of course, the IT group didn't back anything up.

What a spreadsheet it was too. This was my finest hour. The best work, I think, that I had ever done. It was massive and contained over 7,000 figures, all highlighted and colour coded, with bold headlines and sections with pivot tables, graphs, pie charts, and calendars. One could scroll endlessly sideways and down, pouring over remarkable and impressive figures, such as the date and time of Mallory's inception, the number of kilometres on the family car, which they called, 'Bessie 3,' and the number of times they had been camping, the dollar value of Mallory's first bicycle. It was all there in the files, but it wouldn't sum. There was one cell left that gave me an error. There were no numbers left to type in. I poured through all the files trying to find the mistake. I figured that the error was in column xxx cell number 79. I had entered 89.6 in that cell (Dana's average when she graduated high school), but I was not certain that it was correct. The Hepburn P. file that contained the information had a cigarette burn in it, so it was a little difficult to read, but I checked it again and again. That figure had to have been correct. I changed the decimal point, reversed the numbers…and still, nothing…still no sum. 89.6.

I was still in Hell, I still had an error that needed to be corrected, and although the spreadsheet was to be the cornerstone of my PowerPoint presentation to the board on Monday, it was useless to me without a conclusion. I sighed. I needed out of that office. I needed a coffee break.

I wheeled my chair back from my desk, stood, and left the office, locking my cage behind me.

Although there was a kitchen and lunch room at the end of the hallway, the little alcoves and seating areas off the main hallway were chock-a-block full of people in business attire, licking greasy smears of mayonnaise from their lips as they chewed, spilling fountain pops about the floor, and shuddering orgasmically (perhaps from lack of nutrition) as they shoved cheeseburgers and fries into their mouths. The hallway was littered with containers and wrappers from fast food. The whole floor smelled like a heavily used grease trap lined with pickles and processed cheese. The air was so vile that I could barely stand to breathe. Up against the wall, beneath a framed motivational poster of a sailboat, captioned, "ADJUST YOUR SAILS. NOT YOUR DREAMS," a man and a woman were openly engaged in a heavy-petting session.

It was becoming difficult to lift my zombie-bit foot when I walked. I could hear it thudding along the carpet, providing a beat for all the voices coming out of all the offices.

On my left I passed a room full of women. It was one of the boardrooms, but all the furniture had been pushed up against the walls. The group of women were laughing. Well, not really laughing. It was like they had forgotten how to laugh, and someone was trying to teach them how to do it again. They strained, "Ha. Ha. Ha. Ha." And "He. He. He. He." With a tone that seemed angry and witch-like, they went, "Ha. Ha. Ha. Ha. He. He. He. He." And then one older woman, grossly thin with a severe looking pageboy haircut, started making a sputtering sound with her lips and she broke off from the group, sticking her arms straight out and zooming about the room pretending that she was an airplane.

I stepped back in horror and my good foot landed in what I first thought was a pile of excrement but was only a box of half-eaten donuts. A man down at the very end of the hallway was watching me. He was spilling hot coffee down his chin as he bit on a Styrofoam cup. When he noticed that I saw him, he ran off and disappeared.

All this and I hadn't even made it to the lunchroom yet.

A red light suddenly went on at the far end of the hall and people started to disperse. The couple making out did up their buttons and zippers and went opposite directions. One of the green guys, riding a machine that kind of looked like a Zamboni, came steering down the hallway picking up the garbage as he went, sweeping and cleaning the carpet behind him. The laughing women stopped laughing and started gathering their purses and sweaters. Lunch was over.

By this time, I had forgotten what I even left my office for. It was really the only safe place, and I was anxious to get back to it. I practically ran down the hallway. When I reached my cage door, I fumbled for my keys. My hands shook as I went to stick the key in the lock. It was like the game Alice and I used to play when we were teenagers. "There's a killer on our tail. How fast can you get into the house?" I fumbled and fumbled, checking behind me for threats. The cage door finally opened. I hurried inside only to find Betty sitting in my wheeled chair.

"Hello there, big girl," she said. "How are you getting on?"

"How'd you get in here?" I asked, cautiously putting my keys onto my filing cabinet.

Betty's eyes were bloodshot and blackened. The thick layer of makeup and lipstick I had seen her in before was gone, and her lilac-coloured wig was frazzled and askew upon her head. She looked deranged.

"I have a master key. I can get anywhere," Betty said. In her hand, she held a thick binder with little tabs jutting from the edges. She opened it and ran her finger across a page but stopped. "No need to worry," she said. "I've had my colour test. Before I had my latest test, I was an Alizarin Crimson. They've taught me how to be a green. A Chartreuse, truth be told. It's much better."

"There is no chartreuse," I said, prepared to catch Betty in a lie. "It doesn't exist."

"Oh, they just made it up," Betty said. "Professor Norris

came up with it. It's a very sought after sub-colour. Not as good as Yellow Pages, but much better than Melchior Brown, and a million times better than Kink Crimson. Anyway, I am sorry we got off on the wrong foot. I am not here to cause you any pain or interfere with your work in any way. I am here as a representative of the social committee to give you an itinerary of upcoming events. On the 15th, there is a birthday lunch for Ernie in accounting. We're going to Woking on Heaven's Door. Hope you like Italian. It's pay your own way. Rebecca is getting married. We need a present for her. I can take your donation now or come back for it later. You better get a pen and write this down. Jimmy is retiring. We are all donating $20 to get him something nice. The third Monday of every month is the cupcake social. Bring enough for everyone, please. There is a lunch on the 19th for Juanita to celebrate her promotion. She's leaving us. We're so sad. We're also chipping in to get her a gift. That lunch will be at Waste of Thyme, Midtown. Not the one on 6th Ave. Friday is coffee klatch. We meet in the kitchen at break. Bring a knitted, hypoallergenic scarf for the homeless. We're also collecting donations for the United Way. Here's the form to sign. You can have the donations taken directly off your paycheque. If we don't beat last year's total, a young child will be sacrificed to the zombies. That comes directly from the United Way board of directors. On the weekend of the 26th, there is the softball tournament against Lexmar. I will leave you a list of all the games so that you can add them to your calendar. We have to win or Satan will behead someone at home plate. And I actually think She is serious this year. Mandy, you know Mandy, Bev's assistant? She wants to have a practice tonight. What position do you play?"

"I don't play baseball," I said. "I don't know Mandy."

"Fine. You can pitch then. Phil says he has a bunch of spare gloves. Also, what instrument do you play? The talent show for The Boys and Girls Clubs of Hell is on the Monday following."

"I don't play an instrument," I told her. "Nothing. I can't play baseball. I can't play any instrument. I can't. I don't know how. I don't want to."

"Can you juggle? Anything?" We've got a five-minute slot we have to fill."

"No. Nothing. I can't play baseball, and I can't play an instrument."

"You have no talents, whatsoever?"

"Not that I know of."

"Well, rehearsals start tonight. Can you learn to juggle by showtime?"

"No. Probably not."

"What colour are you?"

"Peach."

"Hmm. Can you work on becoming a Sap Green? A team player? I mean, I don't feel that you are working with me here."

"I don't know. I suppose. I can't learn to juggle by Friday, though. It's not possible."

"Fine. The band needs a drummer. Can you keep a beat, Peach?"

"No."

"I'll mark you down for drums. Anyone can play the drums. It's for charity, anyway. No one cares what you sound like."

I stood in stunned silence as I watched Betty close up her giant folder, stand, and sidle past me to the cage door. I took my seat back and wheeled it up to my computer, preparing to start work again, my face wrinkled and tight with tension and frustration as I tried to ignore her shuffling out of my office.

"Oh, by the way," Betty was standing in the doorway holding the bars of the cage open, "I forgot to mention: The laughing group meets daily at noon in the large board room. I've signed you up. It's mandatory for all the women on the staff. Professor Norris says women tend to get moody throughout the day. He says this will help us foster better attitudes in the workplace. Okay? Ha. Ha." Betty smiled at me and forcefully shut the cage door, leaving it rattling as she walked away.

I put my head down on my desk, and I felt a tear stream down my cheek. "I hate it here," I said.

I smelled something burning.

666

"Ag. Come on!" Ben said, leaping from his kneeling position on the floor and running over to the stove. The spaghetti sauce he was cooking was bubbling and boiling out over the pot. "Shit." He went to stir the sauce with the screwdriver that he was holding but caught himself in time. He turned down the temperature on the burner, tossed the screwdriver on the counter, and found the spoon.

"Mallory!" he said.

"..."

When no answer came, he repeated himself, "Mallory!"

Mallory appeared in the kitchen. She was dressed in a long, cool summer dress with a pattern of pretty pink flowers. She held a headless barbie doll in her hand. Ben stirred away at the bubbling cauldron of sauce.

"Can you come and take Todd away?" Ben asked.

Mallory picked Todd up. With a headless Barbie in her hand and hoisting Todd up onto her shoulder, Mallory said,

"Daddy? How much longer till you're done with Todd's cage?" Shiny silver screws, wing nuts, bolts, and cage bars were scattered across the lino of the kitchen floor.

"Soon, honey. The instructions are all in German, but I am doing my best. Take Todd away and keep him on the newspaper. Case he poops. Okay?" Todd sniffed at the air and found me in the room.

"He's doing that thing with his teeth again," Mallory said. "He likes Karen."

"What? Who does he like?" Ben's phone buzzed in his pocket.

Mallory ran back to the living room. Ben set the spoon on the rim of the spaghetti pot and pulled the phone out of his pocket. I sidled up behind him reading over his shoulder. It was a text from Don. The heading was titled, "Reiki. That's her isn't it?"

Ben clicked on the link in the body of the email. A video started playing on his phone.

On the screen a massage table sat empty in front of a wall that was painted (very poorly) to look like the night sky, with planets revolving in a very unscientific random manner. An owl swooped across the foreground in the weightless universe.

Soft music began to play, a pan flute accompanied by a

piano that sounded slightly out of tune. Two women then approached an empty massage table. They stood behind it and stared into the camera, pie-eyed as if they had just smoked the biggest hash joint ever rolled. The volume of the music quieted.

"Hi, I'm..."

"Alexis," Ben finished her statement for her.

"Today I am here with Amber, and we are going to demonstrate the art of healing using the ancient technique of reiki. Amber, if you would disrobe and lie down, please."

Amber peeled her jean shorts from her long white legs. Her tie-dye T-shirt followed. She was standing naked before the camera. She had large pale breasts and a mound of brown pubic hair. She laid herself on the massage table, face up, and closed her eyes.

"What the hell is this about?" Ben asked.

Alexis then removed her own colourful Dashiki shirt. Numerous necklaces hung from her neck and a variety of silver and gold medallions rested in the valley between her breasts.

"In case you are wondering," Alexis said, "there's no shame in us being naked for this. Reiki is an ancient and sacred form of healing that is best practiced unencumbered by the trappings of modern life. If we can revert back to our spiritual core where the only thing left is our chakras that is best. Now let's begin. My name is Alexis, as I have said, and I am a level 17 reiki practitioner. Today we are doing a full body treatment on Amber. And this will include a full energy balancing of her Chi. If there are any emotional blockages or evil spirits, we will be releasing them. We will start by bringing the reiki energy through Amber." Alexis went and stood at Amber's head. She raised her arms, palms towards her face and closed her eyes concentrating hard on the invisible forces of the universe.

(Invisible for a reason, let me tell you. You don't want to know what those forces are.)

"Now, what we are doing here is scanning Amber's auric field, looking for any areas of intense heat." Alexis placed her hands a few inches above Amber's face and began making circles.

As she got down further towards Amber's breasts, I noticed a lump rising in Ben's pants. (No matter how lousy my life was, no matter what happened to me after I died, I was always happy about one thing: at least I was not born a man.)

"No. No. No," Ben said. He paused the video. "Come on. This is Dana's new friend."

I remember wishing there was a way to tell Ben it was all going to be okay. I was going to take over soon. And once I did, the growing distance between him and Dana would not matter. Satan would not only protect the Matthews family, but She would ensure that the family prospered. Ben was soon going to have the whole world at his disposal, tits and all. Being father of the chosen girl child meant mortgaging his future and spending eternity in Hell, but at this juncture in his life, if he continued on the course he was on, he was probably going to end up in Hell anyway, so what did any of it really matter?

Ben poked his head into the living room. "Mallory you are suspiciously quiet in there. What is going on? What have you done? All your Barbies? The heads? What have you done with the heads?"

"But they needed new heads, Dad."

Across the entirety of the living room, headless Barbie dolls were strewn like victims of some ancient Barbie massacre.

"You know, Mallory. We buy you all these toys because you don't have a brother or sister, and you just wreck them. What is wrong with you, child?" Ben said.

"They need new heads, Dad."

"Argh."

Ben's phone buzzed again. He checked it. It was a text message from Don.

"Is that her, or what? Anticipatory (possibly lecherous) smiley face."

Ben quickly and deftly worked his thumbs over his phone. "Yes. We'll talk later."

He brought the video back to the screen. He had paused it on a tight shot of Alexis's hands drifting just above Amber's breasts.

(Oh, to be in my twenties again and not some ancient old ghoul.)

"He put the phone in his pocket and started up the stairs. "I have to go to the washroom, Mallory. I will be down in a minute. You just play. Okay?"

"Okay, Dad." Mallory took the head of a Ken doll and was using clear tape to attach it to the body of a Skipper doll.

At a certain point, I figured, I would have to be of some use to this family. If they were ever going to accept me as one of their own, I would need to show my worth. I mean, I wasn't going to be like Todd. They couldn't keep me in a cage and pet me whenever they felt the need to touch some soft fur. No, not only were they going to have to accept me but also let me live among them, let me take over a large percentage of their daughter's very essence, her core, her personality, her soul. Was there something that I could do to show them how useful it could be having a demon in the family? Just as I was thinking this, I saw the screwdriver on the counter, and at first glance, I wished I could take it back to Hell with me and plunge it into Betty's forehead, but then I started thinking about opportunities, thinking like a businesswoman.

As I learned in the lecture series I attended, "The Guiding Principles to a More Successful You," hosted by Jeremy Storm, lead singer for Easy Lover, a Phil Collins tribute band, "never let an opportunity to shine pass you by."

As you can imagine, everyone in Hell knows how to speak or read at least a bit of German. I picked up a hex socket from the floor, checked the instructions, stood a portion of the cage up, and went to work.

It took all of five minutes to put the cage together.

Ben was coming down the stairs again. "Mallory, what is going on here? Is everything okay?"

"Fine, Dad."

Ben walked right past the cage and to the pot of spaghetti sauce. He stirred and filled another pot with water to cook the noodles and set it on a burner to boil. "Now," he said, as he turned. "I am not letting you kraut bastards beat me. What the Hell?"

"Karen did it." Mallory was standing in the doorway. "Stuff was floating around."

"What the Hell?" Ben said again. "Who did this?"

"Karen did it," Mallory repeated herself. "Do you think she will ever go away?"

"Mallory, what do you mean? Did you put this together? No, you couldn't have. Did I do it? I must have done it and forgotten? Where is my head these days? I could have sworn that I still had to put it together."

"Daddy, you told me everything was going to be okay. Is everything going to be okay?"

"Of course, everything is going to be okay. What are you talking about?"

"Karen."

"Karen. Again. You're saying she did this? Mallory, enough with the imaginary friend, okay? It's getting weird. Oh, I hear Mom at the door. Go! Go give her a big hug. Okay?"

"..."

"Go on. Everything is going to be okay. Let me worry about Karen."

Mallory scooted across the kitchen floor and towards the

mudroom at the back of the house, shouting: "Mommy, Mommy."

"I could have sworn that I hadn't done anything on this," Ben said, with no one around for him to hear. "Karen?" he said softly and hesitantly.

"Yes." I wondered if he could hear me.

"Karen," he scoffed. "The shit kids come up with! Mind's a funny thing. Foolish." Ben took a big gulp of wine from his glass, eyeballed the cage for a moment, and went back to his his spaghetti sauce. As he stirred, I took up the hex keys, raised them high above my head, and dropped them to the floor.

"What the!" Ben turned from the stove quickly, an arc of spaghetti sauce droplets flinging from his spoon and splattering on the kitchen cabinets.

Dana came in the kitchen. "What's all this?" She said as she took her name tag off her hospital greens and stuck it to the fridge with a magnet.

"Jesus, you scared the Hell out of me," Ben said.

"What's that, Ben?"

"What's what? The cage?"

"That's Todd's cage," Mallory said. "Daddy said that Todd has to have a cage and a water bottle, and he can't wander around the house pissing and shitting everywhere."

"Mallory! Language!"

"But Daddy said it!"

"That doesn't make it okay. Can you watch your language please, Ben?"

"Yes, dear."

"Todd?" Dana asked. "Ben, please tell me you didn't!"

Ben stood shuffling his feet and staring at the ground. "Yeah, about Todd. It's been a weird day, okay. And now we have a pet rabbit named Todd. What more can I tell you." Ben leaned over and whispered into Dana's ear. (I could hear because I was right behind them.) "I don't think rabbits live very long if that's any consolation." Then loudly: "Mallory, why don't you go get Mommy a towel out of the laundry basket in the basement. Mommy, you go have a shower, get out of your scrubs, and get into something more comfortable. We are having a spaghetti dinner. And I'll put Todd in his new cage and cook the noodles. Okay?"

"Excellent," Mallory said and ran off to the basement.

"For God sakes, Ben. I told you. What are you thinking?"

"I'm sorry. If you saw her face. She was crying. I thought maybe this would help her out of the funk she is in."

"Oh, my God. She's playing you. Every time she cries, you buy her a toy. You're such a pushover. Call that magician and make him take it back," Dana said.

"I can't. I don't know how to reach him."

"Well, put it outside. I don't want another pet. What about the cat? What about Gregsie? She'll kill it."

"Listen, Dana. I've had enough. This has been a miserable day. Leave me to deal with the rabbit. I will take care of it. Okay? I can take care of it. You just have to trust my judgement."

"Do I, Ben?" Dana said as she bent down to examine the cage. "Do I have to?"

"You know, I was thinking about that email that you sent," Ben said. "Ringo Chan. It was because you needed him to be like you. That is why you were mad at him. He wanted something else."

"Doesn't everyone need an ally?"

Mallory came back upstairs with the towel. "Here you go, Mommy. Can I tell you about my day while you shower?"

"Of course, honey."

And the two disappeared up the stairs.

The family prepared themselves for supper, with Ben finishing up the pasta and preparing a salad (reading the labels on the croutons, making sure everything was dairy free). Mallory talked to Dana and searched her playroom for more Barbies to decapitate, Dana took a long shower, washing the day's literal and figurative filth from her body. I walked about the house looking at the family pictures on the walls. They were all of Mallory in various stages of her life, up until the present. There were pictures of Mallory smiling at the beach, and pictures of her walking away from the camera with a giant bag of chips in her hand, wearing a baseball cap and shorts. Pictures with grandmas and grandpas, and a family picture at the park, in the summer, then another one in the winter, all of them bundled up with the only exposed skin being their faces, smiling from ear to ear, all of them. A family. Yes, now that was really something. I didn't have a family of my own when I was alive. I had my sister, my mom, my dad, but I didn't ever have a husband or children. I didn't necessarily want a family when I was alive, although now that I saw what I was missing, I realized that I had probably made a mistake. This house, where the Matthews family lived, was a real home, and it would soon be my home. Those pictures on the wall would soon be pictures of me, playing baseball, accepting awards at school, singing in the Christmas choir, and playing the flute in the school band. Me. For my time was coming. Karen was coming.

These were the halcyon days in the possession of Mallory Matthews, sweet beyond measure, wonderful to behold, and I was sad to know that they would not last.

Karen is coming.

666

For supper, the Matthews family ate salad and large plates of spaghetti, steaming and smelling so tasty. Ben had even purchased a dairy-free parmesan cheese substitute for Mallory. Mallory complained about not having rare steak, but she ate the spaghetti anyway. They laughed about Todd and the magician from the restaurant. This was the first time that I had seen them happy. It was as if Satan had not waged war to possess their eternal souls.

After supper, Dana and Ben cleaned up the dishes and Ben asked Dana about her day at the hospital.

"Ah, it was fine," was all she said.

"Hey?" Ben queried. "Do you know what your friend Alexis does for a living?"

"I think she is some sort of massage therapist. She runs a clinic out of her house. Why do you ask?"

"Oh, I don't know. I just wondered. I know she's not making any money as an actress, right?"

"Pft!" Dana scoffed knowingly. "We've got rehearsals again on Thursday. Maybe you and Mallory can come watch?"

"Maybe."

"I miss you guys. Seems like I never see you these days," Dana said.

"I know. We miss you too, hun," Ben said, giving Dana a kiss on the cheek before he put the plates he was holding into the dishwasher.

Ben then gave Mallory a quarter teaspoon of probiotic powder, for her 'dairy' allergy, and said: Why don't you two go pick out a family movie. I'll wash these pots up and be right down.

As the girls went downstairs Ben started running water into the kitchen sink.

I sat on the floor beside Todd's cage. Todd came and pressed himself against me, grinding his teeth and staring lovingly into my eyes.

"I know how you feel," I said to Todd. "Trapped. With no way out. There's a way, right? There has to be a way, doesn't there, Todd?"

Of course, Todd did not answer because he was a rabbit, and rabbits are mostly stupid.

"What is it that you want Todd?"

Todd seemed to have shifted his attention to the mess on the counter.

"Ah! The salad. You want that Caesar salad, don't you? Well, if there is something you want, you've just got to take it for yourself. That is how a free capitalist state works. That is democracy. Opportunities abound, Todd."

Ben went into the dining room and came back into the kitchen with more dishes. He scraped uneaten food into the green bin. He shut off the kitchen faucet.

"You want to watch the Lion King, Ben?" Dana's voice from downstairs.

"No. We've seen it a million times. What about Murder She Wrote?"

"Mallory wants to watch a kid's show."

"Okay, well, whatever then. Not the Lion King though. I am sick of it. Columbo?"

"A KID'S SHOW!"

"Well, whatever."

He put the dishes in the dishwasher and went back into the living room.

I unlocked Todd's cage door and let him hop out. He came and sat on my lap. I stood and carried him to the counter where he nibbled on the leftover ends of the romaine lettuce.

"If you want the prize, and you are trapped in a cage, then I suppose you need someone to unlatch the door for you. You need help," I said.

Ben walked back into the kitchen holding the salt and pepper shakers. "How the Hell did you get out of your cage, Todd? And on the counter, no less?" he said. "What are you? super rabbit?"

"I've got an idea. I'll be back for you, Todd," I said. "Karen is coming."

Ben jumped and looked frantically around the room, his eyes as wide as the dinner plates he was cleaning up. "Who's here?" he said. "Who said that?"

"Karen is coming." The house shook a little when I said it, and I raced to the attic and dove headlong into my sick box, plummeting, of my own free will, back to Hell.

"What was that noise?" Dana called from the basement.

"Nothing," Ben said. "Just the pipes shuddering again."

666

"So, you see, I need some help. I was wondering if you could fill me in a bit on Hepburn P. Is there any way I can contact him?"

Professor Norris's office was sparsely furnished and smaller than I had expected. He had one framed issue of S Magazine on his walls, in which he was featured on the cover, shaking hands with Satan herself. The issue title was, "Doing the Deed." Next to that, a motivational poster hung. It read, "LUCK ONLY EXISTS IN THE MINDS OF THE RUDDERLESS. *Douglas Thompson*," and had a picture of a man fiercely focused on kayaking through an enormous rush of whitewater.

I stood in front of Professor Norris as he sat at his desk, which was mostly empty, no computer, no papers, just a neatly arranged brown desk pad and a pen holder with a few pens and pencils in it. The Professor was leaning back in his chair, deep in thought. He had arranged his fingers and thumbs together like a pyramid and kept tapping his index fingers against his philtrum. He stopped. Creativity had struck him, I suppose.

"Hepburn P. Yes. You can localize, by the extensive action items in your workspace, that there are superannuated vortals in play here. To compellingly plagiarize the bleeding edge economics of global holistics and deploy compellingly..."

"Professor," I cut him off. "If I may. Can we take this offline?"

"Certainly, Karen. I am here to assist you in maximizing your potential to succeed. Do go on."

"I can come and go as I please. I can exist with them. Pick things up, make noises, little Mallory can see me. I can communicate with her. The husband is lying to his wife. The wife is lying to the husband. They are at each other's throats one minute, but deeply in love the next. So what does it mean? I mean, what good is any of it? Where do I go from here? If I can't actually take over the child. I have been nibbling on Mallory's heel, trying to find a way to complete the merge, but all I do is make her sick. And the soft rot is getting worse and worse. And to top it off...have you heard of a reiki practitioner?"

"Reiki! Those bastards," the professor said. "What

level?"

"Seventeen."

"Sonofabitch. We have to get moving. She'll have you exorcised in no time. Perhaps the board will have some input. How is your presentation coming along? Monday is almost upon us."

"I almost have the presentation ready," I said, "but I am missing one crucial figure, and I cannot get a sense of what it might be. I think this is the key that will open the doors of Hell. That is why I am here. Hepburn P. knows. He did it. He got there. I have to contact him. Look. Look at my slides."

I set my laptop on Professor Norris's desk. A few deft keystrokes later, and I had the latest draft of my PowerPoint presentation up. I flicked through the slides to show the professor what I had been working on. The first slide showed people running from great walls of fire, screaming, their neckties and torn blouses flapping behind them. The sky was grey, and lightning and tornadoes ravaged the surrounding countryside.

"Wow. That's good. I like that," Professor Norris said.

"And this one," I said. Another slide depicted a majestic dragon bursting from a volcano and rearing up with bloody teeth to roar mightily (again, as people ran).

"These are great slides."

"And again," I said. The next slide was of winged demons flying in the sky like birds. The domed buildings of this futuristic world appeared to be made of glass and cellophane. A great horned beast sat on a throne, and a line of raggedly clothed men and women bound together at the ankles by an endless chain that stretched off into the distant mountains served the beast platters of bloody flesh.

"Excellent again. Where did you get these? The cartoonist is amazing."

"I expropriated them from the Watchtower online."

"Well, Karen. Good work. Good to see you have the ball rolling here. Now, what shall I architect for you?"

"I need to arrange a meeting with Hepburn P. Where do I find him?"

"Hepburn P. Yes. A catalyst for change. A high watermark of proficiency. He was Germanium White, you know. He was the only one. Ever. It's thanks to him that the enthusiasm for this project arose at all. We're being challenged here. We're targeting our lines of communication now. The networks need to be reconceptualized. The IT department is working on leveraging the configurations as we speak."

"Hepburn P. you mean? You can contact him?"

"It's difficult. We need to get back on message with IT about our conveyance logistical transport programming."

"You mean his email's bouncing?"

"Ideally. If we can still get in through the back end, we should have the deliverables ready by spring."

"But this is Hell, sir. Spring never comes."

"Germanium Whites never doubt, Karen. Naysayers, and pessimists become Honduran Blues. Karen, my Karen, my Toasted Sienna. This is our time. Focus on your deliverables. Hyperscale and repurpose. Revolutionize and reinvent. Look at the posters. Winners are not people who never fail, but people who never quit. If you believe you can do it then it has already been done. You are the gift of you. The path on life's journey is a million miles long, a million miles wide, and takes but a universal second to complete. And the path is crowded, so walk with pride and dignity and cherish every footstep. When you bump into someone, welcome the good, ignore the bad, and love the sunsets together. Life is a full of scraped knees, misplayed balls, and bad umpires, but no matter how many times you strike out, always remember that you're going to get another chance to bat. Never stop swinging for the fences. Life is like a taxi ride. You get in, you pay the driver, and if your head is clear, your directions good, you end up where you want to be. It takes less courage to be the mob than it does to face the mob. I believe in only one thing: US."

I started backing away slowly. Professor Norris sat still with only his lips moving. I think his head would have exploded had the door not burst open behind me and two dog-faced men in suits rushed into the room. They were followed by a crew of hornless men wearing white jumpsuits and hardhats. Professor Norris kept on, getting louder. I could smell something burning: "Sooty Rose. Torched Umber. Aqualicious Green. Purple Mauve. Yellow Pages. Turkey Gobbler Pink. "

One of the dog-faced men barked at me (like, really barked). It was quite clear that they wanted me gone. I kept backing away.

One of the men in white took a drill from a doctor's bag and pressed it up against Professor Norris's forehead. I could hear it whizzing as I shut the door behind me.

"Neptunium SILVER," I heard Norris shout. And then nothing but the whirring of the drill and wet splattering of his brains spilling onto his desk.

Even Professor Norris was not immune to restructuring.

I started walking back down the hallway. Well, limping, actually. My entire leg was numb. It still moved, but the zombie infection had made it to the hip. This might be the last walk I ever took down the hallway. How would I ever solve this riddle? I needed one last bit of data. I needed to talk to Hepburn P. Somebody knew how to contact him. But who?

"Something wrong with your leg?" Betty said.

She was standing in the mailroom with a cup of coffee in her hand. Her face appeared to be made of shaved meat, like a pastrami sandwich with hot mustard. She smelled like fresh bagels pulled from an oven. I shook my head to clear it. A drop of sweat rolled down my forehead. In my entire existence in Hell and on earth I never wanted to eat anyone as badly as I wanted to eat Betty at that moment. It was then that I noticed the letter opener conveniently located by the counter. It was calling me.

"I should check my mail," I said.

As I walked over, dragging my leg to the mail slots, I heard a voice behind me. "Esira Live," it said loudly.

"ESIRA LIVE," louder again.

My stomach grumbled with a painful hunger. I needed a snack.

666

"You can't possibly be hungry, Mallory. I already gave you a snack. I gave you the peanut butter and toast. You had the leftover steak. You had the brownie. You ate less for supper."

"But I'm hungry, Daddy. I want a snack."

"I want a snack. I want a snack. Every night before bed you want a snack," Ben said, as he pulled the covers up to her neck. "You know what I think? I think you are stalling because you don't want to go to bed."

"Sleep with me, Daddy. Please. Sleep with me. I'm scared."

Ben sighed. "Scared! Scared of what? There is nothing to be scared of. This is your home. No one is getting in here. This is the safest place in the world. You just need to close your eyes and think nice thoughts. Daddy is always here to protect you. Every night, Mallory. 'I'm scared. I'm scared.' Every night of my life since you learned to speak we have to go through this. I am going to lose my mind."

"Go to bed with me. I'm scared."

"I can't, honey. It isn't grown up bedtime yet. I need to talk to Mommy. Goodnight. You have your stuffy? Mr. Bear?"

"Yes."

"And Todd is here. I put his cage right here. And Gregsie is around somewhere. It's fine. Right?"

"Right."

"Then goodnight. Don't let the bed bugs bite. I love you."

"I love you too, Daddy."

Ben kissed little Mallory on the forehead and walked downstairs. I followed him to the steps. I could still see Mallory in her room, the door open, her little Minnie Mouse night light on, but I could also see Dana and Ben. Dana was sitting on the couch in the living room. I stood on the landing.

"Is she asleep?" Dana asked as Ben came lightly down the stairs.

"Soon."

"You didn't get her a snack?"

"No," Ben scoffed. "She isn't hungry. She just wants to stay up later. 'I'm scared. I want a snack.' Every night.

'Sleep with me.'"

"She's just little, Ben."

"Maybe."

"No. Not maybe," Dana said. "She is little. And she needs our help. Next year, she'll be in grade one. And in fifteen years, she'll be in university. Do you know how fast fifteen years go, Ben? Do you have any idea what can happen in fifteen years?"

Ben paused in thought before he spoke. "No," he said. "What can happen in fifteen years?"

"I don't know. Anything, I suppose. Like, when you woke up this morning, did you think we would have a caged rabbit named Todd in our house?"

Ben laughed. "No."

Dana laughed too. "Like I said. Anything."

"You're tired," Ben said. "Do you want a massage?"

"Sure. Sounds good. Where should I go?"

"Just sit between my knees here."

Ben sat on couch, a bit of retro furniture that someone had in their living room in the '70s. It looked more like the back seat of a 1966 Buick LeSabre than a couch. Dana took her cell phone out of her pocket and set it on the coffee table and nestled herself between his legs. Ben started working on her neck.

I could feel Mallory's eyes staring through the back of my head, and I turned to see her in her bed.

"What are you doing?" she mouthed.

"Spying," I mouthed back.

Mallory started to pull the covers back, so she could get up and join me. I shook my head NO and put up a stop sign with the palm of my hand. Mallory huffed in anger and rolled over.

"Do you remember the prophecy?" Dana asked as she rolled her neck.

"What, the movie with Christopher Walken? Yeah, it was awful."

"No. THE Prophecy."

Ben thought for a moment while he massaged her neck. "Oh, yeah," he said. "The Prophecy. Yeah, that was so strange. What made you think of that?"

"Remember they came into our hospital room. The nurse said we had visitors. They came bearing gifts for Mallory, autographed LPs, CDs, and cassette tapes. The only thing they did not have was an eight track."

"Yeah, some people will do anything for publicity."

Dana let her chin hang on her chest as Ben massaged. "You ever listen to it, Ben?"

"No. NO! Of course not. We threw it out, didn't we?"

"Why didn't we listen to it?" Dana asked. "Do you remember?"

Ben shrugged. "I thought we threw it all out. They looked so weird. Didn't we call the cops?"

Dana sat up a little straighter and turned to face Ben, her elbows on his knees. "I found the CD in the junk drawer the other day. I played it in the car. I used to think it was heavy metal. You know, they were all dressed in black and had those piercings. But I listened to it. It actually isn't heavy metal."

I turned to make sure Mallory was not coming. She had rolled over and was staring at me again. I saw her mouth the words, "NOT FAIR."

Dana continued: "It was all acoustic instruments and flutes. They sing songs about little demons in misty forests and rising cell phone rates. The lyrics are bizarre. They sing songs about cable television bills that rise so high no one can afford to watch TV anymore. It's so weird. There's a song about a world series that no one sees. There is another song called, Lucy Fur Ball. It's got the oddest melody. It goes like (Dana started to sing softly, hauntingly):

"The cell phone signal is out of tune
The horned shepherd raises the rune
Who would be the tamer?

Mouse or cat

Mouse or cat

Who can afford that

NAME HER

Unholy unnamable namer

NAME HER

NAME HER

Hail Lucy Fur Ball Hail Lucy Fur Ball

Welcome Mallory"

"NOT FAIR," Mallory mouthed again.

"Quiet," I said.

"Ha." Ben laughed. "That's funny."

Dana continued: "What's funny?"

"Lucy Fur Ball. Next cat we get let's name it that."

"I don't find it funny," Dana said. "They said Mallory. That's our child's name, Ben. They had no way of knowing that. Not at all. Like, this shit is not funny. It had all this eerie flute music playing and acoustic guitars and fiddles. It was like they were the headlining band at a virgin sacrifice."

"They were just a bunch of freaks," Ben said. "That drum factory opened the same year Mallory was born. It was those damn hippies. Maybe one of the ones your sister met when she got into communal living. Pam knew we

187

were calling the baby Mallory. She always had such bizarre friends. Remember Dalton, or as he called himself, 'Earth Centre Ganpati.' Remember he got his tongue pierced, and it got infected. Like, that kid was demented. I'm telling you. He belonged in a mental institution. Remember he was in a band even. Turn around again. You're tense. You're tired. You're not making sense."

Dana turned; Ben continued to knead her neck muscles.

"I don't think it was my sister," Dana said. "I don't think it was Earth Centre Ganpati, either."

"Well, who was it then?"

"I don't know, but that is kinda the point."

"What. What is the point?"

Dana stared straight ahead. "How come you can't see it?"

"See what, Dana? You're tired. You need to go to bed early tonight."

"You keep saying that. Like that is a reasonable response. It's not. Just because you go to bed doesn't mean when you wake up all your problems will be gone."

"But what problems, Dana? We have no problems. Everything is fine."

"It is? I don't feel fine."

"Why? Because of The Prophecy? You haven't thought

of that stuff in years. There was no trouble with them. They went away. What's the big deal? Stress does horrible things to people's minds. Do you have any vacation days left? We have no money to go anywhere, but you could take a staycation?"

"Do you know what reiki is, Ben?"

"No. Never heard of it."

"It's a cleansing of sorts. Like a spiritual cleansing. You know, Alexis is a level 17 reiki practitioner? She studied in Japan. She learned from a reiki grandmaster. A man named Hirohito Kawasaki."

"Alexis? You two are thick as thieves, eh? That's good. Good to have friends."

"I like her. She's funny. She's smart. And she knows all this stuff about alternative medicine. I've been working as a nurse for my entire adult life, and I think modern medicine stinks. We won't accept the age-old proven benefits of acupuncture, homeopathy, or even something like reiki."

Ben undid the top button on Dana's shirt and started working on her shoulders. "Maybe there is a reason for that, eh?" he said. "Maybe you can't heal a gaping wound with homeopathy or by calling upon the God of the beaten drum to heal us."

"A gaping cut. Like a rabbit bite? You mean?"

Ben's mind whiffed on that curveball, "..."

Dana took a big breath. "Right then," she said as if gearing up for something big. "Ben, I think our relationship is not doing so well. I want to go out on a date. I want you to take me out."

"What?"

"We haven't been out on a date in a long time."

"What about Mallory?" Ben said.

"We'll get a babysitter," Dana told him.

"Who? Your mom's out of town. My sister's getting another divorce."

"What about Alexis?" Dana quickly answered.

"Alexis. How's that going to work?"

"What do you mean, how is it going to work? I will phone her and ask her. She's a nice person. I've talked to her quite a bit lately."

"Yeah, I know she is nice, but you really want her looking after our child? How well do we really know her? I mean, really?"

"I know her plenty well. She's fine and she'll take good care of Mallory. We'll go out this Friday, after I get home from work."

"I don't know," Ben said.

"It's too late, Ben. We're doing it," Dana said. "We're

going to play bingo and have a laugh. No discussion."

"If you trust her. I guess."

Ben quickly undid another button on Dana's shirt.

Dana tossed her head back into his lap.

Ben stopped massaging and pulled on a chain around Dana's neck. "Where'd you get this necklace?" he asked.

It is interesting to think about events, occurrences in the past; in the moment, when something occurs, your perceptions of the event are far different than your memories of that same instance. This is always true. Even seconds later, after you have had time to process the information. What I mean is: When I heard Ben mention the necklace, I thought nothing of it.

Now, when I look back on it, I can pinpoint that very moment as the beginning of a sequence of events that would take me from a simple story about Satanic possession to a dark and distorted, horrible and dishonest place, down a strange twisted and awful avenue that no one could have ever expected.

Not even me.

"Where'd you get this necklace?" Ben asked.

Ben pulled the long chain with a pendant from the hollow of Dana's breasts, moved her hair over to the other side of her neck, and held a pendant in his palm.

"It's a Marvel cross," Dana said.

Ben held the pendant up to the light. It was a single loop that crossed at the bottom to make two more small loops.

"It's to ward off evil spirits."

And Mallory began to shout. "Mommy. Mommy. I want Mommy."

"Where did you get it?" Ben let the cross drop back onto Dana's chest.

Dana turned to him, kneeling between his legs. "She's calling me."

"Yeah, I heard her," Ben said.

"I'm going to have to do this without you, aren't I?" Dana said.

"She called you. Not me," Ben answered. "I took her to bed the first time. Go see what she wants."

"MOMMY. I'M SCARED."

They were staring into one another's eyes. Dana balked first. She stood.

"Don't fall asleep," Ben said as he stood and grabbed Dana about the waist. He held her close to him. "I love you," he said.

"I'll be back in a minute," Dana said. "I want you to listen to the CD. It's in my purse. We need to talk."

"Ok. Don't fall asleep, though."

"Of course, I won't."

"Yeah, of course, you won't," Ben said. "Every time you go lay down with her you fall asleep."

"Oh, my belly. Momma. Momma. My belly," Mallory moaned.

"I won't," Dana said and came running up the stairs past me. She sat on the bed next to Mallory, then laid down beside her and stroked her hair. It wasn't more than ten minutes later that she was asleep and snoring.

As a last act of defiance, Mallory peered at me over Dana's shoulder and stuck out her tongue. She then fell asleep herself, safely, and beside her mother.

666

After Dana left him to go upstairs, Ben sat back down on the couch and picked up a paperback novel that had been shoved between the cushions. I could see the cover. It was an old pulp fiction novel called *Tender is the Knife*. He read it for about fifteen minutes before he stood, went to the bottom of the stairs, and softly called up: "Hello? Dana?"

No answer.

"Shit," Ben said. She had fallen asleep, and he knew it. Ben looked out the front door window. "SHIT!" he said again. He threw open the door and the screen. Standing with one stocking foot in the house and one out on the porch, he yelled: "Hey, can I help you?"

I stood behind him. My stalwart protector.

"I said: Can I help you?"

A shadowy figure with long wispy hair that trailed in the wind stood in front of the house.

"Hey, man." Ben stepped outside in his socks.

I followed. The night was warm, and the air almost had a sweet taste to it. There is nothing in Heaven or Hell that can rival the beauty and ominousness of a warm summer evening.

"Hey, are you the guy with the dog?" Ben said to the shadow figure. "It wasn't my fault that your dog ran away. I'm sorry, but I can't really do anything for you."

The figure did not move or respond. It stood there staring at us.

Ben lowered his voice to its most masculine, authoritative bass. "Listen, buddy. Why don't you beat it before I call the cops. Get outta here."

"..."

"Beat it, I said. I got a sleeping child upstairs. I had nothing to do with your dog running away."

Ben kept mentioning the dog, but I wasn't certain that it was the same guy. I couldn't really tell from the porch, however.

The figure turned and started walking slowly down the street. Ben and I watched him go and were just about to go back inside when Ben started sniffing. After a moment, I smelled it too. It smelled like a skunk was being roasted on a pyre of Life Savers and Sweet Tarts.

Voices, nonsensical mutterings, could be heard from the

side of the house, the dark unused side by the air conditioner. "Oh, man. Fer sure it is. That's B.C. bud, man."

"Yeah, man. My brother from another mother mailed that to me, man. Huh huh huh ha huh. Man. It was in a bunch of socks. Huh huh. Huh huh, Huh ha huh huh huh."

"What in the Hell?" Ben said, grabbing the straw broom that was on the porch. He streaked down the porch stairs and across the front lawn. He turned the corner to the shadowy side of the house where a small gathering of hippies stood passing a joint around and kicking a hacky sack.

"Get out of here!" Ben shouted, swinging the broom like a baseball bat, showing them that he was prepared to strike them down.

The circle of hippies turned their attention towards Ben. Their hacky sack plopped to the ground in the middle of their circle.

"Calm down, dude."

"You're harshing my mellow, man," one of them, or perhaps all of them, said.

"Yeah, man. What'd we do to you?" A young braless woman with a headband holding down her wispy blonde hair said as she bent to retrieve the hacky sack. "We're not hurting anybody."

"What do you think you are doing," Ben said. "This is my house. You're on my property."

"Oh, man. He's hung up on property, man," a slim, handsome young man with a thick brown beard and a floppy denim hat responded,

"Hung up?" Ben said. "Just get out of here, you're trespassing."

The slim boy continued as if Ben had not spoken at all: "Like, this all belongs to the creator, man. Just because you paid for it doesn't mean you own it. You can't own Mother Earth, man. She owns you, dude."

"Right on," the circle said.

"Get out of here before I call the police."

"This guy's tripping. Wendy, grab the radio and let's go."

"Here, man. Want a hit?" A chubby hippy in a purple tie dye shirt held the burning joint out to Ben. "It'll help you relax."

"Get lost, lard-ass," Ben said.

The circle all laughed simultaneously as they gathered up their knapsacks, radios, ponchos, and bongos and walked off down the street together.

"I can't believe I voted yes to that legalization bill," Ben muttered as he came up the steps, seemingly looking directly at me. "I swear to God, I think the whole world is going insane."

Ben went inside and I followed.

He locked the door behind him and started up the stairs. Again, I followed.

Before checking in to find Mallory and Dana fast asleep, Ben stopped to straighten a family portrait in the hallway. He then trudged slowly up the attic stairs to his loft. He sat at his desk, turned on his laptop, and opened his email. There was only one fresh email in his inbox.

The email was from *gary.moon@theheraldtribune.com.* I read over Ben's shoulder.

Dear Mr. Matthews,

Thank you for your interest in the Herald Tribune. Unfortunately, we are not interested in taking on any new staffers. We are a small community newspaper and just do not have the budget. I am sure your advice column, Dear Ms. Vicki, will get picked up somewhere, and I wish you the best of luck with it.

Ben quickly hit reply and began to type:

"Listen asshole, I didn't... "

I couldn't see the computer very well where I was standing, so I reached out to move the laptop screen forward to deaden the glare.

As I touched it the screen went black.

"What the Hell?" Ben said.

After a tense minute, the computer popped back to life. Only, Ben's usual wallpaper (a picture of himself and little Mallory playing in the fall leaves) was replaced by a set of red glowing eyes with a faint outline of a furry wolf face. The eyes seemed to stare right through you.

"Shit!" Ben said. "What the Hell?" His virus protection program started to beep, and a box appeared in the right-hand corner reading: "You have a virus. Estimated time of removal is 666 minutes."

"Goddammit. That's all I need right now," Ben cursed. "A red eye virus!"

A browser window suddenly opened and the number 666 appeared again and again, all over the screen. They computer began typing 666 everywhere. Then it stopped. Alexis's reiki video appeared. She was naked from the waist up.

"We just take all the bad energy, ball it up, and throw it away."

The computer went blank again when Ben's cell rang.

Ben stared around the room, then at the phone on his desk. He hesitated momentarily before he picked it up.

"Hello," Ben said.

"..."

"Who?"

"..."

"No, sorry. There is no Karen here."

"..."

"Well how can I tell Karen that Hepburn P. is calling when, like I said, there is no Karen here?"

"..."

"Listen, buddy, it's been a long day. How do you know my name?"

"..."

"And when I meet this Karen, what is the message that I should give to her?"

"..."

"What's that? Say that again?"

"..."

"Esira Live. What the fuck does that mean? Go play on the freeway, punk. Esira Live. Kiss my ass." And he slammed the phone down.

EVIL ARISE

666

Esira Live. Esira Live. The voice again.

Betty was slouched on the counter with a letter opener jammed into her throat, blood splattering across the countertop in slowly diminishing spurts.

I turned to see the little bald man with the moustache standing in the doorway. He was smiling and whispering eagerly. "Esira Live. Esira Live."

I spit out whatever part of Betty that I had been chewing and turned to him. "Evil arise," I said. "Now, gimme the numbers, shrimp!"

He laughed.

"I just want my old job back," I said, more to myself than to anyone else, as I tore the letter opener from Betty's neck. The little man skipped out of the doorway. I pursued, my dragging leg leaving a trail of blood down the hallway.

Having the drive to succeed in business, having vision, is a lot like being a zombie in pursuit of your next meal.

Mocking you from a few metres ahead, goals taunt, evade, and you only get to eat when fortune smiles on you (a slip and fall, a sprained ankle, a dead end).

The little man escaped me easily. He continued to skip along down the hallways, looking back at me as he turned the corners to make sure I was following him.

We finally reached a dead end, where a row of floor-to-ceiling windows looked out onto the world below. There was a telescope on a stand planted there and a line of comfortable-looking leather chairs. The little man was standing by the telescope. He motioned to me to have a look. I stopped when I saw him and dropped the letter opener. No longer did I feel like eating his face. Two large apple trees grew in pots on either side of the expansive embankment of windows. I had not seen anything this beautiful in a long time. A crow cawed from one of the apple trees, jumping from one branch to another, and a garter snake slithered out from one of the pots, slithering across the floor towards me. It came up to my feet and seemed to say, "Come. See."

The little man pointed at the telescope. I dragged my foot towards him and looked into the lens. Across Hell, tall glass office buildings and condominiums stretched endlessly to the horizon. A network of roadways was filled with busses, service vehicles, overturned and abandoned rickshaws, and thousands upon thousands of cyclists fighting their way through the snow and ice. I watched as one man slipped on his bicycle and fell into a snow embankment. He did not have time to get up before a horde of zombies set upon him, opened his cranium, and ate his brain like a bunch of kids after a fresh pizza. Another man walked past the fallen one, taking a wide berth around the zombie luncheon. This man was carrying a plastic container full of sushi. Ben's words came back to me:

"Probably taking it back to his office to eat. Alone. Again. Like he probably did every day of his life."

It was the man from Ben's vision.

I heard a phone ringing. I backed up. Behind one of the apple trees there was the sound of a ringing phone.

The little man took my hand in his, his fingers cold and clammy in my palm, like breakfast sausages out of the fridge, and he gently walked me towards the noise. Behind the apple tree there was an old black rotary phone sitting on a table beside the line of chairs. I stared at the phone as it rang and rang. The raven shook the apple tree and jumped down to land on the telephone table.

I picked up the phone. "Hello," I said.

"Hey, Don. It's me. Ben."

"No," I said. "It's me, Karen. I need your help, Ben. I need you to let me stay. If you let me stay, I can help you too. I need to help you, Daddy."

"What's up, bro?"

"No. Karen. It's me, Karen," I said. "The man with the sushi. Remember? I saw him. I need to help you. I can help you."

"Listen, Sergio. I need you to do me a solid," Ben said.

I realized that I was, as usual, an interloper in the earthly realm. I was in control of nothing there, not even the soft rot. Neither Don nor Ben could hear me, so I listened.

"Sure, what is it?"

"Dana and I are going for a date night on Friday. I need you to watch my house for me."

"Watch your house do what?" Don said.

"Just watch the house. Sit out front in your car. Alexis is going to babysit Mallory. If you see anything weird going on, call me on my cell. I'll come right home."

Don paused. "Weird? What do you mean, weird?"

"Man. To be honest, I don't really know. But I don't want no naked reiki sessions filmed in my house."

"Well, if you are that worried about it, why are you letting her babysit?"

"Dana insists. Those two are suddenly the best of

friends. They're wearing the same necklace even. I'm starting to worry about Dana. I think she is becoming unhinged. The whole world seems like it is becoming unhinged. You know what I mean?"

"Yeah."

"Listen. I hear Dana. She's coming." Ben sounded frightened. "Just come to my house on Friday. Park on the street and sit with the lights off. If you notice anything strange phone me. Okay?"

"Okay."

"Bye."

"Bye."

"Satan will see you now."

I set the phone down and turned.

A woman stood in front of me. She appeared to be perfectly normal. She had no horns or devil tail, and she wore a nice red dress and high heels. She had on lipstick and blush. I was gobsmacked by her appearance. Her skin was warm and clean, like she had bathed recently, and she smelled of lilac-scented deodorants and perfumes. I wanted to fall to my knees in her presence and worship before her.

"Me?" I said.

"Satan will see you now," she repeated.

"You don't have horns?" I said. "You don't stink? You're

not dead. Are you?"

She smiled. "I'm on contract. Hired through a temp agency. Now follow me, please."

I followed the woman to a large door. She opened it for me, and as I stood there, she said: "Your four o'clock is here."

The great evil that was known to the world as Lucifer, Satan, Beelzebub, The Beast, sat at Her desk working on a crossword puzzle in one of Her magazines. She looked up. Her face was not the same as the one I had seen before. This looked like a different person. It looked like an old man with droopy skin. Satan looked at me and smiled, His teeth too white for a person His age. His skin appeared to be stained orange. And whatever stained His skin also seemed to stain His hair as if the orange hue were spreading like a disease. He wore a nicely tailored, although garish, suit.

"What can I do for you?" He asked.

I dropped to one knee. "All hail Satan," I said.

"And again."

"All hail Satan," I said.

"You may stand." He closed the magazine.

"It is an honour to be here, sir."

"Is it? I mean, I know. It must be exciting for you. To be

in the presence of someone so great. Isn't it."

"It is, sir."

"Yes, it must be. I has to be. Right?"

"My name is Karen Floyd. I am working on the Matthews portfolio."

"Yes, I know. Don't I? I do, right?"

"I suppose so, sir. The Matthews portfolio. The possession."

"Of course. I know what you are talking about. That's high-level stuff. Very high level. How's it coming along? Am I doing well? The company's stock is rising. Isn't it? I must be doing well. I am great. You know it. Don't you?"

Framed copies of S magazine hung all over the office. "Yes, sir."

"That's what I like to hear. My father taught me many important things. The number one thing was that a leader must be feared and admired by all his staff. And as you can see here, Karen, by all these magazine issues and my big desk, and all the old wood in my office, the clean carpet and the books on the wall, I am the kind of man who demands attention. I loved my father. I really did. He would be proud of me now. Don't you think?"

"I do, sir."

"My fame is widespread. People all over Hell love to

look at my picture and see what I am doing. They love to
gaze upon me. It gives them hope that things can change
for them too. While they toil and suffer, they can gaze upon
me and love me. It is mostly the only love they have in
their lives. Isn't it? It's great. I know it is. I know they have
children and husbands and wives and lovers, aunts and
uncles, some people have entire families here in Hell. But
they choose to love me. They all toil, so they can be me. I
am their Horatio Alger story. And they need that. If only to
dream of it, of being me. They need it. They need me.
Don't they? Of course, they do. A self-made man who took
on the world of commerce and conquered. Did you see
them out there? Toiling? In the snow? On their bicycles?
Getting picked off by the zombies one by one as they try
and make a buck. It's marvellous. Very high level. That is
their lot in death; that will never change. If we give them
hope, if we promise to build a wall to keep the zombies out.
If we promise to start wars with other companies, like
Lexmar and Transcorp. We promise we will invade their
corporate culture and install our own people in there, so
Hell will finally be safe, and Hell can prosper again, like it
once did, and they will love me and fear me. My father
would be so proud of me. He would. I know He would.
Wouldn't He?"

"Hail Satan."

"Of course. Hail Satan. The trick, you see, is to convince them that they are not in Hell. We need to convince them that they have an opportunity, when in reality there is none, and I cannot stop the zombies, and any war against Lexmar or Transcorp or Scarlett Inc. would be futile. Do you know why?"

"Why?"

"Because without Transcorp or Scarlett or the zombie horde, they would have nothing to fear. I built this entire place on fear. Fear keeps them striving. Without it, the infrastructure crumbles, the buildings burn, the real estate market collapses, the entire economy tanks, and we end up back where we started: in the dark ages of brimstone and lakes of fire. Trust me. Why am I telling you this?"

"I don't know, sir."

"Do you love me? Do you love me like my father loved me? You are proud of me, right? You fear and love me, right? I am your leader. Right?"

"All hail Satan."

"I knew it. You do. They all do. So, here we are. What can I do you for? You and I, we are at a crossroads. A fork in the road."

"A pitchfork in the road," I joked.

Satan's face turned a slightly brighter shade of orange. "Excuse me?"

"Hail Satan."

"I thought that is what you said. Please don't get any ideas here, dear. I call the shots. It's all high-level business. You wouldn't understand. And let me tell you why. Because I am a success. Because I rose from the ashes of this godforsaken Hell and built this company on my back, with hard work and sweat. It could have been a million years ago. It could have been yesterday, but when I found that sack of money in the alley that day, I took it right out and bought a nice suit and the can of spray tan. I had my teeth done. I then went out and had lunch with my father's friend, Mr. Downey. Do you know him? Great man. Great guy. Great businessman. Very high level. Downey owned this company, and I gave him a quarter of the sack for it. I threatened him with my pitchfork, and he signed the deal. The fool! From there, we built a city. A world. We hired lobbyists, we bribed and strong-armed politicians who made bills that would allow us to build cell phone towers on the most environmentally sensitive, ancient volcanic beds. We extinguished the lakes of fire and bottled the water in them, selling it for one-hundred times the cost of bottling it. And the fools bought it because we put MY picture on it. Even though it causes chronic testicular pain in 80 percent of men, and it causes baldness in women, and the water in the taps is far safer to drink, they still bought it. We raised cell phone rates, we put arbitrary caps on internet usage, we bundled packages for cable television, and we gouged them till they were nothing. And they hated us for it, but then we put out the magazine, and I got a TV show, and I created a personality. I hired a media team and we spun it on its head. They called me The S. I am on every cover of every magazine. I have a hundred different faces, and they grace every cover. And now we want to branch out. We want to do this in other realms. We will start with the earthly realm and go from there. We'll start with telecom and branch out into media and real estate. Then I will get a Netflix series and build my empire.

"There will be nothing that I do not own. And they will love me for it. I will become friends with celebrities, movie stars, and rock and roll stars alike. The people will worship me, and I will buy expensive clothes that look cheap and ill-fitting and fly in jet airplanes. I will find a cure for myself, for evil, and I won't be Satan anymore. No longer will I be the fearsome beast of Hell. I'll be just like them, although I will be immortal. The Earthly plane is dissolute. We must change it. So, how do we do this? Is that what you have come here to ask? The key here is this: the balance of power. We must tip that balance and break through the quantum force field that She created to keep us out. A great war is going to be waged in the telecom industry. You ever hear of 5G? I didn't think so. Very high-level stuff. My face will be everywhere. They will love me. They must love me. I am a Bright Red! The only one. A born leader. A type A personality. What are you, dear Karen?"

"I am a Peach. Creative and artistic. But I signed up for a twelve-step program, and I am working on healing in my spare time."

"And?"

"Hail Satan."

"Good. Good for you. High-level stuff. Very high level. I like it when a person recognizes their shortcomings and shows initiative. I like the cut of your jib, Karen. Of course, I can trust you. We need you to break through. This child that you are possessing. She is the key? She is, isn't she? You take over her body and then when you graduate high school you will meet Hepburn. Paul Hepburn. And you two will marry. Little P., as I call him. Because he is my friend. And he loves me. He does? Right? Of course, he does. He says I can call him Little P. because he is my friend. You must push him, my dear. Because behind every good man is a great wife. Together you two will be unstoppable, and when the orange dragon bursts forth from the volcanic ash, I will join you and we three will rule for eternity. And we will make Hell great again!"

"All hail Satan."

"All hail Satan," Satan said, wiping away a drop of orange sweat from His forehead.

"There is just one thing, sir."

"And what is that?"

"I cannot get through. There is a piece missing, and I do not know what it is. I need to speak to Paul."

"Well, that shouldn't be difficult."

My heart started beating more quickly.

"Just check the staff section of the website."

No. Was it that easy? All along. I just had to search him on the staff page.

"All his contact info should be on there. We're still sending him cheques. So, if that is all you need to know, if you don't mind, I have a conference call with Pete Rose scheduled." Satan looked at Her watch.

"You are saying that I can just dial his extension, and I will reach him. It's that simple."

"Bingo."

666

"Bingo."

"Really? Bingo? I haven't played bingo in a million years. That sounds fun," Alexis said. "Mallory is in good hands, I promise."

Ben leaned down and kissed Mallory on the forehead. "Mom and I won't be gone too long. You be good for Alexis. Okay?"

"Yes, Daddy," Mallory said.

"Thanks, Alexis," Dana said. "You have my cell number, so call or text if you need anything. Anything at all. There's chilled white wine in the bar fridge downstairs. Beer. Help yourself. Ben left some dairy-free cookies in the Tupperware on the counter for Mallory."

Ben motioned to Dana with his head. "Okay, let's go."

Dana hugged Alexis tightly and leaned to whisper in her ear, so only Alexis (and I) could hear: "You're a dear friend. Thank you for doing this. Be safe."

Be safe? I wondered as I watched Dana and Ben leave the house. Alexis shut the door and ran to the window to watch the driveway. "What is going on?" I asked Mallory.

Mallory shook her head. She didn't know either.

As soon as the car pulled out of the driveway, Alexis scurried over to gather her large purse that was sitting on the steps. She tore off the plain green blouse she was wearing and undid her bra. She stuffed the shirt and bra into her purse, pulled out a Grateful Dead tie-dye T-shirt, and whipped it on. She then rummaged through the purse, pulled out necklaces and silver wristbands with bells and hanging talismans, and put them all over her body: neck, wrists, and ankles. She tied a bandana around her forehead, lit a stick of incense, and began waving it around the room.

"Oh, shit," I said to Mallory. "I think I get it. She's going into good witch of the west, high-priestess mode."

"With this peppermint sage incense, I plan to cleanse this house of all the evil within it," Alexis said, "and lay the foundation for the good vibes that we will be bringing here tonight."

Mallory turned to me and raised her arm, her balled fist towards me, her middle finger jutting straight up.

"Why have you come to this house, evil spirit? Tell us your name."

666

"Oh, snap. When they get all up in your grill, don't tell them your name. Telling your name to the exorcist is, like, hella bad."

"Is this really you? Hepburn P.?" I said.

"No. Duh. Waz up? Just call me Proper." He had the cracking voice of a teenage boy. "And you're Karen, I know. The prophecy foretold it. Do you have big boobs? Will you? I can't wait till we get married and hook up. Where will we chill on our honeymoon?"

"I have to get there first, Paul."

"Proper. Proper Paulie. Or Little P. Word up. It's nothing, Karen. Just don't tell the exorcist your name. That's the most important thing. Once you're in, it's gravy."

"But how do I get there? Where you are? How do I stay? How do I find you? I'm so confused."

I could hear Paul shuffling the phone from one ear to the other. "It's like getting new kicks, girl," he said. "You just gotta work them in." I heard a loud crash on the phone, and it crackled and spit as Paul spoke.

Someone started shouting. "What the hell are you doing! Get back to work! Those cable boxes aren't going to refurbish themselves."

"I got another five minutes on my break," Paul yelled.

"And who said you could use that phone? That's for emergencies only."

Paul shouted back: "Yo, bud. Check it. I got five left on my break. Step off."

"Listen here, you annoying little shit. I got news for you. It's not 1985, and if your daddy wasn't a VP I'd fire your sorry ass. Now get back to work!"

"Don't make me open a can of whoop ass on you, Larry," Paul said. "I'm gonna be running this show one day, and I'm gonna fire YOUR ass. You watch. You got a problem with me talking on the phone, you can speak to my dad about it, narc."

"Who's that?" I asked.

"That's Groundhog Larry. We call him that cause he's got the face of a groundhog. He's a stooge, thinks he's a magician, but somehow, he got a manager position in the warehouse. So why you tripping, girl?"

"..."

"You're cracking up," Paul said. "Your voice sounds all whack. Did those zombies get you?"

I could see my reflection in my ever-rebooting, grey computer monitor: My face was sallow, my eyes hollowing, Betty's drying blood was smeared across my cheek and chin, and my head was tilting sideways on my neck. By God, yes. I was turning into a zombie and fast. I stood and shut my office cage door tightly, openly flouting the company open cage policy. They would find Betty soon; they would come for me.

"Shut up," Paul said. "You're turning zombie on me. You need to motivate and bounce outta there. If you turn zombie, you'll never finish the report. So are you hot? Or is your host hot? Like, will she be hot? Do you think? I want a hot wife. That'd be dope. No fat chicks, okay? I never even got married when I was alive the first time. I lived with my mother my whole life.

Then the psycho bitch got all religious and poisoned me. She put Ajax in my swiss steak. People always say to me: How could you not taste Ajax in your food? It was a TV dinner. They all taste like Ajax. You know? Don't they? Like, how is that legit? She kills me, and I am the one who goes to Hell. Oh well. Here's to second chances, eh?"

"..."

"I wish you would stop growling, baby. You sound whack. You gotta finish your spreadsheet. You feel me? Once you do that, you'll be golden. You can just forget about your body in Hell. Whatever happens to it. Who cares? You're gonzoli. You'll be like, "Wicked. Talk to the hand. I'm outtie." It won't matter if you are a zombie. So, whadya got left to do? Let me guess: There's one figure you are stuck on? I got stuck on it too, baby. And if you don't hurry up and figure it out, you'll start to slip into the shadow world. And that ain't cool. It happened to me too. You know that feeling you get when you see a baby, and it's, like, hella cute, and you just want to pinch it, or bite its cheek, just nibble on its cheek? You're all like, "Wicked. Time to mange." That feeling is almost too much, but you're all like, "hold up," and stop yourself before you bite it. Like, you want to, but you're like, hold up. Where's the beef? And you just can't bring yourself to do it. That's what being a zombie is like. Except you want to bite all the living flesh you see, and you want you eat it because it looks and smells like a juicy big hamburger, and you feel like you haven't eaten in a hella long time. Your work is the only thing that is keeping you from turning."

"Proper! Let's go. Break's over. They're starting up the line."

"Listen, I gotta bounce," Paul said.

"But what am I supposed to do?" I asked.

"Just finish the spreadsheet and get your hot self up to Earth. Fulfill your prophecy. Satan would not have put a dream into your heart if She hadn't given you everything you need to fulfill it."

"Well, tell me what the answer is," I said.

"Hang up that damn phone. NOW. Or I am writing you up!"

"Word up, Karen. The answer is mega easy. The answer to the formula is: What brought you to Hell? Why are you in Hell? Just write down the word or number, the formula will sum, and the spreadsheet will stop giving you an error. And you need to do it quickly. You are turning."

Click.

The phone went dead.

A snail crawled over my computer screen, leaving a trail of slime.

There was a low rumble in the hallway, the sound of many feet. "Get the master key," someone shouted. "She must be in there." I heard my cage door rattle as I grabbed my mouse and tried to get my computer to boot up.

"Let us sit in on the gossamer drum circle, little miss moon. I bequeath you. "

666

Someone was chanting.

Mallory's room reeked of incense, marijuana, and patchouli oil. There was something wrong. My freedom to move about had been stifled. I felt pinned to the wall. I could see Mallory floating in space above her bed, stiff as a board and her nightgown trailing down in the empty space, her neck twisted 45 degrees to face Alexis as she led a group of shirtless women dancing and chanting, "Groovy doobie groovy doobie groovy doobie." Naked men with their flaccid penises were sitting on stools and playing guitars and bongos and also chanting, "Groovy doobie groovy doobie groovy doobie." A terrified Todd cowered in the corner of his cage.

"Swines!" I started shouting. My growling angry voice filled the room. "You're going to kill her! It's all right, Mallory, I won't let them hurt you. I won't let them take you from me!"

But the soft rot made it all come out in German, so what the hippies heard sounded more like this: "Swimes Es ist alles in Ordnung, Mallory..."

"Groovy doobie groovy doobie groovy doobie." The chanting got faster and the women's breasts bounced furiously as they danced and shook and flapped about the room.

"Opal saturation!" Alexis shouted. "I call upon you! Time stands still! You need to get it together and split, man."

So there I was. Caught up in some hippie version of an exorcism, and, just my goddamn luck, it was actually working. I could feel myself being pulled away, I could feel the swirl of some centrifugal force churning and pulling me out of the house.

Alexis held up an amulet, the Marvel cross, towards Mallory and said: "Oh, unloved spirit, death is falling fast. Be groovy and bestow upon us your handle. We can help you. Dig it?"

"Groovy doobie groovy doobie groovy doobie," went the chant, and the bongo drum was beating at a frenetic pace as the men now stood and danced with the women.

"Go fuck yourself, bitch," I said (for some reason it came out in Hawaiian: *Hele anal oe ia oe iho, bitch*). The old plaster walls cracked and crumbled as I spoke, the plaster dust raining down on their pale naked bodies.

"Oh, sisters and brothers of the spirit world. Tighten up your centre, dudes. Remove yourself from the velveteen cosmos. You are harshing our buzz. Please be cool and depart upon us your unholy handle. It's far out, man," Alexis said.

I watched as poor Mallory's ankles cracked and bent sideways with a horrible popping sound. Her back arched in a lurching motion until she almost looked like a triangle and she floated higher. "You're killing her!" I cried, and a cold wind blew through the room. The chanting and dancing were reaching a level of feverish hysteria.

One of the hippies, caught up in the moment, dropped his hash pipe on Mallory's bed. The embers of the burning hashish spilled on the bedspread and glowed fiery orange. "Groovy doobie groovy doobie groovy doobie."

"The time is now. You must enter the vortex. Lay your handle on us. Settle your chi. I can feel your bad energy. I am a healer. I can meditate upon your chi and balance you. I just need your name, dude or dudess."

The bedsheets started to smoke. Mallory opened her mouth wide and belched out an odour so foul that two of the hippie women fell to their knees gagging and vomiting.

Good girl, I thought. *Fight them.*

But that did not stop the chanting. "Groovy doobie groovy doobie groovy doobie."

Slithering snakes began pouring out of Mallory's toy chest and coating the floor. Mallory began barking like an angry dog. Smoke began to rise from the bed.

"Groovy doobie groovy doobie groovy doobie."

It did not stop them from chanting and dancing and playing their instruments.

This was when I realized it. The hippies would sacrifice anything to get rid of me, including Mallory. They would keep dancing and chanting until the entire house burned down. They were using terrorist tactics, taking hostages, and they would kill the little girl to get what they wanted. I had to just give it to them. The jig was up, and all the work I had done in Hell would be for naught. I would have to go back to Hell and face eternity as a zombie. The Cheezie report would never be finished. The Sick Box Prophecy would remain unfulfilled.

"Your mind is blown away with our wonders. Lay your name on us," Alexis said. "All we want is your name, man. Mushy, melty, drippy, trippy darkness. We balance you with the night owl and the spirit marten."

Maybe I deserve to be in Hell with Satan and the rest of

them, I thought. Who was I kidding? This promotion was not for me. I couldn't handle the responsibility. Who was I to think that I was better than Glenda or any of my co-workers in the cubicles, Mary the ZSW, or even Betty? The name. They wanted my name. I started to speak it, "*Ka...*" but I heard the front door slam open. A familiar voice filled my heart with joy. "GET THE FUCK OUT OF MY HOUSE, YOU GODDAMN HIPPIES."

"BEN. BEN." Dana pleaded with him. "Stop. This has to happen! You have to let her finish."

"BEHOLD TRIBAL SATURATION! UNIVERSE UNITE! TELL US YOUR NAME!"

And chaos ensued. Everything was happening at once. The shit was hitting the fan, as my father used to say

In Hell, an angry crowd rattled my cage door.

In the Earthly realm, Ben was smashing guitars and chasing the naked hippies around his house.

Mallory's ankles and back righted, and she crashed down to her bed as smoke from her mattress filled the room. The fire alarm started going off.

"Oh, my God. There's a fire! Mallory! Mallory!" Dana was calling.

"Get the fire extinguisher!" Ben yelled at Dana.

Dana took off down the stairs.

"Dudes. Let's get out of here, man. The place is an inferno!"

Alexis grabbed Ben by the shoulders. "Mallory's chi is being overwhelmed by a bad spirit, Ben. We need to save her."

"BEN! Where is it? I can't find it!" Dana called from the bottom of the stairs.

"Go help Dana," Ben said. "The fire extinguisher is in the basement by the old wood stove."

Alexis looked into Ben's eyes. "You have to believe me, Ben."

"I do. I believe you. Now go!" Ben said.

Alexis turned and ran.

I was the only one who could stop this. And I could only do it from Hell. I rushed up the attic stairs and dove headlong down into my sick box, landing in my demon body just as the angry mob, thirsty to avenge Betty's death, kicked open my office cage door.

I typed the reason I was in Hell on the computer.

Alice.

And I pressed enter. Alice. Just as Little P. said to do. That was all it took. "The reason you are in Hell." Alice. The errors went away, and my sheet summed. The answer (in case you haven't been paying any attention at all): **666**.

Alice. It all came back to me, like some unrelenting nightmare. I was just making a joke. I didn't mean to hurt her. I remembered it as clearly as if it were happening right in front of me and not countless years ago. We were children for God sakes. She was sitting in my dad's lap, crying. He was consoling her, hugging her tightly. "It's okay, baby." My father looked at me with eyes full of hatred. "Look what you've done! Did you really think that would be funny?"

"But Dad?"

And with that, Mallory and I were one.

Ben rummaged through one of Mallory's drawers, grabbing a sundress and some underwear. He threw us over his shoulder in a fireman's carry, tossed a blanket over our head, snatched Todd out of his cage, and brought us out to the garage. He opened the garage door. I lifted the corner of the blanket to see naked hippies scattering up the street. Dana and Alexis were nowhere in sight, but I could hear Dana shouting Ben's name, "BEN. WHERE ARE YOU! BEN."

"I love you, Dana," Ben said to himself as he set us all down. "God help me. God help me, I love you."

And Mallory and I collapsed into a deep sleep until a warm rush of morning wind greeted us through the chill of morning dew. We were moving.

"DADDY?"

I felt it; I tasted it: freedom. Esira live.

"DADDY!"

Evil arise.

6

"Daddy?"

"Yes, honey?" Ben said in forced breathy tones.

"Where are we?"

Ben's legs churned as he pedaled his bicycle, the wheels silent on the asphalt and kicking up bits of road dirt into the screen of the Chariot bike trailer he was towing us in.

"Who wants to know, baby? You or Karen?"

The sun was just beginning to rise over fields of sorghum, yellow canola, and mustard. Long dirt driveways led to distant farmhouses where I envisioned women shuffling around their kitchens, starting the day's baking. In our lap, Todd slept peacefully as we stroked his ear.

"Tell him that there is no Karen," I said.

"There is no Karen, Daddy," Mallory said.

"Tell him you were just teasing him."

"I was just teasing you, Daddy."

"I know, dear," Ben said, sounding very sad. "I wish you

would have told Mommy that. Your joke has caused a great deal of trouble."

"Ask him where we are going."

"Where are we going?" Mallory asked.

"We're taking a little holiday."

"And where's Mommy?" Mallory asked.

"We'll call her later, okay?" Ben replied. "Maybe she'll catch up with us."

"I hope not," I said.

"You're mean," Mallory scolded me in our head.

We crossed a small bridge. The stream beneath us rushed through the forest where birds flitted from tree to tree, making an awful racket, and not another foreign noise within hearing range.

Ben brought the bicycle to a stop just past the bridge.

"If you tell him I am here, he'll send me away and our vacation will be cancelled," I told Mallory.

Ben reached behind him and pulled a map from the saddlebags. He spread it open on the handlebars of his bike. Ben took off his sunglasses and started pointing, making trails on the map with his index finger.

"We are going to have some fun!" I told Mallory. "A real vacation. This is great. After all that has happened, we need it."

Mallory just slumped back in our Chariot and petted Todd.

"Your mommy will come back to you," I told her. "It is prophesied. We are to be a family."

"Daddy? What *is prophesied* mean?" Mallory asked.

Ben mumbled something and pointed towards the sun, "West. East. North. South," he said turning his head and pointing each time he gave a direction, tragically confused and disoriented.

"Geography is not his strong suit, I take it?"

"Daddy? What *is prophesied* mean?"

"Hold on a second, Mal." Ben turned and sniffed the air, licking his finger and holding it out to feel the wind, as if somehow his impossible quandary could be solved by a saliva-coated index finger. "No, wait. What is it, again?" he asked himself. "Sun sets in the east and rises in the west? That's right. Isn't it?" He pointed towards the rising sun. "WEST!" he proclaimed.

"Ferdinand Magellan he is not," I said. "Tell him he's cracked. Tell him it's east."

"Now what was it that you wanted to know, Mallory?"

"You're cracked." Mallory said. "East. The sun is east."

"It is? How do you know that?"

"Sesame Street," Mallory said without prodding.

"Are you sure?"

Yes, east, you hapless dope, you dumb but lovable man. The miasma of orange and pink sky caused by the rising sun was perhaps the most beautiful thing I thought I had ever seen until I looked at my hand. It was unblemished and soft with no wrinkles nor hirsute patches below the knuckles. I could hear the honest, beautiful, untainted blood coursing through the veins to the fingertips and back down. My blood, pumping through my new flesh, my second chance, with no talons nor stains of dried zombie blood or gore beneath the fingernails.

"You should go back to sleep, baby girl," Ben said. "It's really early."

Sleep. I had years of sleep ahead of me; years of sleep behind me. This was no time for sleeping. I scratched Todd behind the ears. "Will we eat?" I asked Mallory.

She shrugged. She didn't know.

Someone was coming up the road towards us. It was a black horse and black buggy. It looked like something Satan would ride in. No. She couldn't have been coming for us already. I still had to meet Paul. We'd be married. We'd lay the groundwork for the takeover. It couldn't have been for me.

Ben was folding his map as the buggy approached.

Riding high on the buggy's seat, a rotund young boy sat holding tightly onto the reins of his black horse. He wore a straw hat with a wide brim, a striped short-sleeved dress shirt, black pants, and black shoes. We had entered Mennonite country".

The boy did not look at us as he passed. He did not wave, nor nod, there was no gentle country greeting for us, as I think we all expected; instead, the boy's horse began sniffing the air and fighting to see beyond its blinders. Great gouts of snot issued from its nostrils as the horse twisted its neck against the tightening reigns, but it was all happening too quickly. Spooked, the horse shot off into the ditch, the buggy trailing behind it. The dip in the ditch caused the springs on the buggy's seat to absorb the weight of the corpulent rider. When the horse came up the other side of the ditch, the springs on the buggy thrusted back to their original shape, acting as a catapult and launching the Mennonite boy into the air.

Sailing across the sky like a blackened ham, the boy reached the apex of his flight, and with arms flailing and legs churning, he twisted himself in just such a way that the arse of his pants split from belt to crotch, exposing an expansive creased moon of white jiggly buttocks, and he plummeted back to earth and out of our sight. We heard a grunt and a splash.

"My GOD!" Ben exclaimed.

"Holy shit, did you see that?" I said.

"YOU SWORE!" Mallory scolded me.

Ben set his bike down and tore off after the boy.

I started to laugh, rocking back and forth in our seat and clutching our stomach. Mallory was not laughing.

"You're mean," she said.

"He must have flown 20 feet in the air." I could barely stand it. It felt like a swarm of butterflies were tickling us all over. "And his butt. HA HA HA. Did you see his butt?"

Todd got off our lap and hopped around a bit, kicking his back legs out and rubbing himself on us.

"The boy is hurt!" Mallory said.

"He's fine," I said through bursts of uncontrollable laughter.

"He's fine." Ben was suddenly back picking up his bike and putting his leg up over the crossbar. "Did you see that, Mallory?" Ben said, chortling. "That was crazy. He rolled right into that stream. Ha."

"I told you it was funny," I said.

"Is the boy okay?" Mallory asked.

"Of course. He'll be fine. He's got to ride home without his pants though. They split right in half."

"With a bare bum?" Mallory asked.

Ben laughed.

Mallory laughed.

I laughed.

Todd sat staring blankly at us.

This is going to be the greatest vacation ever! I thought.

As Ben pushed off and started pedaling again a snail slithered over the lip of the Chariot and into our enclosure.

"Ew," I said. "Squish it."

"No," Mallory said, watching the snail move slowly towards our foot. "Kill it," I said.

"No! I like him."

"I am sorry, child, it must go."

"NO!"

I half expected Ben to turn and scold us for fighting in the backseat, but he could not hear us.

666

I am not sure how much further we travelled, but when Mallory and I woke again, the sun was brighter, and it was getting hotter. We were stopping at a countryside cafe. Our stomach ached with hunger, and we smacked our dry lips and stretched ourselves awake. As we pulled in, we noticed a number of thin, ropy farmers milling about the front of the store, sitting on picnic tables, eating sandwiches. They all had long beards and wore the same black garb that the little flying butterball child wore. More Mennonites.

The Mennonites had their horses and buggies parked off to the side beneath the shade of a hitching area. A few cars were parked in the lot as well. Leaning on the hoods of the vehicles were tourists with wide-brimmed hats who snapped pictures with their cell phones. If I had not known better, I might have thought that the Mennonites and their buggies were some sort of stage show, like Tina and Tony's wedding, a presentation, dinner theater for the alabaster tourists to enjoy as they lapped up their ice cream cones.

They were tourists of the worst sort: gawkers and antique hunters who pack themselves into cars and travel hundreds of miles to stay in rundown motels. I knew the type. Waking their children at dawn they take them out to local markets, and after exhausting the aisles and aisles of crocheted wonders, quilts, apple dolls, used VCR tapes, and the broad selection of cured meats, pickled delights, and preserves, they pack up their cars again and move on to spend the afternoon oohing and aahing at the wonders inside the fenced barricades of whatever pioneer village is close by. The kind where employees dress as if it were 1870, and in-between cigarette breaks, demonstrate how to make candles out of beeswax.

Meanwhile, the children of the vacationers, utterly horrified at the thought of yet spending another vacation day watching a blacksmith with a Red Hot Chili Peppers tattoo pound iron, beg to be taken back to the motel and it's swimming pool. I had been there before. These were our vacations when I was a child.

"I don't like this place," Mallory said to me.

"Quiet. They have ice cream!" I said.

"Daddy says I can't have ice cream. It's got milk, remember, stupid? It's your fault. You made me sick."

"But it isn't the dairy, dear," I told Mallory. "It was me that was making you sick; that is over now. We are one! And we can have ice cream again."

"Daddy, can I have ice cream?" Mallory asked.

"No, honey. It has diary."

"Kar..."

I stopped her: "No. No. No. Not yet, Mallory. What did I tell you? He'll take us home. The vacation will be cancelled."

"What's that, Mal?" Ben asked.

Mallory ignored the misstep and pitched on: "I won't get sick. I promise. I know I won't."

"No, honey. I am so sorry. The doctor said maybe when you are older you can have it."

"You're mean," she said.

"Sorry, Mallory," I said.

Ben walked his bicycle (and us in the trailer) across the parking lot and leaned it against a tree. Before retrieving his cell phone from his saddlebag, he pulled up the protective screen on the bike trailer to let some air in. "Don't let Todd run away," he said.

A gust of warm, fresh country air enveloped us. A man with a fishing pole and a tackle box walked past and into the woods.

"Hello. Dana," Ben said, cell phone to his ear.

"He's calling Mommy," Mallory said. "You're in trouble now."

"..."

"Of course," Ben said.

"..."

"Dana, calm down."

"..."

"I did not kidnap her."

"..."

"Don't be ridiculous."

"..."

"Just be quiet for a minute. Calm down. She's fine."

"..."

"No. I won't."

"..."

"No, you calm down. Is the house okay? Did you put out the fire?"

"..."

"Okay. Fuck it," Ben said. "I don't have much battery left. I don't know what Alexis told you, but you are acting crazy. Please listen to me, honey. I love you. What is she telling you?"

"..."

"This is insane. You really think your daughter is possessed by an evil spirit? You can't be fucking serious?"

"..."

"You need help, Dana. Dana, do you know how crazy this sounds? Please. Please stop. You're losing it. You need to see someone, Dana."

"..."

"I'll say it as many times as I want. Dana. Dana. Dana. Dana."

And again. Those two with the bickering. It was enough to drive a person around the bend. "They sound like a clacker on a duck's ass," I said, a favourite expression of my father's. "How can you stand it?"

"Sometimes I hate you," Mallory said.

"No, seriously, Dana," Ben said. "Don't you dare. Leave the police out of it. What do you expect to tell them?"

"..."

"Possessed? By the Devil? Where is this coming from? Please don't tell the police that. They'll lock you in a mental institution. Then we will have serious problems.

"..."

"Stop saying that. I did not kidnap her. We are on vacation. That is all."

I craned our head out of the trailer and met the gaze of

one of the farmer men on the picnic tables. He was old and slim, with a long, hooked nose and a white beard. He wore black suspenders and a blue shirt. He was eating ice cream out of a tub. As our eyes met, he abruptly plucked his spoon from his mouth and handed his tub of ice cream, spoon and all, to the man sitting next to him on the picnic table. He stood and pointed at us.

The man who now had the ice cream tub took no notice, for he immediately accepted his new position as ward of the ice cream tub and began eating the ice cream with such zeal that I wondered if perhaps the fate of all Mennonite-kind was to be determined by his spoon-licking skills.

"Daddy says you are not supposed to share spoons," Mallory said.

"It's gross," I said. "Even in Hell, you get your own spoon. What do you think he wants?"

"Daddy says you can get sick from sharing spoons."

"Dana," Ben was saying, "I don't know what to say to you right now. She's a kid. Her behaviour was that of a child. She has an imaginary friend named Karen. So what. She drew on the wall. Big deal."

The bearded man approached us, and sheepishly bent to look into our trailer. His long beard bristled like straw upon the canvas of the Chariot.

As I stared into the man's brown eyes, I wished for his neck to snap.

"Make him go away," Mallory said.

Ben spat into the phone, "I don't care what Alexis said! She's got you wrapped around her finger so badly you can't see the forest for the trees."

The man continued to stare. I could almost smell the blockages in his arteries; I could almost taste the heart attack he was going to soon have. It tasted like peppermint. Like the other man in the hospital who could see me, this one was also dying, yet I doubt this one even knew it. There was a good chance he had never seen a doctor his entire life.

"Let's stick out our tongue," I told Mallory.

"Okay."

A long, forked tongue shot from our mouth, like a snake, followed by a loud rattling hiss. The man fell onto his ass and scurried backwards, his legs slipping in the grass like he was Scooby Doo trying to evade the three-headed minotaur ghost. His hat fell off his head as he finally achieved some grip and he turned and ran, past the front of the store and into the woods. His farmer friends turned to each other and shrugged as they watched him go. If I could read minds, I bet I would have heard them thinking: *Good. More ice cream for us then.*

"I can get plenty far on a bike," Ben said. "And you know it."

"..."

"Listen, this isn't healthy, Dana. Call the cops then. I have done nothing wrong. We are just on vacation. A cycling tour. You can meet us if you like, but you have to give this stuff up. Our daughter might have some behavioural problems, but she is not possessed by evil spirits. *That* is ridiculous. If you really believe *that* maybe you do need to check yourself into the hospital. Tell them that you think your daughter is possessed by an evil spirit. Maybe that is for the best. They can prescribe antipsychotic medication for you."

"..."

Ben held the phone back from his ear as a barrage of expletives exploded from his cell phone.

"I'm not doing this. We are on vacation. I will call you in a few days when things have calmed down." Ben hung up and immediately typed out a short text with his thumbs, before announcing: "Let's get something to eat."

666

"I don't like sandwiches."

"But I do," I said.

"Well, that's all they have, Mallory," Ben told us.

"Let's just get a sandwich," I entreated the child. "With lots of meat."

"I want a treat," Mallory said.

"Good idea. We'll have a pie," I tried to speak for Mallory, but the words came out of Mallory's throat in a low growling rumble that barely tripped off our tongue.

The bonneted waitress's lip crinkled up in a sneer, as if she were doing an Elvis impersonation, and she took a step backward.

"Mallory, would you please clear your throat?" Ben did not even raise his gaze from the map that he had laid out on the table, once again running his index finger along it, drawing out potential routes in his mind.

"Are you people ready to order or should I come back?"

the waitress asked.

"Of course. Of course," Ben said. "We're here, right?" He pointed to the map. "Right? By this Ament Line, here?"

The waitress moved in to look at the map, holding a pot of coffee in one hand.

"Would your dad let us have coffee?" I asked Mallory. "Order one and see what he says."

"I don't like coffee."

"Well, not really," the waitress said. She pointed about six inches east of where Ben had his finger. "We're here. Three Sisters Cafe. See the old trout stream? You can follow that to Ament Line," she said.

"Ah, I see," Ben lied.

"There's an outlet right beside you," she said, "If you want to plug in your phone. Now what would you like to order?"

After we determined the dairy freeness of the various menu items, Ben ordered sliced meat sandwiches and apple pie. Ben marvelled at the fact that Mallory ate most of everything. "You sure were hungry, weren't you?" he said. We were not allowed coffee, however. Ben was a good dad. I really hoped that nothing bad was going to happen to him.

As Ben fiddled with his charging phone and pointed at

the map, he mumbled to himself about finding places to stay.

"Looks like there is a lake not too far from here," he said. "Maybe they rent cabins?

Whadya think, Mallory? Does that sound fun?"

"I want Mommy," she said.

"I'll talk to her again when the phone charges, okay? Maybe tonight? You can call her."

"Okay," Mallory said.

"Sorry. Hello. I couldn't help but overhearing." An attractive young woman with poker-straight long blonde hair was looming over us. She wore jeans and sandals and a baggy tie-dyed T-shirt. Across her braless and expansive bosom there was a hyper realistic (I mean like a photograph) picture of a grey kitten strapped to a large wooden cross. Behind the kitten, tiny alien saucers, also driven by grey kittens, hovered in the psychedelic print of the tie-dye.

We stared at the woman but did not speak.

"I don't mean to interrupt. I was just sitting behind you," she said as she pressed her long index finger at a spot on the map. "That's Rat Farm Lake," she said. "It's very nice. It even has a little beach."

"Rats!" Ben gagged.

She sighed, "You know what happens when you let farmers name things."

Ben nodded, *yes, he did,* although I highly doubted the veracity of his nod.

"Is it teeming with rats?" Ben asked.

The woman sighed again. "No. There are no rats there at all. So, if you look up here," she said in reference to the map. I leaned in closer to see where she was pointing; I knew Ben would never figure it out. "There is a motel. I happen to know the owner. He rents out cabins by the lake. Let me show you. If you just go down the road here, up the second line, turn left at the rendering plant, and the motel is there on the fourth sideroad. The owner goes by the name Mr. Marbles. You can tell him that Misty sent you. He'll give you a good deal on a room."

Ben stared at the map for a moment. "So, just a little east of here?"

"West," the woman corrected him. "Here, let me show you."

She took a pen out of her back pocket and drew a route out on the map.

"Well, that sounds fine. Perfect. Thank you." Ben's cell phone buzzed and chirped simultaneously, and he picked it up to read a text.

Misty swung erratically towards us, bent low, pretending to pick something up off the floor and said, "Hope you have a nice vacation, Karen."

What fresh misery was this?

"If you like, I can give yous guys a ride," Misty said as she stood. "I have a truck out back."

Ben set his phone down. "Well, thank you very much, but no thank you. We need to get back to Todd," Ben said.

"Be seeing you, then," Misty said as she went back to her table.

"She's up to no good. I know it," I said to Mallory. "Tell your dad we don't want to go. Tell him to take us to Disneyland. It can't be that much worse than Hell."

"No," Mallory said. "I want to go to the beach. You always get your way."

"Listen, Mallory. We are one entity now. We have to make compromises."

"Daddy, what is a compromises?"

"Never mind," I cut her off. "We just have to get along. You see, we are like sisters now. Even better, like twin sisters, and we have to find a way to live here together. So, I am thinking Disneyland. You are thinking motel in the middle of nowhere. Can we meet in the middle somewhere?"

"No."

Ben paid the bill, and we left the restaurant. As we made Todd scooch over in the bike trailer seat, Mallory said, "Sister?"

"Who me?"

"Sister," Mallory said. "If you really are my sister, you have to play with me then. That's what sisters do."

"Sure," I said. "I can play with you."

"Okay," Mallory said. "Let's pretend we are taking a trip. I'll be a nurse, and you can be a lady who babysits bunnies."

666

As we cycled towards the motel, the farmhouses became further and further apart. The tiny Mennonite schools with the bumpy baseball diamonds became fewer and fewer. Ben was tiring. He was pedaling slowly. He kept muttering to himself, "*Why didn't I take that ride?*" To keep her occupied, I played with Mallory. We were sisters who were nurses, and bunny sitters, and princess warriors, keepers of a special breed of single-horned bunnies who had magical powers, and sisters who became flying birds who also owned a motel, sisters who cooked food in a restaurant that sold no milk, sisters that owned a shopping centre, sisters, sisters, sisters, until I wanted to pummel and choke the first person who looked at me sideways.

The smooth paved roads soon turned to potholed and hard compact dirt roads, and Ben's legs pumped harder and harder over the rougher terrain. All the cars disappeared, and roadside mailboxes became even further apart. Dead frogs, snakes, racoons, and one porcupine, all squished dead, littered the roads, despite the apparent lack of vehicles. It was like they had all gotten together to make one final decision and then flung themselves flat and bloody upon the sacrificial altar of, "THE ROAD."

I had a bad feeling about where we were heading. Something in our stomach (and it wasn't dairy) was telling me that we were moving towards a darkness even more miserable than the Nakara Corporation.

After about three more hours of cycling, and about a million, "Daddy, how much longer?" questions from Mallory, a sign loomed up ahead. It was on a white pole and read, simply, "MOTEL," and in smaller letters beneath it on another sign, "VACANCY." I suspected the NO, as in "NO VACANCY," had never been used.

"This place is a dump," I said to Mallory. "We should keep moving."

"Let's pretend that I am a doctor, and we are sailing on a ship. You will be sick."

"Do we have to? Let's just be normal sisters for a min..."

"No," Mallory stopped me. "You said you would play with me, and we have hardly played at all. Tell me that you have been sick."

"Okay, fine. Doctor," I played along, "I have been sick.

My stomach hurts when I drink milk."

"No. You say you have pains in your butt."

"Oh, come on!"

Ben turned the bike into the paved lot of the motel and coasted up to the office door. He stopped the bike and hung his head on the handlebars, breathing heavily. He'd been biking all night and half of the day. He must have been exhausted.

A boy sitting in a Muskoka chair was eating a slice of pizza.

"No. Say it. You are going to have to play with me, or I am not going to share with you," Mallory scolded me.

Where'd he get a pizza out here? I wondered. *Do they deliver all the way out here? We should call.*

Ben got off his bike and leaned it against a pole. "Hey, there," Ben said to the boy. "Is there a person named Mr. Marbles around here?"

The boy turned to us. Behind thick glasses his crossed eyes appeared to stare off into a film of perpetual bewilderment. His dew worm lips were wet with saliva and pizza sauce.

Smacking mightily upon a mouthful of good taste, he garbled out of his phlegmy throat, "In dere."

"In here?" Ben asked, pointing to the office.

"Yeah. Budd-head," the boy said. "Dere waiding for you." He stood and tossed the bit of crust he was holding out into the parking lot. "Don'd dell Marbles," he said. "De birds will ged id."

Ben undid our seatbelt and helped us out of the trailer. A cool breeze ruffled our summer dress. I felt pretty and free. Our legs were stiff. I wanted to run.

"The boy's parents are obviously cousins," I told Mallory.

"Don't be mean," Mallory said.

"Maybe he's the missing link. Who knows? Raised in a nuclear waste dump? His entire community abandoned by the government and left to rampage in a lawless, atomic wasteland? It happens you know."

"Let's pretend we are queens and we own a motel."

"I am sick of pretending. Can't we do something else? I'm hungry. What is there to eat? Ask your dad."

"No. You be Janet, and I'll be June. Queen of this land. We ride flying unicorns and have rainbow powers."

"Not now. Let's check in, then when we get to the room we can play more."

Ben zipped the trailer up, like zipping up a tent flap, trapping Todd inside.

A bell rang as we followed Pizza Boy through a door

and into the motel office. Inside, a man stood behind the counter, reading a newspaper. He did not even look up as we approached.

"Scuze me," Ben said.

"By God," the man said, startled, folding up his newspaper quickly, as if we had caught him ogling his sister in a pornographic magazine. "Customers," his face reddening with embarrassment.

He had a heavy moustache and broad nose. His eyes were brown, and he was wearing the same strange shirt that Misty had been wearing, with the crucified kitten and spaceships. His hair was long and brown. I guessed his age to be mid-thirties.

"A woman named Misty told me to stop by here," Ben said. "She told me that you rent cabins?"

"I do indeed," the man said. "They're down by Rat Farm Lake. Don't let the name fool you. It's a nice place. Got a beach and everything. There's a full cord of wood there. You'll just have to split it. The axe should be plenty sharp. What else we got to offer ya? A generator, so you got your lights if you need them. We can set you up with a can of gas, even. No charge. We got a propane barbecue. I tell ya, it's as good as home. We run a cash only operation. Or cheque, I suppose. $250 a week. How long do you plan to stay?"

Mallory and I wandered over to the souvenir section.

"I'm not real sure," Ben said. "Couple weeks for sure. Cash is good for us. I hit the bank before we left."

A shelf affixed to faux-wood panelling on the wall was full of bric-a-brac and souvenirs: bookmarks in the shapes of cats, coffee mugs with painted on whiskers and curvy cat tails for the cup handle, cat keychains, cat stuffies, cat pens and lighters, cat everything. And in a glass curio cabinet, there was a display of Egyptian cats, countless gold and onyx (looking) statuettes, ranging in height from a few inches to one that had to have been a foot tall.

"I like dis one," Pizza Boy was standing next to us, his breath smelling of oregano and garlic. He was pointing at a gold cat with a red pendant around its neck, his glasses, as thick as pop bottles, gleaming in the lights of the curio cabinet.

"I hate cats," I said. "They're creepy."

"No dere nod."

The boy could hear me.

"You can hear me, Pizza Boy?"

He nodded yes.

"You should fear me then, for I am a scout of the Great Beast. Her age is coming and with it, She will bring plagues, and pestilence, and zombies. Why are you not scared?"

"Let's pretend we are superheroes who are cats, and we are fighting the orpians who guard the pyramid," Mallory said.

"Whad's an orpian?" Pizza Boy asked.

"She means scorpions. Satan will bring them too." I said, trying to sound menacing. "Scorpions as big as wiener dogs! They hide behind toilets and burrow into tucked-in motel bed sheets; and with neither a warning hiss, nor venomous rattle, they attack. Keenly intent on ending a life, the scorpions aim to pierce your flesh with a massive aculeus dripping with a poison that is released from its anal glands. So, what's your game, Pizza Boy? What say you? If you stand in my way, I will crush you like a snail. Why do you not fear me?"

"Cads," he said.

From some hidden doorway, four or five cats came streaming through the lobby. A big tabby jumped on the front counter and laid down where Mr. Marbles was writing out a receipt. Mr. Marbles pushed the cat aside, but it came right back again. The others waited by the door circling each other like a meowing tornado. Pizza Boy went to open the door for them.

A shiver ran down our spine.

"Well, I guess we're set then," Ben said, turning to us and smiling.

"ORPIANS!" Pizza Boy yelled as he bounded out the doorway, waving an imaginary sword.

"We must follow him," Mallory said out loud.

"Let's just leave these freaks," I said to Mallory. "We can run off into the woods or something. I've heard of kids running off into the woods. We can be raised by wolves or coyotes. It happens all the time where I am from."

"No. No. Mallory," Ben said. "You can play with your new friend later. We're going to spend the night here, and in the morning, Mr. Marbles will take us to Rat Lake."

Mr. Marbles was petting the purring tabby cat on the counter. "We're going to have a great time," he said, smiling at us like some evil villain in a James Bond movie. "Charles," he shouted at Pizza Boy. "CHARLES! Take our guests to room six."

"We're going to have a great time. We? What does he mean, WE?"' A fear, a numbness, a creeping anaesthetic, started in our heel. I don't know if Mallory felt it or not, but I did. An infection that would begin working its way towards our heart, taking over and ruining all my plans. "Why is your father so FUCKING oblivious?"

"HUH! Mallory gasped. "You said a swear. I'm telling."

"No. Don't tell. Please don't tell. I won't do it again."

"CHARLES! ROOM SIX! You're in room six," Mr. Marbles said as he handed Ben the keys.

"Let's pretend we're on a spaceship, and we are teachers, and we are teaching aliens how to plan parties," Mallory said.

"Oh, God help me."

"You can be called Lexie, and I will be called Janet."

"Dhe orpians god me!" Pizza Boy shouted as he ran in circles and fell in a cloud of dust in the parking lot.

The sun was hot on our faces as we headed to room six. A trickle of sweat dropped from our nose.

"Do they have any food around here?" Ben asked.

666

Ben arranged for Mr. Marbles to drop off two pizzas. Apparently, Mr. Marbles had invested in a restaurant-grade pizza oven some years ago, thinking that fresh homemade pizzas would bring in customers. It had not been as successful a venture as he had hoped. One pizza with olives, pepperoni, and cheese was made for Ben and another with pepperoni and no cheese was made for us. After Ben ate, he fell asleep. He slept all afternoon while Mallory and I watched television.

Initially, this seemed like it might be fun. However, the advancements in television had been slim since I died. In fact, the only difference that I really noticed was that there was a channel on the television called, "The Beehive Channel," that played nothing but children's shows, all day and all night. (What children were up at midnight watching television anyway?)

And, of course, this was what Mallory wanted to watch.

"Why can't I choose a show?" I asked.

"Daddy said that I could watch Beehive," she said as she stuffed the converter under the sheets, hiding it from me.

There was no arguing with her.

So, we settled into watch this endless dreck of brightly-costumed men and women bouncing about like simpletons on parade as they sang songs and spoke calming words of assurance in saccharin voices. And the shows weren't fun at all. They weren't stories. Each and every show was a life lesson, a teachable moment about how to listen and make good decisions. It was complete shit, but it held Mallory captive, worming into our brain.

By hour four, Ben's persistent snoring shook me back to consciousness, and I struggled to pull myself free of the Beehive dimension that Mallory had us locked in. I noticed Todd shitting on the floor, rabbit poo pebbles piling in the shape of a pyramid on the carpet.

'Never mind,' I said to myself. It was probably not the first time that feces had touched this carpet.

I surveyed the room as a cartoon child with an ill-fitting ball cap and a bald head pranced about the television screen. Ben was snoring loudly on the bed beside us. His body had given up on him. Lying shirtless and comatose atop the sheets and blankets of the strange bed, he rolled onto his side to reveal a hunk of pizza crust intertwined in the long coarse black hairs on the small of his back.

The lack of luggage in the room was going to be a problem. I wondered how we were going to get around this. Ben had grabbed one dress and some underwear from the dresser when we left, but we had no clothes to change into and Mallory did not have a bathing suit. How would we go to the beach?

It was dusk. It would soon be completely dark, and we would be alone. Whether Ben woke up or not, we would be alone, for we had crossed that threshold. We had checked into a motel. We had become vacationers. Travellers, like the ones we had seen in the parking lot of the Three Sisters Cafe. People whose initial concept of fun and good times had become a reality of pizza crusts stuck to their backs and dwindling billfolds.

Bugs swarmed in the flickering lights of the vacancy sign outside our window.

We found ourselves downstream, in some place on the earth so foreign to most people that I am still not sure it even ever existed at all, for it all seems like a nightmare now. A place that could do nothing to even raise the interest of the world's most fervid collectors of cat souvenirs; a place that the hungriest pizza eaters would drive right past; a place where intrepid hunters of fat, bespectacled, slow-witted man-children would not even break long enough to fire a single shot.

I remembered it when I was alive. These were our family vacations, with Dad and Mom, and Alice and me. We were people searching in a fog, feeling blindly for a horizon of good times and looking for a spark of light in a foreboding darkness of loneliness, reaching our tremulous hand out in search of good time papa, only to be bit by reality. It might seem melodramatic, but we all felt it. I know that Ben felt it coming, the rising pressure, the filthy motel carpet, the stress of travel.

What next? What will we do tomorrow? Can we just go to bed and sleep till it's over? I wondered.

We all felt it, the impending doom, the fear that this vacation was actually going to suck and not be any fun at all. It didn't help that Dana was undoubtedly hunting us down, coming to haul us back to reality: me back to my patchouli-drenched executioner and Ben to a possibly long stint in prison.

Ben slept like a man who was trying to shake a great burden from his shoulders. He snored and shifted and thumped about the bed.

I was suddenly very depressed.

On the television, the bald boy had removed his cap. He was backed into a corner and swinging a knife as he grimaced and threatened. His father wore a thick yellow sweater and was holding a stick. The boy growled at the father and ran at him, biting his leg ferociously as the father struggled to wrestle him off, whacking him with the stick.

"What is this?" Mallory said.

The mother appeared in the doorway stripped naked, her curvy figure and breasts gleamed in the light of the kitchen.

"It's soft rot," I said. "It's hard to explain. Do you know what fake news is?"

"Fake what? I don't know what you are saying."

"Never mind. All hail Satan."

"Why is the mommy showing her boobies?" Mallory asked. "Who's Satan?"

"We need to get up, Mallory. Stand up. Go to the door."

"Why?"

"We need to leave here. Go to the door."

"No. Turn off this fake news and put my show back."

"Yes. Please, yes. I just need some air."

"No. Turn my show back to what it was."

If she wasn't going to move, I'd move her. I fought to make her muscles work on my behalf. I fought for control. I moved our leg off the bed and set it on the floor. I started working the other leg.

"Fine! I'll go!" Mallory said. "Just to the door though. For your air." And we stood and walked past the sleeping Ben towards the door of room six. Todd hopped out of the way as we reached for the door handle.

"Ew," Mallory said and pulled her hand away.

"What is it now, child?"

"Ew. Look. A snail."

There was a snail sliming its way around the door handle. "Kill it," I said.

"No."

"Yes, you have to. Just squish it."

"No."

"Mallory!"

"You are not the boss of me."

"Aren't I?"

The door suddenly swung open, and on the other side, Charles stood with another missing link. This link wasn't as muscular, or tall as Charles, but his face was as lumpy, and he was just as ugly. The boy's teeth were all askew, some grown-in adult teeth, others still baby teeth; and beneath the brim of his greasy John Deere Trucker hat, long bushy eyebrows, like nests, seemed to cover the majority of his forehead. If he had been a cartoon drawing, the exclamation, "Duh" surely would have appeared in a speech bubble beside his head.

"Great, more kissing cousins," I said.

"I dold you," Charles said to the link.

The link scratched his forehead just beneath the brim of his hat, leaving a white mark where dirt used to be. "Well, there ya have it," he said.

"Wanna come oud and play?" Charles asked.

"What should we do?" Mallory asked.

"Do you see that letter opener there on the dresser?" I asked her.

"Uh huh."

"Slowly reach over and grab it."

There was a sudden eruption of snoring, and Ben awoke with a start. "I didn't even know there was a goose there," he said, obviously still half in his dream.

The boys turned and ran off into the woods.

A small black cat sauntered into our room and jumped up on the bed.

"What time is it?" Ben asked.

"Next time," I said as Mallory set the letter opener back on the dresser. "Next time."

"What time is it," Ben asked again.

666

That cat slept on our bed all night, curled up in Mallory's arm. I asked her not to touch it for fear it might have fleas. I told her that I was concerned for poor Todd's safety and she should let it outside, but Mallory refused to listen. It seemed like anything I said Mallory just did the opposite.

Friggin' kids.

In the morning, the cat nudged its head against our cheek, purred, and asked to be let out the door. We let it out.

We showered, had some leftover pizza for breakfast, and checked out of the motel. Ben packed the bike and trailer into the bed of Mr. Marble's pickup truck, and we climbed into the front. Ben did not have Mallory's car seat, so Mr. Marbles propped us up on pillows to make certain that the seat belt would not choke us. He then set Todd in our lap. Ben sat in the middle seat, and Mr. Marbles climbed into the driver's seat, holding the door open for a large orange cat that seemingly levitated straight up off the ground and into Mr. Marbles' lap.

"He likes to go for rides," Mr. Marbles said.

"Look, Mallory," Ben said. "He's like a dog. Hold onto Todd tightly."

We followed a dirt road to the cabin. The forest of maples, cedars, ash, and a few paper birches surrounded us. The road was so straight it felt like we were falling down a hole.

"What's this road called?" Ben asked.

"Line 75. It goes straight from the motel down to the lake," Mr. Marbles said.

We travelled this way for many kilometres, mostly in silence, other than the odd yawn, until Mr. Marbles slowed the truck down.

"It's up here somewhere," he said. "I nearly always miss the driveway. HERE!"

He turned the car down a narrow pathway only wide enough for one vehicle. The truck rocked and pitched as we drove through massive muddy potholes. Eventually, we came to a clearing where we saw a cabin with a freshly built front porch. Mr. Marbles stopped the car.

"I don't like it here. It's too secluded. What if something were to happen?" I said.

Mallory did not respond. She jumped out of the passenger side door when Ben opened it.

Ben slid out after her. Mr. Marbles opened the driver side door, set his orange cat on the grass, and got out. The cat sniffed around for a bit before it slunk off into the woods.

Ben smacked the back of his own neck.

"I believe there is some mosquito repellent inside," Mr. Marbles said. "Case you don't have any with you. This time of year, it doesn't seem to do much though. It's like gravy to them."

I felt a pinprick as Mallory smacked our arm where a mosquito had been feasting.

"Look, Mallory," Ben said, walking towards a bunch of trees. We followed. He could obviously see something that we could not. Cutting through a stand of cedars, we came upon Rat Farm Lake. The water was still and black, and cabins dotted the opposite shoreline. Somewhere in the haze clinging to the surface of the lake came a familiar sound. It was an eerie tremolo, reminding me of the call to prayer in Hell.

"What was that?" Mallory asked Ben

"Yeah, what was that? Ben asked.

"Loons," Mr. Marbles answered.

We walked out to the end of a rickety old dock. The wooden planks that kept us from falling into the water had been slowly rotting over the years, and the dock seemed ready to collapse. Were it not for Mr. Marbles' fearlessness and obvious confidence in the soundness of the structure, we probably would not have continued to the end.

"East?" Ben said, pointing towards the opposing shore as we all stood at the end of the dock, trying to keep our balance. I held onto Todd tightly.

"South," Mr. Marbles corrected him as a small fishing boat slowly drifted by.

The fisherman waved and said, "Good day," to us. He was only about twenty meters from the end of the dock.

"Line 75 south, straight from the motel," Ben repeated to himself.

"Catching anything?" Mr. Marbles shouted out to the man in the boat.

Just as Mr. Marbles said this, the fisherman's pole came to life, and he scrambled to reach it. We watched as he fought with the pole, reeling in whatever was on the other end.

"Looks like he's got a big one, " Ben said, trying to sound like a man who knew about fishing.

The fisherman's bucket hat (with all the pretty fishing

lures on it) fell off his head as he gave a jerk of his pole, sweating and cursing underneath his breath, calling the fish a "dirty whore" and a "filthy bastard," as if it were his mortal enemy. Finally, reeling the fish to the surface of the water beside the boat, he set his pole down and reached out to grab his line. He hauled up the fish, and we all watched as the hooked beast swung there, captured.

The fish was fat and long, grey and slimy, with a flapping maw, and long sharp little teeth, and big black eyes. There was no beauty to it, no thoughts of filleting it and frying its flesh in a pan (it was far too ugly for that). This fish was just something grey and slimy that might bite you.

We watched as the man dropped the fish into the bottom of the boat, reached into some curved recess in the hull, took a large wooden mallet, and began pounding upon the fish's head, undoing God's failure. It was a murder. Nothing but. And then the fisherman took the fish by the gills, held it over the water, and with his filleting knife, he gutted it, sending entrails and a sizable amount of roe plopping into the lake. When he was through eviscerating the fish, he dropped the carcass into the lake. It splashed lifelessly, floated there for a second, then sank.

The fisherman kneeled in the boat and dipped his

hands into the water, washing away the blood. When he noticed us staring at him, he spoke up: "Invasive species," he said. "Taiwanese rat fish. They're destroying this whole damn lake."

An unease spread through our body, and a lump of vomit rose to our throat.

"Well, I gotta get back before Charles burns the place down," Mr. Marbles said. "You have my number. Give me a call if you need anything."

Mr. Marbles got in his truck and drove away, without the orange cat.

"Can we go swimming, Dad?" Mallory asked.

666

"Swimming? Are you crazy?" I am not going in that water. It's full of Taiwanese rat fish," I said.

Mallory sniggered at me. "Fake news. Don't be silly. They are just pretend."

"No. Not fake news. That was not pretend. That happened. That was real."

"Fake news. It's like the TV show. It's not real. You're silly, Karen," Mallory said as she slapped our forehead, killing a mosquito.

"Ow," I said. "Buggers."

"You're funny, Karen."

"Kill that thing, would you?" I said, in reference to a snail cresting a rock in the tall grass.

"No," Mallory said, slapping our calf as another mosquito looking for its lunch was smeared off to meet its maker.

"You have no problem killing the mosquitoes. Kill the

snail."

"The mosquitoes are bad. The snail is good."

"It's not that simple, Mallory. Just kill it. What kind of god would invent such a disgusting creature anyway?" I asked.

I fought with all my power to stomp on the snail. Mallory would not let me. She would not allow me control of the body, and she was strong. She fought hard.

"No," she said, again and again. And she was sticking to it. She would not allow me to move.

Ben was pacing down by the dock (it was the only place he could get a cell phone signal).

We heard distant murmurs and laughter.

"Yes, line 75," he said, and started laughing.

I wondered if maybe Dana was coming around, assuming it was Dana that he was speaking to.

"Kill it," I said, referring to the snail.

"He's done nothing to hurt us. You shouldn't kill things. It's not nice."

"Well, let me kill it then. It will give me great pleasure and satisfaction if you allow me to kill it."

"No."

"I will get control over the body one day. You cannot hold out forever."

"No."

"I cannot go back to Hell," I told her. "I won't, Mallory. I won't. Do you know what that means?"

"..."

"Well, do you, Mallory?"

"Daddy will save me."

I laughed manically.

"He will!" Mallory insisted. "He's my daddy, and he loves me."

One little girl in a floral dress and her directionally-challenged father versus the Nakara Corporation and all its subsidiaries. It almost didn't seem fair.

"What are we going to do, Mallory?" I said.

"Go swimming."

"No, I mean..."

"What are you looking at, honey?" Ben walked up behind us, smiling, holding his cell phone at his side.

"Nothing."

"Are you watching that snail?"

"Yes."

"Okay. Don't hurt it, though. Remember, it's never done anything to harm you. Just because you are bigger than it doesn't give you the right to kill it."

"I know."

We heard something crunching on the gravel road. A car was approaching.

666

An old mint green Ford Taurus with tinted windows turned into the driveway. Ben was smiling from ear to ear. He ran over to the car and slapped his hands on the hood as it pulled to a stop. The driver's side door opened and Don, Ben's friend from the restaurant, got out.

"You are THE WORST direction giver that I have ever known," Don said. "The motel was east on line 86, not north."

"Well, whatever, Mr. Aragones. It's good to see you. Did you bring the stuff?"

"I sure did."

"Mallory, come here." Ben called. "Come see what Uncle Don brought."

We ran over and stood at the trunk of the car while we waited for Don to open it. The truck sprung open and inside we saw what Don had brought: groceries, a suitcase full of clothes for us, sundries, a cooler full of meat, and another one full of beer and liquor.

Ben laughed and his smile nearly split his face. He took his friend's hand and shook it. "And you're sure no one saw you?" he asked.

"I'm sure."

"And no one followed you here?"

"I'm sure. I'm sure," Don said. "You owe me 300 bucks though. And you have to talk to Dana. I don't want to be an accessory to this. She's going to call the cops. She's left, like, a hundred messages on my phone. This is serious, dude."

"I'll call her again. She'll calm down. I promise. That friend of hers, Alexis, has her turned all ass backwards." Ben paused momentarily. "Well, whadya say, everybody? Let's have some lunch and head to the beach."

"Yah!" Mallory shouted, bouncing up and down on the lawn.

In the cabin window, beside the front door, a ghostly grey face with black eyes, a yellow toothy smile, and a giant mop of blue hair was peering out the window at us. Mallory stopped bouncing when she noticed it.

"Who is she?" Mallory asked.

"What's she doing here?" I said.

"Is she fake news?"

"I don't know. Soft rot. I think. Kind of like fake news. Her name is Betty."

"So, is she real or imaginary?"

"I don't know," I said. "Maybe this is what happens to a downsized employee."

I felt Mallory shrink a little, retreat deeper into her body, and when she did, I raised our hand, moved our fingers one by one, and smacked a mosquito on our forearm. The sun disappeared behind the clouds as ghoulish Betty disappeared behind the curtain.

Don smacked his cheek, killing yet another mosquito.

"Insatiable little fuckers," Don said.

"Easy with the language!" Ben said as he too smacked at a mosquito on his cheek.

666

After we unpacked the car and put the food and the coolers away, Ben put some hot dogs on the barbecue. The orange cat that had been left behind by Mr. Marbles came bounding out of the woods when he smelled the hotdogs. It wound its way around Ben's legs as he cooked, purring and stopping intermittently to paw at Ben's calves until he dropped bits of hotdog for it to eat.

"Why's this cat so crazy for hot dogs?" Ben asked.

Don picked a playing card from the picnic table and nested it in among his own. "There is an acceptable amount of ground rodent in all processed meat. It's government sanctioned."

"Oh, that's nonsense."

"Do you have a nine?" we asked.

"Go fish," Don said. "No, it's true. Read the Schmansky Report. You can download it. It's no big deal. It won't hurt you."

I picked a seven from the pile, and because Don was distracted by his conversation with Ben, I threw the seven back into the pile and turned over a few cards until I found a nine.

"I'm out," we said.

"Again?"

"Rodent dogs are ready. Let's eat inside," Ben said, smacking a mosquito.

The cabin was dreary. It was clean but still a dank, dreary place that smelled like creosote and chopped wood. Ben opened some windows to let the air in but closed them quickly as blackflies and mosquitoes came pouring into the cabin from large holes in the window screens.

Over in the corner, by the fireplace, Betty was glaring at us with such terrible hatred in her eyes. She attempted to pick up an axe, but her hands kept passing through the wooden handle as if it were nothing but air.

"Why is she staring at us?" Mallory asked. "What did you do to her?"

"Nothing. Absolutely nothing. She was already dead when I killed her. I have no idea what her problem is."

"I don't like her. Make her go away," Mallory whimpered.

"Trust me, I've tried," I said. "Ignore her. The nasty old

bitch is just trying to ruin our vacation. I don't think she can hurt us."

After we ate and cleared our paper plates into the fire pit outside on the lawn, Ben smacked a mosquito on his forehead and announced: "Get your swimming stuff on, guys, we're going to the beach."

Mallory ran off to our room to get dressed. We put on a one-piece bathing suit with a frilly midsection and a picture of Minnie Mouse on the belly, flip flops, and heart-shaped sunglasses. Don, equally as excited, ran off into his room and put on his vintage cabana wear: red/white/black Hawaiian shirt with matching, tight-fitting shorts, aviator sunglasses, a straw fedora with a band on it that said 'Miami Beach USA,' and the token flip flops.

"Ready," he said as he came bursting from his room.

"You look like a simpleton."

"Think there'll be chicks there?" Don responded.

"Other than the thermos full of piña coladas, he looks just like my own father did," I told Mallory.

"Was your dad a simpleton too?" Mallory asked.

"Good one," I said. "Grab our towel and let's go."

We all basted ourselves with mosquito gravy and sun repellant and we headed out.

To get to the beach, we followed a path from the

cottage. The path had not been used for a very long time and was overgrown but still evident. As we walked and smacked countless mosquitoes and blackflies flat, I couldn't help but feel as if the forest surrounding us was alive. I got the feeling that it was not only watching us pass but also watching with a very particular and unreasonable kind of hatred akin to bigotry. It was a living malevolence that breathed and sniffed and contemplated our deaths just because we were there, and it didn't like the looks of us. I thought for a moment that perhaps the swarms of mosquitoes and blackflies that buzzed around our heads searching for a soft place to land and bite or sting were there warning us.

"Bzzzzzzz. Get out. Bzzzzzzz."

And just as a crushing iceberg of claustrophobia hit me, and I said to our self, "Mallory, to hell with this shit. We're getting the fuck out of here," the path broadened, and we heard voices ahead.

Mallory started to bounce us up and down with excitement.

We came out of the forest to a sandy parking lot where a few cars and trucks were parked. There, before us, lay the beach, a curved section of fine sand about the length of a football field and about fifty yards deep to the tree line.

There were lots of spots to sit. Before we did, however, we all (well, everyone except for Mallory because she could not read) stopped to read a giant sign resting on cedar posts in the sand.

BEACH COMMANDMENTS
1. **N**O PERSON INFECTED WITH A COMMUNICABLE DISEASE OR HAVING OPEN SORES ON HIS OR HER BODY SHALL ENTER THE BEACH AREA
2. **N**O PERSON SHALL CAVORT WITH CANINES ON THE BEACH AREA
3. NO PERSON SHALL POLLUTE THE BEACH WATER WITH SHAMPOO OR SOAP
4. URINATING OR DEFECATING ON THE BEACH AREA IS STRICTLY PROHIBITED
5. NO LIFEGUARD SHALL BE PROVIDED IN THE BEACH AREA
6. NO ALCOHOL SHALL BE ALLOWED ON THE BEACH AREA
7. NUDE BATHING IS STRICTLY PROHIBITED
8. HAVE FUN BUT DO NOT BOTHER THINE NEIGHBOURS

9. THIS IS A RECREATIONAL BEACH.
BAPTISMAL CEREMONIES ARE STRICTLY
PROHIBITED

10. SWIM AT THINE OWN RISK

In case of emergency, please call Beach God, Gary
Whittaker, at 666-457-1949. Paid for by the friends of Rat
Banks Beach.

"I plan to break all ten of the Beach God's
commandments," Don said.

"Even number 7?" Ben answered him.

"Yep. I fear no man. Maybe least of all Beach God,
Gary Whittaker. By the way, did I ever tell you about my
new invention?"

We started walking along the beach, the sand warm on
our feet. "Mallory, did you put Todd inside the cottage
when we left?" Ben asked.

"Yes," Mallory lied. She was not certain where Todd
was.

"It's called the Skinny Dip Buddy," Don continued.

Small groups of people sat silently staring out at the
water and reading books. Some were methodically tossing a
softball or a Frisbee back and forth.

"It's for skinny dip enthusiasts. People like me," Don

went on.

"God help us," Ben said as he picked out a flat place for us to sit by the water's edge, away from the other tourists, and he started laying out a beach towel for me.

"Essentially, it's a dressing screen that you can take out in the water with you. Once you are out there, you can disrobe, hang up your trucks, and swim unencumbered by archaic conservative rules and..."

"Can I go play in the water, Daddy?" Mallory asked.

"That's the stupidest idea I've ever heard," Ben said.

"There's more of us out there than you think. You just watch. I have a patent on it. I plan to quit Radio Barn in two years. I'm taking it to Dragon's Den."

"Daddy, can I go play in the water?"

"What? Sure," Ben said. "Stay close to shore, honey. Where I can see you. We don't have your life jacket."

"Shall I pour us a piña colada?" Don said.

"Please do," Ben replied.

Mallory ran into the water, laughing and splashing.

"Hey, stop splashing," I said. "It's cold."

"No, it's not," Mallory said.

"Yes, it damn well is."

The sun disappeared behind some clouds, and a cool wind came ripping down from the sky.

"It's going to rain," I said. "Let's go back and sit on the sand."

Mallory splashed some more and tipped backwards, falling into the water, the cold fresh water shocking our arse.

"It's freezing. Let's get out and go play in the sand before the Taiwanese rat fish get us," I pleaded with her.

"Fake news," Mallory said, rolling onto our stomach.

"I'll do it myself, Mallory. I am going to control this body eventually, and you won't have a say at all. This water is like cold tap water."

"Ha. You're funny, Karen. Let's pretend we are getting married. In one hour, we will get married on the beach. Then we will have a fight and make up. Then we will have a divorce. Then let's pretend we get married to other people, but the other people die, and we get remarried again when we are old and we have childrens and then we die. But then our childrens have childrens, and they all live for thousands and thousands of years until the last one is a woman who has a baby in her tummy, and she is hit by a car and dies."

"Oh, come on. How long is that going to take? I'm cold. Let's play restaurant on the beach. The sun is behind a cloud. I am cold."

"Oh. Please. Please. Please. Please play with me. You promised."

"Promised what? I never promised anything."

"Please. Please. Please. Please."

"Quit begging, Mallory. It's annoying. It's going to rain. Let's get out of this water."

"Play with me."

"Arg. Okay, fine."

"I'll be Mary. And I'll talk British. What is your name going to be?" Mallory asked.

"I don't know."

"You have to pick a name."

"Glenda."

"No. You be Alex."

Is she trying to drive me insane? Drive me back to Hell? I wondered, getting a little angry with her then and raising my voice: "No. If I am playing, I get to pick my name. I am not playing unless I get to pick my own name."

"Fine," Mallory said, and added, "sucky baby!"

Sucky baby. How dare she? I had been nothing but kind to her. I had treated her like gold through this entire possession. No other demon would ever have been as kind as I had been. This was a friendly takeover. We were working together to get this proposition hammered out. If I had launched a hostile takeover, I bet I could have taken her entire body, mind, and soul, and sent her packing to the daycare centre in Hell within a week of meeting her, but I was being nice. I was patiently sharing with her until the time was right. "I'm not a sucky baby. You're a sucky baby. I am protecting you."

"No, you're not."

"Yes, I am. I am protecting you from that lady in the cottage with the blue hair. I am protecting you from those hippy witches back home. I am protecting you from that forest. For God sakes, Mallory, I am protecting you from Hell itself. And you are being nothing but shitty to me."

"NO! You swore. I am telling. DADDY!"

"No. Hold on. Wait."

"DADDY!"

"What is it, honey?" Ben called from the shore.

"Fine. I'll be Alex," I conceded.

"Never mind," Mallory told her father.

"Tattletale!" I said. "You shouldn't do that, Mallory. No one likes a tattletale."

"Okay," Mallory said, ignoring me completely, "let's get ready for our wedding. I'll talk British starting now."

We played wedding and living and dying and motherhood for what felt like an eternity, at least until our lips turned blue and we started to shake and shiver uncontrollably. I could hear our teeth chattering. I became worried that we might freeze to death when Mallory suddenly looked up at one of the sunbathers, and I felt her poor little heart drop to her feet. The woman she was staring at looked like her mother: dark-skinned with long black kinky hair. The atmosphere of the beach turned a stagnant blueish-grey wash, and everything appeared to stand still. The modern-looking sunbathers with bikinis and smiles on their faces had turned into fat old men wearing striped singlets, and the women were no longer wearing bikinis with half their arses hanging out. They wore bathing costumes down to their knees and sunbonnets.

The vacationers stood ankle deep in the placid water, not speaking, just staring, vaguely interested in a setting sun that may or may not have been the last one they ever saw.

Hell was never going to leave me.

"Can we get out now?" I asked Mallory. "Please? I am cold and depressed."

Mallory snapped from her gloom with a cheeky, "Cert-ten-lee, me lady. Will you be having tea on the beach then?" We walked out of the water, passing the men with singlets, and the blue world turned normal again. The sun came out, and I felt its warmth on our back. I sighed as the tableau shifted back to reality.

Ben jumped from his chair when he saw us approach. "By God, child, you're blue." He laughed and wrapped our towel around us and hugged us tightly, rubbing our back to warm us up. "Just sit in the sun for a bit. Warm up."

Ben took a gulp out of his solo cup and sat back down quickly.

"You have to," Don said.

"I can't," Ben said. "How can I?"

"Call her, man. She's your wife."

A soccer ball came rolling to a stop a few metres from us. We looked up to see a boy, about ten years old, staring.

"Ball," he said. "Pass it over." Mallory stood and dropped the towel.

"Let him get his own ball," I said. "We're not his slave."

Mallory did not listen to me, of course, and picked up the ball.

"Bring it over," the boy said.

"Tell him to piss off," I said.

"You're mean," Mallory said as she walked the ball over to the boy. She stretched out her hands and handed him the soccer ball.

He was a slim young thing, with buggy whips for arms and a gawky smile, teeth jutting everywhere. "My brother wants to speak to you," he said, as he took the ball and ran off down the beach.

Before I knew what was happening, a boy of about sixteen grabbed hold of our wrist. He was pulling us towards the tree line. We struggled to dig our heels into the sand, but the boy was too strong.

"Karen, help," Mallory pleaded.

"Shout for your dad!" I said.

"DA..." Mallory began to shout, but the boy stopped and turned to face us.

He tightened his grip on our wrist to make it hurt, and with his free hand, he put his index finger against his downy teenage moustache. "Shhh," he said as he got down on one knee. He had a red ball cap with a wide straight brim on, and he wore numerous long gold chains around his neck, all of them looking like something he got out of a bubblegum machine. The chains hung down over a pink shirt cut off at the navel that said, "RELAX," on it.

"Take a chill pill. It's me, Karen."

ME!" I said, "Mallory, ask this punk who ME is?"

"Who are you, punk?" Mallory said as we pulled back on our wrist, wresting it away from the boy.

"Yo. Karen, it's me. Proper Paulie. What's your damage? You have to bounce out of here. You're in danger."

666

"I don't want to talk to you," Mallory said. "My daddy said I am not to talk to strangers." Collectively, we all looked to see Ben and Don laughing on the beach, pouring more drinks from the thermos.

"Listen up, baby girl," Hepburn P. said. "They'll be here soon, 'kay, and they will take you. The prophecy will, like, not be fulfilled. You feel me? Let's bounce. Now." He took his fist and smacked his heart in a show of peace and love. "I'll hide you in my closet until you grow up."

"Who is he?" Mallory asked.

"Your future husband," I told her.

"Ew."

"I know," I said. "Grody to the max, eh?"

Paul grabbed our wrist again. "You're my heart, baby," were the last words he got out before the tree line seemed to burst open, and a flood of slack-jawed missing links brandishing all sorts of crude weaponry issued forth with the battle cry of "ORPIANS!"

666

Leading the charge was Charles from the motel. He raised a large stick that looked like a shillelagh and hit a stunned Hepburn P. over the head, dropping him like a sack of potatoes. Blood poured from the split in Hepburn P.'s head and soaked through his hair into the beach sand.

Charles turned towards us, breathing heavily through his nostrils, his eyes behind his Coke bottle glasses black with murderous rage.

"Easy now, Charlie," I said. "Easy, big boy." I made a motion with my hands like a mime trapped in a glass cage.

Across the beach, sunbathers dropped their cans of beer, scooped up their children and ran for their cars, leaving behind their coolers and beach umbrellas. Chaos was the new order of the day, and the sudden eruption of violence and strange shouts of "ORPIONS!" made for widespread panic.

Ben and Don ran towards us, but Don was tackled from

behind by a tiny link with a head like an eggplant and enormous buckteeth. He started punching Don with his tiny fists, shouting "You want a piece of me?"

Don squirmed and bucked the link off just in time to scramble to his feet and intercept a line of five links moving towards Ben. They were running on all fours like gorillas. The gorilla links trampled Don and sent him rolling in a cloud of sand, his fedora and aviator classes crushed in the melee, but it slowed them down just enough to allow Ben time to reach us. As Charles was about to grab our hand, Ben scooped us up by the waist and started running towards the parking lot.

The parking lot and a good Samaritan with a fast car might have been a route to safety had it not been for the black horses and buggies that had converged there, blocking the path. The Mennonites were in league with the links. When Ben saw them, he tripped in the thick sand, sending Mallory and me somersaulting away from him. Charles was behind us, running, with the other gorilla boys right behind him, sweat glistening on their upper lips and brows. The eggplant headed link was facing us, closing in. "You want a piece of me?" he cried. A line of black buggies were to the left of us, the deep dark woods behind us. We were surrounded.

There was only one hope for escape. I stood and brushed the sand off us. The horses in the parking lot reared back slightly and shook their heads when they saw me. I wrinkled our brow and glared at the beasts, giving them the crook-eye, the stink-eye, and the evil-eye all at once. I didn't know for certain whether this would work or not. I saw it in a movie. I raised my head to the sky, lifted my arms, and called upon Hell for help.

Muttering in a low voice, I recited: "Melchior Brown, Yolk Yellow, Ochre, Plump Sienna..."

The sky suddenly became dark and lightning struck over the open water. An unholy chorus of demons began singing in something that could be Latin (but probably was just some made up nonsense, knowing demons as well as I do) and sounding sort of like, "Dos dos. Occide inimicum! Dos dos. Dos. Dos. Occide inimicum!"

"Bathrobe Blue, Pickle Green."

The sky blackened some more, and the horses were spooked, rearing up on their hind legs. Lightning struck again. I furrowed my brow and stared harder. The beasts charged across the beach, their black buggies trailing, bouncing across the sand behind them. The missing link attackers scattered to get away from the horses. Lightning struck again. A wild howling wind attacked from the sky.

"Dos. Dos. Occide inimicum!"

Ben grabbed me by the waist, and we ran towards the woods.

The music stopped when we hit the tree line. Ben set us down on our feet. We turned back to the beach, searching for Don.

In the chaos of the missing links trying to figure out how to put out a fire that had somehow erupted in one of the buggies, we saw Don charging towards us. Ben waved him on, but just as Don was within a few feet of us, Charles recognized him. Holding his staff up over his head, he let loose a screeching battle cry, "ORPIONS!" and started bounding towards the tree line. Ben threw me over his shoulder in a fireman's carry, and we ran.

666

We finally stopped in a clearing in the woods. Charles was not behind us, at least he was not close enough that we could hear him or see him, and Ben and Don collapsed, breathing heavily. We all lay in a soft bed of pine needles, a buzzing swarm of mosquitoes blanketed us. They were relentless.

"What the Hell was that?" Don huffed.

"I have no idea. We have to get Mallory out of here."

"Out of here?" Don said. "Piss on that. I'm phoning Dana."

Ben paused before he said, "Dana? What is she going to do? She's a two-hour drive from here."

Don popped up from the ground and started smacking himself all over as if he had lost his mind, killing mosquitoes five at a time with his open palm.

"I can't take it anymore, Ben. I feel like I am being eaten alive. I'm stuck in the middle of nowhere being chased by some inbred hillbillies, for God only knows what reason, running through this forest with flip flops on. There are strange voices coming from the sky. Your daughter cheats at cards. Don't think I didn't notice," Don shouted at me. "This is some vacation. You know, I've had enough." He pulled his cell phone out of his pocket.

"Gimme that phone," Ben said.

"No."

"Give it to me!"

"No," Don said, holding the phone against his chest.

"You can't call Dana. I won't let you," Ben said. "She needs to clear her head first. I'll talk to her."

"Clear her head? Ben, look at what is going on here. Does it not seem a little strange to you?"

"Gimme the phone," Ben said.

"No."

"There's nothing strange about anything. We are on vacation. That's all."

"Maybe you are the one that needs help, Ben." Don said. "You ever think of that? You ever wonder if maybe there is something going on with Mallory? The rare meat? The body odour? The strange voices coming from the sky? She talks to herself incessantly. Her complexion? Look at her complexion, Ben. Does she not look a little green to you?

Maybe Dana is right. Maybe something is wrong with her. Maybe Alexis can help expunge whatever is going on inside of her?"

"Expunge? Don't you mean exorcise? Fuck, man. You too? What are you people smoking? There is nothing wrong with my daughter. She's fine! She has a dairy allergy!" Ben said. "Now, where is Dana? Tell me that you didn't call her."

"Listen, man."

Ben snatched the phone from Don's hand. He turned it on and started scrolling through the text messages.

"I'm sorry, man," Don said. "This is rigoddamndiculous, though."

"You've been texting her all along, haven't you? What's this? *Dana: I'll be there in an hour.*' How could you do this, Don?" Ben dropped the cell phone and swatted at the mosquitoes hovering around his face.

"This has gone too far," Don said. "You and I both know that this isn't right."

"You Judas. What isn't right? What isn't right about it? How would you know the difference between right and wrong, Judas? There's a simple explanation for everything that is going on here. Mallory, come here," Ben said. "Take Daddy's hand."

"Mallory, don't," Don said. "Your mommy's on the way. She'll take you home."

"Mommy?" Mallory said.

"Don't do it, Mallory," I told her. "She'll send me away."

Mallory stood and started walking towards Don. I fought her, pulling her leg towards Ben, so she was frozen in the middle.

"Here, Mallory. Come to Dad."

"No, Mallory. Come to me," Don said. "I'll take you to your mom.

It looked like a dog calling contest, a final showdown to determine who the real owner of Lassie, or Thunder, or Benji truly was.

"We have to go, Mallory," I said. "I can't let you do this. The witches will get us. They will send me back to work, and I will be a zombie forever. You can't do that to your sister."

The sun was beginning to set, the mosquitoes buzzed ever louder, and an eruption of birds flew from a distant tree.

"Leave me alone, Karen," Mallory said.

"Come on, Mallory. Let's play a game. I'll be a teacher, and you can be my sister from France. We'll open a pet store that sells cupcakes."

"No. I want my mommy."

"You can talk British."

Mallory took a step to turn towards Don.

"NO!" I shouted as loudly as I could, and it came out of Mallory's mouth in a spewing volcano of reeking green vomit. "No. No. No. No." It felt like someone cracked a warm egg on our brain, and it ran down through all the crevices and cracks of our personality, wetting all the connections between the lobes, and Mallory was suddenly gone. Something had broken. By sheer will I had torn through, and the body was now mine. It was me. Only I was left. I mean, Mallory was there somewhere, maybe in our big toe or in a few strands of hair, but it was me who was finally in charge.

I turned slowly and skipped towards Ben.

Ben wiped the vomit from my chin with his shirt and we hugged.

"Dude, this isn't right," Don said.

And then he fell to the ground in a heap, replaced by the hulking figure of Charles from the motel, breathing heavily, holding his stick like he had just hit a three-run home run.

"Orpions," Charles muttered, and the grove was suddenly bustling as dark figures began stepping from the shadows.

666

"Charles, I don't know what you are angry about, but I think you should go back to the motel to play with your friends. Mr. Marbles would not like this."

We were surrounded by missing links, all slack of jaw and crooked of eye, big-lipped mouth breathers with dumbo ears and eggplant heads, and filthy fingernails. With their John Deere hats slightly askew, they slowly crawled from the edges of the woods into the dying light of day.

"What do you want from us?" Ben said.

Charles approached, pointing at me. It was clear what they had come for, and there was no escape. The noose tightened as they closed in.

Great, I thought. I get one minute, maybe two, with a brand-new body to call my own before I am beaten to death (or worse) by a bunch of inbred dimwits.

Ben picked me up and charged at them, trying to burst through their line, but they just shoved him down to the ground, laughing stupidly, 'Huh. Huh. Huh." Ben hugged me tightly, covered my face and head as he tried to hold them back, but they were creeping in closer like a slow-moving flood.

"Get back, you dumb shits," Ben said.

"Orpions," the chant went up, softly at first. "Orpions. Orpions. Orpions." They were getting louder and louder as they converged upon us.

I closed my eyes. There was a struggle. I ended up on the ground. I could smell pizza and Dr. Pepper and cow manure and body odour as I felt their hands touch me. I could feel their breath and a tear slipped from my eye as I prepared to die (again).

"STOP!" a voice came like a gunshot.

Everything was suddenly still and calm. The smells dissipated, and the hands left my back. I opened my eyes.

"Holy shit, am I glad to see you," Ben said, straightening from his karate stance.

I could not see over the crowd until the sea of links parted and made a path for the voice.

I saw his orange cat before I saw him: Mr. Marbles, from the motel, approached us. He was wearing the same T-shirt he wore before, along with white linen pants. His long hair flowed over his shoulders and shifted in the breeze as he walked towards Charles.

Mr. Marbles snatched the stick from Charles's hands and said, "What did I tell you about taking your games too seriously?"

Charles hung his head in shame.

"Mr. Marbles," Ben said, "we need to call an ambulance. Charles hit my friend Don on the head. Is he okay? Can someone check him?"

Mr. Marbles stepped over Don's body and walked up to us. "Are you okay?" he asked.

"I'm fine," Ben said. "But my buddy, Don. We need to call an ambulance for him. What's with these kids? Charles, you are in big trouble!"

"I wasn't asking you," Mr. Marbles said. "I was asking her." He looked at me. "Are you okay, Karen?"

Oh, shit.

"Karen?" Ben said. "What the Hell are you talking about?"

Mr. Marbles sighed, "You know, I am just going to come right out and say it," he addressed Ben. "Either you are one stupid sack of shit, or you are THE most oblivious bugger on the planet." He turned to me. "She can't wait to see you again, Karen."

666

Before I knew it, the missing links were all over us, and we had bags over our heads, our wrists were tied, and we were corralled into the back of a van. I could hear the links breathing, chortling, and guffawing as they farted loudly and blamed it on one another. "That was you, Charles."

"No, it wasn'd. Id was Ronnie."

"You're a liar."

"Whoever smeld it deald id."

The van stunk like the sulphur manufacturing district in Hell.

Ben struggled and stood up to lunge at his captors every once in a while, shouting at them and calling them "crazy assholes," but he was easily subdued and eventually, sick of wrestling with him, they stopped the van and hogtied him. For the rest of the trip, Ben lay on the floor whimpering, crying over his misfortune, and shouting, "What the fuck do you people eat?" after every stinky fart. At one point I believe that he was praying to God for help.

As the teenagers say, "Yeah. Good luck with that."

The van slowed and pitched and rocked as the driver eased our way through giant puddles. Charles and another boy were playing rock paper scissors, arguing over what beat what. Charles was insistent that matchbox firebomb was an option and that matchbox firebomb beat everything and only he could use it. Yet somehow, in the end, Charles still managed to lose the match.

The van finally stopped, and the back doors opened. A rush of sweet fresh air came pouring in, blowing out the farty ether that was gagging me.

"Where are we?" Ben demanded to know.

"You're home. Finally, home," Mr. Marbles said. "Charles, take him to the altar and prepare him for the sacrifice."

"Get your hands off me!" Ben began writhing on the floor and shouting out Mallory's name, screaming, weeping, and gnashing his teeth, fighting against the ropes that bound him, but it was as useless as fighting against death itself. I heard the sound of a few sets of feet and felt the shocks on the van compress and then release as the pleading, "Please don't hurt my daughter!" became fainter and fainter.

"Remove her hood." The sun had all but set.

I saw Mr. Marbles standing there at the open doors of the van. A number of people (thirty, maybe forty) were standing behind him, some women, some children, and they were all wearing the same clothes: the T-shirt, the one with the crucified cat and the spaceships, wispy white cotton pants, and sandals, their long hair fluffed up in piles of curls or trailing straight and long down their backs. Standing beside Mr. Marbles was the woman we had met at the sandwich shop, Misty, when we first stopped to have lunch.

"Welcome to the order of the Grimalkin, Karen," Misty said.

666

I was helped from the van. A sign above the entranceway said, "Welcome to Camp Gobaith."

We walked, Misty on one side of me, Mr. Marbles on the other. My bathing suit was uncomfortable, and I wanted to get out of it and put on a dress.

"It's an old KOA camp," Misty said, matter of factly. "It was abandoned after an outbreak of Legionnaires disease."

An orderly row of cabins, more like barracks, stood to the right of us. They were rickety, but all the rotting wood had been replaced. I looked up to see a ragged child peering at me from the window. Her blonde bob cut framed her filthy cheeks. When our eyes met, she ducked out of sight quickly.

"Can she speak?" another child, a bold boy of about 9 or 10, asked as he came running up from the parade of people behind us.

"What did I tell you, Shadow?" Mr. Marbles said,

shooing him away. "Get back in line."

"It's a fair question. Can you speak, Karen?" Misty asked.

Not to you, bitch, I wanted to say, but I kept quiet, feeling that anything I said might incriminate me. These people seemed crazier than a bunch of shithouse rats, but I had learned while drafting the Cheezie report that, although it may seem contrary to newspaper and television reports, statistically speaking, very few people are crazy enough to kill a child. So I figured that as long as I left some doubt in their brains as to who I truly was, I might be able to keep my head attached to my neck, or my heart inside my rib cage, for a little while longer.

"Well, I don't suppose it really matters much," Misty said. "We know who you are, Karen. It has been prophesied. The Teacher has great things in store for you."

I smelled something like ammonia. It stung my nostrils.

"The Teacher's cabin is right up here. Follow me, if you will." Mr. Marbles held out his hand in a sweeping gesture as Misty took me up a flight of steps. We stood there on a rickety old porch, and Misty put her hands on my shoulders and turned me to face the crowd beneath us. They stood silently watching us, now about a hundred men, women, and children, and what seemed like hundreds of cats of all shapes and sizes and colours, glaring at me.

That's what that smell is, I thought. *Cat pee.*

666

Misty massaged my shoulders in a friendly, gently way, as if she wanted me to feel comfortable. She began to speak:

"I am so glad to see you all here today. Welcome, family. Welcome, my Grimalkin family. Today is the most holy day in our calendar. The prophecy is as the Teacher told it to us. We have been good students on this planet, and our mission here is about to come to a close.

Karen has arrived, and tonight is the night we return whence we came.

(A few cheers of hallelujah erupted from the audience, along with some clapping.)

"The Kingdom of God. We came here thousands of years ago with the express purpose being to offer a doorway to the Kingdom of God in this age, this millennium, to these people on this planet. And now on this day the prophecy has come to pass. The child has arrived. And our job is done. We can go home, people. We have gathered all the Grimalkin we can. All those that were born into the chassis of flesh and bone and blood; we used it to hold our celestial spirits in a pattern of harmony. Now it is time for us to leave these bodies, that, truth be told, and we all know it. We all know it don't we? The Teacher has told us a million times. We all know it. Come on, we know it."

The crowd laughed knowingly and cheered and clapped.

"It is time for us to leave these containers and to call out across the heavens to our Grimalkin brothers and sisters and say, dear family, it's time. Can you pick us up?"

The crowd cheered loudly.

"We are coming home again. Our mission here is ended, so go now, my Grimalkins, my family. Go now and prepare for our interstellar journey. Our brothers and sisters are coming tonight. The beacon has arrived. Across the space time continuum, we will travel. Home. Home, people. My brothers and sisters, we are going home again!"

A great meowing came from the crowd. Shockingly, they all sounded like cats, and even more shockingly, the cats themselves joined in, and the entire crowd was meowing together.

Misty took me by the hand and opened the door to the cabin.

666

"The Teacher will be with you shortly," Misty said, shutting the door behind us and locking it.

I wondered if I could rip her throat out with my bare hands. It didn't seem likely, considering my hands were that of a five-year-old girl. I checked around for a weapon, but it was dark, difficult to see. The windows in the cabin were all blacked out with spray paint. The only real light coming from a number of aquariums. As I moved closer to the aquariums, I noticed they contained no water (I guess that made them terrariums), and each one was a little world, a scene composed of rocks, dirt, plants and moss. Each one was different, a tropical mountainscape that looked like King Kong might be hiding somewhere inside; another looked like the mossy moors of Scotland with a model cabin painstakingly placed on a hillside, a rock path leading up to it. I bent to get a closer look. At first, the scenes appeared wanting, lifeless, so a person could only make it come to life through one's imagination. As I looked closer, I saw something move, ever so slowly, a snail, with its mucus-coated underbelly shifted towards me from the top of a rock in a Japanese garden, turning its tentacles in my direction, its globular eyes staring right at me. I checked the other terrariums. It was not immediately obvious, but all the terrariums housed snails, slithering along the sides of the glass, living the life of Riley with beautiful, magical surroundings and food and water. I immediately reached my hand into one of the terrariums to snatch a snail out, the vile spreader of rare diseases, the French delicacy, the asexual abomination, and toss it against the wall smashing it to pieces. Just as my thumb and index finger touched the snail's shell, I heard a voice.

"No, Karen."

A familiar voice.

"Not again, Karen. Put it down."

It couldn't be. It wasn't possible. I let go of the snail and turned. "Alice?" The Teacher? My sister?

666

There stood my dear sister, Alice. No longer youthful and vibrant, playing games, escaping the orpions on the backyard lawn. She was older now, much older, all grey and slim with stooped shoulders and a walking cane. Her breath was visible in the suddenly freezing cold room.

"You may leave us, Misty," she said, her voice shaky yet sure and confident. "God you stink, Karen. Have a seat."

As Misty opened the door to leave, I noticed a desk with two chairs placed in the centre of the room.

"You don't mind if I sit, do you? I am old now," Alice said. "I get tired so easily. And I have to save my strength for tonight."

I opened my mouth to speak, but only a dry whisper came out, my throat like gravel. I tried again, my words a gargling mess of phlegm and demonic rot. "I've missed you so much," I said.

"Here, have a drink. Clear your throat. Coke, wasn't it?

You always loved Coke." Alice reached into a bar fridge below her desk and retrieved a can of Coke. She poured it into a glass and set it in front of me.

I drank the sweet caramel goodness, the delicious carbonated bubbles popping at the back of my throat.

"Thirsty?"

"Alice," I said, my voice low and gravelly, more like a growling dog than a voice. "Sister, why am I here?"

Alice scoffed. "Why are you here? That is what you are asking me? I mean, that is it, isn't it? The point of all of this. Why are you here?"

I shrugged my shoulders.

"Don't you remember, Sister? Don't you remember what you did to me? Think back. Tell me why you ended up in Hell."

I knew exactly what she was talking about, but I was not going to give her the satisfaction of admitting it.

Alice stood. "Hurley! Burley! The Twins! Raymond! Francine! Does that ring a bell?"

"Not really," I lied.

"Hmmm. Even though their blood is on your hands?"

"Alice. It was a joke," I said. "Why can't you take a joke?"

"A joke, was it? A joke? That was funny to you? That is

what is funny to you?"

"We were children for God sakes," I said.

"Murderer. You remember then, murderer? My sister, the murderer."

"Oh, lighten up."

"You remember how I cried?" Alice said. "How Dad held me tight? He rocked me in his arms and said, it's okay, baby. It's okay. Do you miss him? Dad? And Mom? Do you miss them? 'Cause you'll never see them again, DEMON! That is what you get for being so cruel. Your cruelty sent you to Hell in the first place, and now it has brought you full circle, here, back to me. You remember it? Think how horrible it was."

The scene flipped on in my head, like someone was playing an old home movie on a super 8 projector, the film reel clicking. There she was, Alice, with her cute little pigtails and tanned legs, sitting in my dad's lap, crying. He was consoling her, hugging her tightly. "It's okay, baby." On the floor, there was an overturned fishbowl with bits of grass and leaves and some dirt half-spilled out of it. Alice's pet snails Hurley! Burley! The Twins! Raymond! Francine! Or what was left of them, their shells, lay still in the spilled dirt.

My father looked at me with eyes full of menace and

anger. "Look what you've done! Did you really think that would be funny?"

Alice glared at me with eyes so much like my father's, but sharper, the hatred legitimate.

"You told me they liked it!" I could hear Alice say. "You told me it would be good for them. Now they're dead! They're dead, and they're never coming back. I hate you, Karen. I hate you! I'll never see the Twins again. Because of YOU!"

"This is ludicrous," I said (I had just learned the word in a Nancy Drew book two days before), but the glaring eyes of my father and sister let me know that they did not appreciate my sense of humour.

My mother, not knowing what had happened, came in from the kitchen, wiping her hands on her apron. "Has anyone seen the salt?" she asked.

Alice let loose a howling mournful wail, the likes of which I have never heard since, nor do I ever hope to hear again, and I laughed because it all seemed so ludicrous.

"Murderer," Alice said, the old Alice in the cabin, with the same black hate-filled eyes, some 80 years later. "You told me that salt was good for them. You murdered them, Karen. You remember? The salt sizzled their poor little bodies. It melted them. They melted alive. You remember, don't you? You said that they liked it. I was just little. I didn't know any better. Snails love salt, you said. It was a joke to you. And to think, you would pay with your eternal soul. Some joke. How's it feel to be a broken turd in Satan's toilet? I call you that because that is what you smell like."

"Well, it sucks," I said. "But you think life's not fair? You think it was mean of me to play a joke on you and sizzle your snails with a bit of salt. Try judgement day on for size, Sister. Given all the shit that's gone down over the course of human existence, you'd think God would have a better sense of humour than that. I thought we were all going to have a laugh about it."

"Liar. You were just being mean, and you got what you deserved. You're mean."

"You're stupid."

"Dad never loved you after that," Alice fired.

"Well, my new sister is better than you anyway," I blurted. "My Mallory is nice to me, and we have fun. I hate you compared to her. My Mallory is my new sister, and together, we will rule the world, along with Hepburn P. And Satan is going to rise from the ashes and start a monopoly and charge exorbitant amounts for internet services and cable television and cell phone plans. 5G! You ever hear of it? I didn't think so! So poo on you, my dear sister. I'm getting our dad, Ben, and I am leaving here now. You all belong in a mental institution. And I swear, if anyone tries to stop me, I will rip their throats out with my bare hands. I control this body now, and I have the power of Hell behind me. You big cry baby with no sense of humour. I hate you. I hate you. I hate you. You're the one who belongs in Hell. Not me."

I stood from my chair, but my legs were like jelly. I collapsed to the floor, all woozy and disoriented. The room was spinning.

"Dear sister," Alice was immediately standing over me. "I've drugged you, in case you are wondering why you are so dizzy. I can't let you go. You see, we're having a concert tonight. The Prophecy is playing. The band. Not that terrible movie with Christopher Walken. And we are going to use your evil energy to summon God's spaceship, and when we are through with you, we'll send you back to Hell."

"God's spaceship?"

"God will take us home."

"You're nuts." I tried to reach out for her throat, but I could barely lift my arm. "How," I squeaked. "How did you know about me? How did you know I was coming?"

"Hope I didn't give you too much. Seems like it is

working pretty fast," Alice said, watching me fade. "The Prophecy came to me before you died. They brought me the sick box. They told me to put it in your room. They knew everything. And they taught me. They taught me the mastery of an old and nearly forgotten form of witchcraft. The Prophecy never ages. The Prophecy never dies. They gather thousands of people for their concerts, but they have never even had a single in the top 100. It's called an underground following. Their power is almighty, and when the chosen ones, the order of the Grimalkin, leave our bodies tonight, The Prophecy will stay behind to keep order on Earth, to guard against demons, to play to sold out festivals across Europe and North America. The Prophecy will continue to rock and protect the earth long after you and I are gone."

"I heard their music." My eyes fluttered in my head, and I felt my breath flutter in my chest.

"And what did you think?"

"It sucked."

"Go to sleep, dear sister. You'll need to save your strength. For you will be our beacon tonight. Our sacrifice. Now sleep. You have some more dying to do."

"I'm going to kill you all," I muttered, "and feed your souls to the hungry beast."

666

And I was out like a light, dreaming. I had a nightmare about a handsome man that lives in the cosmos...somewhere...and he loved me. He was king of the universe and all things in it, and he was coming for me. And I told people that this was the case. I told Lucy, the Zombie Safety Warden, Mary, Betty, and Professor Norris. I told anyone that would listen about this king of men, and they laughed at me. They told me that I was full of shit. I might as well have told them that I was the living reincarnation of Napoleon Bonaparte or that my tinfoil hat protected me from aliens who were sending me messages from outer space. In the dream, a crowd gathered, an angry crowd, and they locked me away in a dark cage in a mental institution where I cried salty tears and longed to be hugged by my beloved father, Ben Matthews, and the king of men never came.

"No," I shouted in my sleep. "No! NO!" And I woke

myself up shouting "NO!" and I found myself being raised from a prone position to an upright position, raised high up in the air, my little girl arms out to the side, my feet resting on a platform. I was bound at the wrists and ankles, chained to a crucifix. Someone had stripped off my bathing suit and dressed me in a long white robe. I heard a generator start up and gears turning. I could smell gasoline. It was dark, completely black, but I sensed a presence below me, a murmuring shadow, a crowd moving and shuffling well below me, and I heard someone say, "two minutes."

I shook my head trying to knock the cobwebs loose. "Two minutes to what?" I needed out of this. Things were suddenly becoming too real. I wondered if this was going to be the end of me. A tear slipped from my eye. I'm not sure if it was a remnant of my dream or a legitimate tear for the moment. Why did things always end so badly for me? It wasn't fair. So I killed some snails that belonged to my sister. I played a mean joke. So what? I should be tortured for all of eternity for a joke?

"Two minutes to midnight."

A spotlight beam flashed over my shoulder and hit the ground beneath me. My blood sister (Alice) suddenly appeared in a spotlight. I heard the crowd began to cheer and shout things like, "Praise you, Teacher," and "All hail the Teacher."

"Quiet. Quiet down now," Alice said into a buzzing wireless microphone. "Tonight is our night, Grimalkins," she continued, pulling a piece of paper from the folds of the white cassock she wore. "Tonight is the night that we have been waiting for. Tonight is the night that the prophecy is fulfilled. Tonight we leave Earth. And I want all of you to know that I love you. And although this might appear strange to the rest of the world, just know that you have all made the best choice. Some people say that only the bravest can sacrifice their vessels to a greater cause, but we know this isn't true. We know that leaving the vessel and letting the spirit continue on is no different than changing your socks in the morning. Only a fool would think it any different. Let us pray, Grimalkins. Let us pray."

A murmuring sound came from the crowd as they spoke in unison:

"Heart to heart

Grace to grace

Captain of my soul

Celestial winds of promise

Paw to paw

Together we ride

Holy of holy

Journey beyond journey

Together we ride

Mine captain and I

Soul to soul

to the other side

Prrr"

"You people are fucked in the head," I said.

"And now, without further ado," Alice continued, "here to play us their new album, The Eresurection, I am pleased to welcome back, The Prophecy. Give it up for them, people."

The world was suddenly flooded with light, pinks and blues and purple, as the stage lights kicked on, and a group of hooded musicians, dressed like monks, began playing this tuneless music. There were sitars and acoustic guitars and tambourines and fiddles and flutes backing the warbling singer who was jumping all over his scales. He sang: "Telephone ringing pickle blossom murder."

"You suck!" I shouted from my perch behind them, the stage lights beaming all around me making me sweat from the heat. Moths, mosquitoes, giant bugs of all the most bizarre configurations swarmed the lights while the crowd flailed their arms and grooved clumsily along to the tuneless music, most of them stripping off their clothes to let their droopy parts jiggle and flop in opposition to the beat-deaf bongo player who was now soloing from his seated position on a carpet.

"Good Lord, make it stop!" I heard someone shout.

I looked around to see where the voice came from, and I saw Ben. Stage left, he was chained about the neck like a dog. Dressed only in his swimming shorts, his sunburned back was visible in the stage lights. He ran at the bongo player with his fist raised, but his chain yanked him back. Ben looked up at me and raised his arms out, as if there was some way that I could just break the chains that bound me and float down into those loving arms.

I struggled and growled and gnashed my teeth and sent a hailstorm of vomit down onto the stage. I laughed and cried at the same time, and my eyes burned a fearsome red. I screamed out to Satan to release me, to set me free and give me the power to smite mine enemies with bloody force. But nothing happened, and I remained chained to the crucifix no matter how hard I struggled.

The crowd began getting wild, and sweat glistened on their dancing bodies.

The jam session continued, going on and on and on for what felt like an eternity. I searched the stage for Alice, but she was nowhere to be found. It was only in the second half of an hour-long sitar solo that I finally found her.

"Beautiful, isn't it?"

She was with me, high above the stage, standing on a platform to my right. I noticed a set of stairs behind the stage that lead up to the large platform.

"Why? Why are you doing this to us?" I asked. "I loved you, Sister. How can you do this to me?"

"You are our beacon. They are coming. Look. I can see them now. They want you."

"For what? What do they want me for, Alice? Who wants me, sister dear?"

Alice just smiled at me like a lobotomized mental patient and turned away to stare off into the sky. My eyes followed. I could see nothing but a muddle of stars. "There's nothing there, Alice. You're crazy!"

"It is time," Alice said. "The spaceships have come for us." From the folds of her cassock, she pulled her wireless microphone and a little snub-nosed Saturday night special. She turned the microphone on. "They are here, people. It is time to board. Prepare the elixir."

A group of men carried a table out and set it in front of the stage. Another group of men carried out some big water cooler, the kind sports teams used. One man unscrewed the lid, and another dumped a jar full of white powder into it and stirred.

"Poison Kool-Aid. How original," I said. "And the gun?"

"That's for you," Alice said.

"Mallory," I said, "I know you are scared, but you need to come out of hiding and say goodbye to your daddy. I think this is the end." I couldn't feel her or sense her anywhere.

"The Beacon is in place!" Alice shouted.

"One of these days, Alice." I said. "One of these days…"

"Pow…to the moon." Alice remembered the drill from childhood. "I am not sorry, Sister," she said and fell to her knees, her hands clasped in prayer but still holding tightly onto the gun.

A mostly white calico cat with a big belly walked onto the platform. It looked like it had swallowed a football. Slowly and timidly, it walked towards me and rubbed its nose against the base of my crucifix. I could hear its claws scratching on the wood. The band continued to play, but the Order of the Grimalkins had stopped dancing. They were lined up for the poison. The cat scurried up my crucifix and then rested itself on the crossbar by my neck. It took a deep breath, purred once loudly on the exhale, almost like a sigh, and gently eased itself down, curling around my neck. She went to sleep. I could feel Her soft fur and purring throat against my own neck. I could smell Her fishy breath, and I understood. Everything suddenly made sense to me. I knew I was in the presence of The Lord.

God is a cat. I know this now. God is a perpetually pregnant calico cat with a missing fang, the result of some long-forgotten battle with a lesser, yet still dangerous, foe. God's breath smells of fish, and She buries Her feces in garden beds. God roams at night, searching in the shadows for mice and rats to kill. She skulks behind trees and in bushes and waits for birds to land near her and she pounces. God is a cat. And although She cares nothing for the plight of humans, She offers me the hope that one day, if I can offer her a pleasant place to sleep and a can of sardines to eat, she will allow me into the Kingdom of Heaven. There I too will be a fisherman. Giveth She, unto Her new servant, peace and hope. Speaketh She to her flock: Prrrr. Blessed is Her that uses a mouse as a toy until all its legs are broken and it can no longer run and hide and escape. Then, tiring of Her game, blessed and holy is the sleep that follows as the mouse is left to die, broken, bruised, stunned and bloody. For WE, you and I, are these mice. For nigh upon nigh the end slowly stalketh. Unto you this is the one God, your master. Unto you I giveth Her blessings. Unto you She beareth the children of paradise. Unto you let each one understand Her superiority. And unto you glory be to the one God. And all the children borne of Her, the rulers of the earth, of the heavens unforetold. To Mother and children: dominion for ever and ever. Prrrr.

And as the Lord slept and purred in my ear, I felt more alive than I have ever felt (and that includes the years that I was not even dead), and I watched a scene unfold. The naked Grimalkins began arguing in the lineup for poison. A little fight broke out. The Prophecy stopped playing when blood-curdling shouts filled the campground.

Leading the charge through the woods was Dana, mother lion, smashing a shovel over the head of the first Grimalkin she encountered. With her eyes fixed on me, she tore through the crowd like a whirling dervish of contusions, hammering every Grimalkin in her way. Behind her was Don, still in his cabana wear, a bandage wrapped around his head, and Alexis, and an army of hippies with swinging beads and long flowing hair, kung fu kicking and smashing guitars over the heads of the Grimalkins as they charged. The battle was on. I saw Don grab Charles by the collar and smack him repeatedly about the head until he got him down on the ground and then he pressed his butt up against Charles's struggling face, Don screaming at the top of his lungs, "How you like me now?" Eggplant head and the gorilla boys came charging in with the other links, but they were outnumbered by the hippies who, with their kung fu skills, sent them packing.

Alice stood there, muttering to herself. "No. No. No. This was not in the prophecy. No. No."

Then the Lord woke, casually, and came around to stand on my arm. She started pressing Her paws on my bicep, left and right, left and right, each time sticking out Her claws and digging into my skin.

"Stop it," I said. It felt like little pins.

After a minute or two of this, the Lord rubbed Her cheek against mine and reached out with Her paw to pull gently back on my lip.

"Ow, that hurts," I said. "Stop it."

She did it again.

"What do you want, my Lord?"

I looked below and noticed that the fight between the hippies and the Grimalkins had slowed down quite a bit. They seemed to be standing together in groups now, talking, gesticulating wildly, flashing the peace sign at each other. A few of the hippies had begun walking around the stage picking up instruments, strumming chords, beating out rhythms, talking with The Prophecy, and the jam session began anew with an orchestra of ill-tuned instruments, a cacophony of amateur musicians weaving in and out of one another's musical patterns with no conductor in sight to stop them from tripping all over one another. The smell of marijuana smoke filled the air.

"No," Alice said. She pointed the pistol at me. "You!"

The Lord casually clawed at my lip again. Then got Her face right up close to mine, licked my nose with a tongue like sandpaper, and bit down gently.

It was then that I knew what She wanted.

"No, I cannot. Please don't make me," I said.

The Lord rubbed Her chin against my own and purred.

"I won't leave her," I said. "You can't make me. She's my sister."

The Lord bit me on the nose once again.

And I knew what I had to do. I had no choice.

"OW!" Mallory said as She bit us again. Dana ran up behind Alice and shoved her off the platform, sending her plummeting, screaming, to the stage where she landed with a dull thud, like a basketball bouncing on concrete.

And together we (Mallory and I) shared a vision: the weeping face of Dana, holding Mallory's cheeks, gently in the palms of her hands.

Dana turned away for a second to look down on Ben. "I

told you!" she shouted.

"Mommy?" Mallory said.

And the Lord hopped down from the cross and sauntered away, and it came to me in a swell of emotion:

"ONLY THOSE WHO RISK THE PERILS OF THE JOURNEY CAN REACH THE HEIGHTS OF SUCCESS."

I knew that I must follow Her. I must serve Her at any cost. I was now an agent of the Lord. That was why I was back on Earth. A corporate spy who was working the other side of the merger. And with that, I said my name aloud, "Karen Floyd," and I left Mallory's body. It was not a violent extraction, just like a simple pop, as if I were a soap bubble and someone had burst me. I hung there momentarily, an outsider, and watched as mother and daughter were reunited.

"Be seeing you, dear sister," I said to the crumpled mess that had been Alice. Her neck was bent in a very disturbing way, and she was either unconscious or dead.

I started floating away. Without a host, I did not belong there, and I could feel myself fading, as if I were holding my breath, and we all know that a person can only hold their breath for so long. I had to find a way to stay. I could not serve Her in Hell. I had to stay.

Without an in, without a sick box and an unbaptized host, however, I had no idea how I would find sanctuary. I took off into the woods, searching for an evil twig or tree or ant, anything that I could possess, even momentarily, until I got back on my feet again. I was fading fast, getting weaker, dropping back into the blackness. I could hear the growling of the zombie horde, smell the rotting flesh of Hell, the taste of Mike, the night shift janitor in charge of cleaning the urinals, on my lips.

I started falling towards the earth where I knew I would be sucked down, swallowed whole, and sent back to Hell. But there in the darkness of the woods I saw something white, a beacon for me, shining there like an angel, calling me, something white and fluffy. I couldn't believe my luck…Todd, or a reasonable facsimile, was sitting in a clearing eating grass. With my last bit of demonic energy, I flung myself, rudderless in the wind, careening and twisting and falling right out of consciousness at Todd's large ear. If one were watching the rabbit, one might have seen him shake his head, and with his hind leg, scratch his ear and then go back to eating grass.

666

It was a strange state to be in, I assure you, not having the proper motor skills to do anything but hop, eat, and poop little rabbit pellets, but I was on Earth and not in Hell, so it was good enough for the moment. A comfortable and spacious body. The new Todd immediately relinquished control too, so there was no power struggle. The night air was warm and sweet. They would come looking for me soon. I was AWOL, after all. Satan would send someone to find me. I was sure of it. I moved from the clearing in the woods, hopping down a trail, to find a wide-open pasture, and I sat in this open pasture, munching on blades of grass and dandelion heads as I took breaks from chewing to stare up at a full moon. This was the Earth that I wanted. This was the experience I wanted. It was pleasant to be alive. I wondered if I could live in the body of a rabbit forever. I wondered if that would be enough. The calm simplicity of life as the dumbest of beasts, with nothing to do but procreate, eat, and sleep. And when this Todd died, I could just hop into the body of another Todd. Simple enough.

It seemed like a good idea at the time.

In the distance, miles away, I heard a pack of coyotes howling and yipping. The rabbit began to shake, and his small brain fired shots of warning and fear like a machine gun fires bullets. His brain was still functioning in an instinctual manner, always fearful and wary, always concerned that the next beast that was going to murder and eat him was skulking around the corner. It did not seem like the danger was imminent, but I supposed that the rabbit probably knew something that I did not. I backed up and hopped into the glade where I first possessed him, and he calmed down. I suddenly felt like I was all alone on the Earth and that no one cared about me. I missed Mallory.

I'd have to find some shelter soon, a warren or tree hollow to sleep in. I heard the distant howl of coyotes again, an eerie horrible howling that seemed much closer than it had before. From the edge of the glade, behind some trees, I saw yellow eyes staring at me, and I heard some rustling in the fallen twigs. The dark yellow eyes peered out at me from behind a tree and then disappeared again. Another set of yellow eyes was on the other side of me. I was surrounded by something, the coyotes, or worse. My rabbit instinct told me to flee to find safety, it screamed loudly in our brain, telling us to run run run run…but I did not. There was nowhere to run to.

They had found me. Already. The yellow eyes with the black pupils stared at me.

I heard voices, and footsteps on a path.

"Yeah, so I call it the skinny dip buddy."

Don.

"Oh, man. That's so cool." And a woman. "People are so hung up nudity, man. Like, you know, man, we're like a society of robots, man. We gotta break free."

"Yeah," I heard Don say. " I have the patent, and I hope to have it in the stores by Christmas. Should bring in a good profit. What about here? Is this a good place to *ball*? … Hey, look! It can't be. Todd, is that you?"

The yellow eyes disappeared.

6

Months passed until everything was sorted out. With the help of Alexis Warrington and some nude reiki sessions, coinciding with nude couples counseling and a new form of emotional therapy created by Alexis called The Whole Person Matrix (also performed in the nude), Ben recovered from the trauma of his capture at the hands of the Grimalkins and the corresponding PTSD that followed. Ben and Dana eventually reconciled. In one breakthrough session, under a thick blanket of marijuana smoke, his testicles resting on a thin pile rug as he sat in the lotus position, Ben even admitted that there were forces beyond his understanding in the universe, that the existence of bipedal cats who travel the cosmos in spaceships was a possibility, and that his beloved daughter Mallory had indeed been possessed by a fat and ugly evil spirit named Karen. He even considered the possibility that Karen might still be out there and could easily come back to torture them again. Due to this fact, a family decision was made: Dana would quit her job and the family would sell all their worldly possessions, tithing the proceeds over to the New Order of the Grimalkins (a hybrid of the remaining old Grimalkin family and the hippie commune), headed up by their new Teacher, Alexis Warrington, or Ms. Vicki, as she had begun calling herself. Now a level 21 reiki master. The Matthews family would seek shelter in the Grimalkin commune, and the New Grimalkins would protect the Perfect Child, Mallory, promising that as long as she lived, Mallory would stand as living testament to the efficacy of their new world order.

I lived in a cage throughout this dark period, finding no peace in the teachings of Ms. Vicki, no solace in the fact that Mallory and I were together again. I needed out of this rabbit body that shook with fear every time a door opened or closed, or lightning struck and thunder shook God's great earth. I wanted a meat sandwich too. Or a ribeye steak. I was sick of eating carrots and grass. It was enough to drive a person mad.

Mallory had just turned six, and the Matthews family, dressed in white robes and wearing their long necklaces, were having a garage sale, selling all their books and VCR tapes, old bikes, anything they had. A FOR SALE sign was sitting on the front lawn of their house. Ms. Vicki had a booth set up in the driveway, advertising reiki healing sessions and eternal peace at $45 per hour. My cage was sitting on a folding table alongside the rest of the worthless items they were selling. I had presumed that they were just taking me out for some air, as they sometimes did.

A man in a suit came up to the table.

"Hey, buddy," he said. "How much for the rabbit?"

Ben turned."Oh, he's not for sale. He's my daughter's rabbit. We're just getting him some air."

"Bullshit," the man said. "Everything's for sale. How much you want? I'll give you fifty bucks."

"No, sir. Sorry."

"A hundred?"

"Who pays a $100 for a rabbit?" Ben asked.

"My son wants the damn thing, buddy. What can I tell you? He's waiting in the car." The man, with his perfectly coiffed swoop of yellowish-orange hair, obviously died to hide the grey, and his gleaming silver Hugo Boss suit, motioned over to a Mercedes-Benz station wagon with tinted windows parked on the street.

"Listen, pal. I don't really care. Money is no object. My son wants the damn rabbit. So I'm willing to pay whatever. How about $200?"

"Mallory, can you come here please?" Ben called.

Mallory was standing beside Alexis at the table where customers paid for their items.

After Alexis took their cash and put it in an old tackle box, Mallory would hand them a flyer on their way out. She skipped over to Ben with the flyers still in her hand. "What is it, Dad?"

"Well, I know you will say no, but I thought that I had better ask you. This man would like to offer you $200 for Todd. Now, that is a lot of money, Mal."

Mallory wrinkled her nose up, looked at Ben, then at the man, then back to Ben. "How much money is that?" she asked.

"For a rabbit? A lot," the man said.

"No, like, what could I buy with it?" Mallory asked. "Or do I have to give it to the Grimalkins?"

"No," Ben said. "I think you can keep it. We don't have to give everything to the New Order. You'll need some toys to play with at the commune anyway. It's, like, ten Barbies, or twenty new books, or maybe forty of those little stuffies you collect."

"No," I thought. "I don't like this. Mallory. No."

Mallory pondered for a second. "You mean the unicorn fairy dragon family?"

"Sure, yeah," Ben said. "But you would never see Todd again. He would be gone. Is that worth it to you?"

"Come on, kid," the man in the fancy suit said. "Think of all the unicorn monsters you could buy. I'll throw in another 20 for the cage."

"Is it worth it, Mallory? You love, Todd. Don't you?"

"No. Not really," Mallory said as she stared at me and smiled a most wicked, crooked, knowing smile. "I'll take it," she announced very sweetly, shaking the man's hand, taking the $220 from him and completing the transaction by handing him one of the flyers she was holding.

"Mallory, no!" For I feared something far worse than being a rabbit was waiting for me in that Mercedes with the tinted windows.

But that was it.

The man picked up the handle of my cage and walked towards his car. On my way out, I passed Dana standing at a table, laughing with a customer. As she handed over my sick box to the customer, a woman with a two-foot-high dyed green mohawk and an enormous blister-like pimple on the side of her head, Dana said, "Enjoy it. Whatever you are going to do with it," and she laughed.

Ben and Mallory, dressed in white robes, standing in the driveway, waved good-bye to me as I was carried away, a fat wad of bills rippling in Mallory's fist as she waved. Don sidled in behind them and also waved goodbye to me. The cat, Gregsie, was there as well, milling about Mallory's feet.

The man hurried to his car, as if he had just committed a crime, and opened the rear passenger side door. He put my cage on the seat and hurried around to the driver's side.

"There, I got you your goddamn rabbit," he said as he plopped himself down into the driver's seat and shoved the keys in the ignition.

"Chill out, dude. You don't have to be such a buzzkill, Dad," a familiar voice said from the front passenger seat. Paul, with a big white scar on his forehead and a neck brace, craned around in the seat to face me. He put his index finger and his long middle finger to his lips and made a kissing sound, mouthing the words, "My heart," to me.

The car started up, its German motor purring with efficiency, and I checked the seat beside me. There was Betty, a ghastly Betty, with rotting teeth and rotting lips, rancid bleeding wounds, and blue hair piled high on her head. She growled at me like a monster. And beside her, Mr. Marbles, with his long hair trailing down over his shoulders. They were all staring at me as the car started down the road. The man who purchased me, Dad, as I heard Paul call him, pulled up to a stop sign. He muttered something beneath his breath, like "such bullshit," or something like that, and tossed the flyer that Mallory had given him onto the floor of the back seat. He turned right, away from the Matthews house forever.

From where I was sitting, I could read the flyer through the bars of my cage. A typewritten page read as follows:

"I was possessed by very bad and evil in my body.

I was very sick.

I could not eat.

I threw up on my toys.

I lost my family.

I lost faith.

I tried to find help.

But no one could help me.

The evil power was controlling my life.

Ms. Vicki was my last hope.

After six visits I am completely cured."

To hear the rest of Mallory's story, please join us at the Melgage Legion Hall auditorium on November 6 at 6:00 pm. Admission is only $20. ($26 if you choose the dinner option.)

Be seeing you. Peace and Love. Ms. Vicki

A foul and disgusting stench filled the Mercedes, and

everyone crinkled their noses, gagged and wretched and frantically rolled their windows down, shouting simultaneously, "CHARLES! YOU REEK!" as the link Charles, the dimwitted one, popped his head over the back seats of the wagon where he had been sleeping in the trunk and said, "Was'nd ME!"

And the end is as it should be.

Prrr.

Made in the USA
Middletown, DE
14 September 2021